39

© 2011 McSweeney's Quarterly Concern and the contributors, San Francisco, California. INTERNS & VOLUNTEERS: Ryan Diaz, Ted Trautman, Seph Kramer, Becca Cohn, Courtney Drew, Jennifer Florin, Rebecca Giordano, Victoria Havlicek, Jordan Karnes, Magnolia Molcan, Alexandra Slessarev, Angelene Smith, Libby Wachtler, Mark Waclawiak, John Wilson, Valerie Woolard, Rebecca Power, Megan Roberts, Scott Cohen, Molly Elizalde, Daniel Gumbiner, Gilbert Lawson, Sophie Nunberg, Shelby Rachleff, Jim Santel, Nate Mayer, Hannah Doyle, Matt Gillespie. ALSO HELPING: Chris Ying, Eli Horowitz, Michelle Quint, Russell Quinn, Jill Haberkern, Andi Mudd, Walter Green, Sam Riley, Rachel Khong, Em-J Staples, Ethan Nosowsky. COPY EDITOR: Caitlin Van Dusen. WEBSITE: Chris Monks. SUPPORT: Sunra Thompson. OUTREACH: Juliet Litman. ART DIRECTOR: Brian McMullen. ASSOCIATE PUBLISHER: Adam Krefman. PUBLISHER: Laura Howard. ASSOCIATE EDITOR: Chelsea Hogue. MANAGING EDITOR: Jordan Bass. EDITOR: Dave Eggers.

Printed in Michigan at Thomson-Shore Printers. Cover photo by Tabitha Soren.

AUTHOR .... TITLE .... PAGE

LETTERS .... *From Benjamin Cohen, Marco Kaye,*
Dicky Murphy, Elizabeth Sankey,
David-Ivar Herman Düne, Avery Lee,
and Stephen Elliott 4

JULIE HECHT .... *They All Stand Up and Sing* 17

JENNIE ERIN SMITH .... *Benjamin Bucks* 43

ROBERTO BOLAÑO .... *The Neochileans* 67

TOM BARBASH .... *The Shah's Man* 85

VÁCLAV HAVEL .... *Politics and Conscience* 121

E. C. OSONDU .... *Bumsters* 149

TABITHA SOREN .... *Running* .... INSERT

ELMORE LEONARD .... *Chick Killer* 161

YANNICK MURPHY .... *Secret Language* 167

AMELIA GRAY .... *Fifty Ways to Eat Your Lover* 185

JESS WALTER .... *Anything Helps* 193

TABITHA SOREN .... *Running* .... INSERT

BENJAMIN WEISSMAN .... *Louella Tarantula* 209

ABI MAXWELL .... *Giant of the Sea* 225

J. T. K. BELLE .... *Carlos the Impossible* 243

DEAR McSWEENEY'S,

I promised I'd be in touch soon after my last letter, but the year blinked past, time evaporated, and so I apologize that "soon" evidently means "more than a year." We're moving, that's one thing. Figuring that out has been taking a lot of time. Believe me, too, it brings out the neighbors, who now pay us all kinds of attention and offer loads of advice about what we should be doing. The driveway needs more gravel, the front railing could use another coat, things like that. We should weed the lawn better. I'm told.

Since my last note, our one neighbor (the trampoline house) lost her battle with cancer. She passed away. We actually didn't even know; we were so used to ambulance sounds that it didn't occur to us for a while that the last visit was just that, the last visit. I was getting the mail when I saw Billy's car drive by with REST IN PEACE and birth and death dates soaped onto the back window.

Half the time I beam with pride at how much I pay attention; that's the key, right? You just have to pay attention to others, acknowledge the humanity of those around you, and society will prosper. So okay, but the other half of the time is this embarrassing ignorance of the world and everyone in it. If pressed, I have to admit I spend a lot more time there on that other half than a healthy self-image can allow. Not to mention that when your neighbors use the attention you do give them to dole out unsolicited advice it makes you question the whole equation.

But the neighbor catty-corner to our backyard? I finally saw him. For the first time in five years I saw him. How's that. They're making a big deal right now out of how the people in Abbottabad didn't know who was living in that high-walled compound, but even though there are any number of questions I might pose to Pakistan, that wouldn't be one of them. I have no idea what the guy across the way has been doing for the last five years, sixty feet from my kids' swing-set. I mean, I can't tell if this is his summer home, if he has family, if he has one car or two, if that wire-fenced garden that's somehow growing something is maybe secretly tended to in the middle of the night.

Not long after I spotted him, maybe the next week, my wife, C—, was looking out our back kitchen window trying to get a peek at him herself.

Instead she saw Billy with his dogs waddling under our swing-set on a long leash, scratching at the dirt, about to crap. She's seen him walking the property line out back for years, not to mention the front walk. I think I mentioned that in my last letter. Depending on her mood, this has caused surprise, irritation, anger, and seething rage. We've had to live here, though, so what can you do?

But this time his dogs were ranging way into our yard, obviously past the property line, not just dancing along it to leave you wondering, Well, I dunno, is that crossing the line, too? This was more blatant. And so, not even thinking, my wife yanked the sliding door open and blurted out, "Oh, come on already with the dogs, Billy! My kids play there!"

His head snapped up, and that gruff smoker's voice said, "Okay, oh, okay, okay." Then he jerked them back to his side.

C— surprised herself, being so brash, and then got embarrassed that it might be disrespectful, given his circumstances. She was out picking weeds a few days later up by the street when Billy drove by on his way home, slowing his car as he approached our drive. REST IN PEACE was long faded off the back window, no doubt washed away by the rain. C— was a little nervous, dirt-covered dandelion leaves in hand, when he stopped. He's a big guy. Like, car-leaning-to-the-side big. But he just propped his arm out the window and said, "You know, I respect you just came right out and told me that. You didn't call the cops on us or nothin', you talked straight to me about it. I want you to know I respect that."

That was all. Then he drove on.

I guess she'd kept the order in our neighborhood. Maybe it was easier for her to do it, then; she wasn't worried about paying attention to the universe except to notice what was right in front of her. Maybe she blurted that out because it's not our home anymore, not for much longer. I don't know what I'm supposed to think about it or anything else, really, but I have this hunch that the next time I write, from our new home, in another state, with a new job and new schools and new neighbors, I'll probably romanticize our life back here. It'll all be so beautiful and clear.

Take care, for now,

BENJAMIN COHEN
CHARLOTTESVILLE, VA

DEAR MCSWEENEY'S,

Here's what I want to know: when you don't realize that a crime you committed was a "real" type of crime, and so you fail to tell a prospective employer about it, is that tantamount to covering it up? I didn't think so, but this human-resources company seems to. When I told their guy, Reed, that "maybe it was a 'you had to be there' kind of thing, but I bet you wouldn't have realized it was a misdemeanor, either," the voice at the other end of the line was far from sympathetic, and not nearly as musical as the name I've made up for him might suggest.

Trespassing, I have come to understand, is something that will show up on a background check. Legally, I am not at liberty to say where I applied for this job, but I'll divulge that the company is involved in "searching" the "internet." Given the place was founded on background-checking everything in the entire world, it was probably a little foolish of me not to make a mental sweep of the dusty corners of my life before I sat down for the interview.

And of course, the I-9 application I filled out a few days days later wasn't *designed* to help me remember

my criminal record, but wouldn't it have been nice if it had been? "Have you ever been convicted of a misdemeanor or felony? Caught red-handed in an unlucky moment of public urination? No judgments here; we've all done it from time to time. Or maybe you and your friends were looking for a secret swimming hole five years ago, and the only path just so happened to cut through some property owned by the Girl Scouts? Think really hard before checking Yes or No. *Think*, Marco…"

An impractical vision, sure. But consider, to use the internet developers' term, the basic *usability* of those employment forms. Reed said I had to complete them on a PC, and since my parents live too far away for me to use theirs, I went to my public library. Once there, so many pop-up windows interrupted my experience that I might as well have been filling the thing out while driving and texting. After each page loaded, I received a warning: *This page contains both secure and nonsecure items. Do you want to display the nonsecure items?* The first fifteen times, I selected No. Then I thought, What if the nonsecure items are really important? So I clicked Yes the next thirty-five times. Unlike

6

with the law, there seemed to be no right answer.

More boxes demanded my attention, pop-ups within pop-ups. As I finished each page, I was asked to electronically sign it. This brought up another box: *To the best of your knowledge, is the information contained herein true and correct?* Once, with this box, I accidentally clicked No, confusing it with the nonsecure-items box. Luckily, the startled grunt I let out didn't disturb any of the library's other patrons, and I was able to change my answer.

But can I really blame my carelessness on pop-up windows alone? A good deal of culpability rests on the soft shoulders of a woman whom I'll call Trixie. Trixie with her long legs, interestingly dyed hair, and mild acne. Unlike Reed, her fake name is telling. She was our travel agent to this secret brook, talking up its amenities, describing imaginary photos from an unprinted brochure. On our hike to the spot, we passed two girls hightailing it back down to the banks of a sunny river wherein scores of law-abiding citizens floated, contented people who didn't want any more secrets in their lives. "Mum's the word," one of the retreating girls said, "but I wouldn't go up there."

Trixie pressed her for more information, but we all knew what was waiting ahead. For a moment, we stood at that spot—what I now think of as my "line of liability"—and somehow Trixie convinced everyone that the girls were lying. They were trying to protect the swimming location, using an antiquated British idiom to throw us off. Though she'd forgotten their names, Trixie admitted that she'd had an altercation with one of them in the past. The police couldn't *possibly* be hiding out up there, she insisted, only sixty feet around the bend.

Seems to me that the dumbest sins are the ones you have to atone for again and again. Lesson learned.

Yours,

MARCO KAYE
HOBOKEN, NJ

DEAR MCSWEENEY'S,

In the book of Civil War hero David Glasgow Farragut, a man was either "young" or "old" and nothing in between. "I say do away with all this talk of eighteen or seven or thirty-two years old. Of forty, twenty-nine, seventy-six," wrote Farragut. "These numbers are useless to me. The only thing that matters is this: can you perform a handspring?"

This is all backed up in the annals of history. Wrote the historian Shelby Foote (whom Farragut would certainly have classified as "old"), "Farragut was known to be stout-hearted and energetic; every year on his birthday he turned a handspring, explaining that he would know he was beginning to age when he found the exercise difficult."

But this test did not come without its pitfalls. For one, it cost Farragut "the loss of a good 338 quote unquote young sailors who are sadly, in fact, quite old." These 338 sailors, all under the age of twenty-five, had been commissioned to join Farragut in his 1862 fight for New Orleans, but after they "failed to complete any semblance of a handstand," they were immediately "cashiered and sent back to old-ville." It wasn't until word reached Lincoln of this blow to the navy that the 338 sailors were reinstated, so long as they could "prove their youth by running one hundred yards while balancing an uncooked egg on a wooden tablespoon." (Lincoln had his own measurements of "young" and "old.")

A mere ten months later, Farragut, having captured New Orleans, Baton Rouge, and Natchez, experienced his own handspring pitfall. "It was a cloudy day in New Orleans," wrote one of his young, handspringless men. "We had just returned from Natchez to regroup before taking Vicksburg. It was to be a great day, as our Flag Officer David Farragut was celebrating his birthday. The good Farragut baked a seven-foot Orleans-style cake, the word YOUNG spelled out in so many candles across its chocolate frosting. We sang a spirited 'Happy Birthday,' followed by the enjoinder, 'How old are you now? How old are you now?' at which point Farragut raised his hand for a show of silence. What followed was one of the saddest sights I have ever seen; surely one of the saddest of the Civil War yet. For Farragut commenced a handspring, but instead of landing on his feet he stalled in midair, like Euclid's parabola, with nary a way back home. Then, with a wail, he tumbled sideways into the Orleans-style cake."

Farragut's response was swift. A letter of resignation found its way to Abraham Lincoln's desk within a week. "I am too old for war," it said, and nothing more.

But Lincoln could not afford the loss of his all-star naval commander, and so he commanded Farragut to make his way "forthwith to the White

House, where we shall settle this age issue once and for all." Much to Farragut's surprise, he passed Lincoln's fitness test, was proclaimed "young" once again, and was sent back to New Orleans, where in subsequent months he fought with a youthful "damn the torpedoes" élan. For Lincoln's part, he later admitted to Secretary of State Seward that he had "horse-glued that old man's uncooked egg to that damn wooden tablespoon." Yours,

DICKY MURPHY
LOS ANGELES, CA

DEAR McSWEENEY'S,

The *Twilight* books have ruined my life. They've cast a light onto my own sad existence; not a soft, comforting twilight, but a bright yellow fluorescent light that illuminates my blemishes. Before, I was happy to kiss boys because they were funny, clever, or didn't spit when they spoke. Now my standards have changed.

My friends just think it's funny. They keep teasing me for fancying the anemic boy from school: "*Ooh, Elizabeth, here's a bright red apple, why don't you take it to Charlie and talk to him about forbidden love?* I think he's in the nurses' office because he didn't have any protein at lunch." I know it's a teenage cliché to say "Nobody understands me," but seriously, nobody understands me.

Like Bella, the female protagonist of the *Twilight* books, I moved to a new town last year, and just like Forks, where Bella lives, it's really rainy. (Although, to be honest, most towns in England are rainy.) But this place has rain that's heavy and leaves the air moist and thick; rain that feels ominous and fantastical, you know? I also live with my dad, like Bella, although he isn't a surly police officer. He works in advertising. And the idea that I would have to cook him dinner each night because he can't look after himself is laughable. That's what he's marrying Carol for.

Recently, anyway, this boy called Simon asked me to the cinema. He's nice and always has gum, but what's the point? His mum's definitely not beautiful enough to be immortal. She wears saggy beige Ugg boots and gets her hair dyed ginger by a man who calls himself Giorgio but definitely isn't Italian. I guess maybe if Simon got a tan he might look like Jacob Black, the werewolf, but Jacob Black always has his shirt off and Simon has to wear a vest in PE because of his pigeon chest.

When I say this stuff to my friends, they joke that I need therapy. Do you think I need therapy? What would I say to a therapist? "I'm depressed that when a boy I like walks into the sunlight, his skin isn't going to sparkle"?

I was thinking about all this on Wednesday, when I cut my hand. Not on purpose; I was cutting a carrot for dinner—I'm on this sort of intense diet—and my finger started bleeding. I remembered this thing my gran had said about how your own saliva is the best way to clot blood, so I put my finger in my mouth. And suddenly, there it was. The taste.

It was warm and salty, just like Stephanie Meyer said it would be in the books. I know it's silly, but I found it kind of exciting.

After about five minutes, the blood stopped coming, and I didn't think of it again until a few days ago. I was in the house on my own and I just started *craving* that taste again. I know I'm not a vampire, because you can't turn yourself into one just by tasting your own blood, otherwise everyone who ever cut themselves would now be a vampire, which they're not. But maybe it doesn't happen like that? Maybe the vampire urge was always in me, inert and waiting for the right moment to erupt? Like racism?

Yesterday I googled "real-life vampire" and found this woman who says her name is Redangel. She lives in Cornwall, and she says she has a contact at a hospital who gets her all her blood. "It's not ideal, but at least I know it's clean," she writes. She says she's not sensitive to light, the way some vampires are, but she's definitely "more of a night owl." She wants me to visit her and her friends over the summer, but I'm not sure I should. Carol would totally freak out.

Maybe it's my parents' fault for splitting up when I was young. That and the fact that they took me to Disney World repeatedly when I was a child and highly impressionable. It's completely ruined real life for me. I look out the window at my stupid street in my stupid town in this stupid country and I think, There must be something more. The idea of spending the rest of my days with nothing fantastical ever happening makes me so depressed I sometimes stay in bed for a whole day. Carol says it's just growing pains, and rubs my back in a way that she probably thinks is comforting and maternal. But it's not, it's just creepy.

ELIZABETH SANKEY
LONDON, ENGLAND

DEAR MCSWEENEY'S,

It was in the midst of a full-on terrible heat wave in Paris that I moved with my gal into a flat with three balconies—three blocks from Père Lachaise cemetery and far more from any other point of interest.

I first went to see the place with my brother while he was visiting from Berlin. We walked from the horrible street where I was staying at a friend's aparment for a few weeks. My brother was carrying a six-pack of Heineken with only three beers left in it; he opened one the minute we met, and lit a cigarette.

We walked uphill for ten minutes, halted to open another bottle, and then my brother smoked another couple of cigarettes as we started the steep trudge to where my cell phone said the apartment was. This was two years ago, and two years ago I wasn't familiar with navigation applications, and also I was very self-conscious about using that kind of device around my brother, who thinks they should be classified as weapons. Anyway, I got us lost, and my elder brother took over.

The climb became so steep that I vowed never to go back down if we ever made it to the top. Eventually we found the right street, along with an oh-so-typical street-corner "Café Des Sports," where we sat and ordered two pints while my brother lit another Benson.

We had a block left to walk before we got to the building, a three-story-high yellow-brick structure with baby-blue shades and plenty of balconies. I called the number I had, and the owner let us in. I felt drunk and sweaty, but my brother was all right.

When I'd seen the balconies, I'd known that I was going to live there. Inside, I realized that despite the day's blazing heat the corridors felt fresh, although it was probably impossible that the place would actually *be* fresh, because France ignores air conditioning like a horse ignores its dung.

The bedroom, anyway, looked wonderful. A glass door opened from it to a sort of narrow terrace that ran all along the north side of the building, reminding me of New York City's fire escapes, which had once made me very happy. The owner didn't seem too pleased with me smelling of beer and my brother smoking at the kitchen window, but he went ahead and asked me if I was a Jew. When I said yes, he smiled gently and I knew he wouldn't let me down.

I called M. and said I had found a great place, where she would have a room to draw, where it stayed fresh enough that we could have roses, and where there was an oven with which I would learn to bake bread for the Sabbath. A week later, she was there with me, back in her hometown, up on the highest hill in the city. We moved in with nothing but my ton of records, my two guitars, two chairs, and her million shoes.

The sheer wonder of moving our two chairs around! Moving them from the balcony, where we'd sit with our glasses of pinot, staring at the big fat dirty golden moon, to the empty living room with its record player cranking Amy Winehouse, where we'd eat coconut-flavored "Pasta à la Yaya" from a bowl on the floor. It was perfect.

And then we met the neighbors. I hate having to do this; worse is having to say hi and ask stupid questions, or having to be thankful because they so nicely accepted your UPS package for you. Truth is, neighbors only want to snoop around. They tell you they love music when they see your guitar just so you'll let them play terrible dance hits when they're high on speed at 3 a.m. Maybe they throw a few

dirty looks at your girlfriend during their visit, too.

But despite my misgivings, our downstairs neighbor trapped us inside his filthy flat for a welcome drink where he did all the drinking. He seemed to be drugged out of his mind, but through the muddy chitchat, the grunts, the hysterical laughs that I suspect were hiding farts, I heard something interesting.

"Some place you got! Some place! Some owners before you!"

I'd met the owner, I told him.

"No, no! Their son you met! What a prick—little rabbi scum! The *owners*, they're a couple like you! Beautiful spouse—" and, to M., "—not so handsome a husband!" Then he winked.

"He died at 105!" he went on. "Last year! And she's now 108! They... they used to work at the Muséum d'Histoire Naturelle, in the fifth district! Together! Searchers!"

I couldn't help following that lead. "Searchers?" I said. "You mean they were working in research? What field?"

He said, "*Spiders!* Big, big spiders! With hair! And fur! *Grrrr!*"

It was hard to understand him, as the gin didn't seem to mix well with whatever he was on. But I tried hard, as it was the first time in what felt like forever that I actually wanted to listen to what he was saying.

What I understood of his story was that both Mr. and Mrs. Smolarsky, former owners of the third-floor apartment at 30 rue Boyer, used to head up the arachnids department at the Museum of Natural History. Along the way I figured out that what was now our bedroom used to be their vivarium. It made sense; after all, it felt so fresh in there, right at the apex of an incredibly hot July. They used to keep all kinds of spiders in that very room, our neighbor explained, from little common tarantulas to the biggest, meanest eight-legged specimens.

And then, as he was almost falling over drooling, his yellow eyes in the dark kitchen of his filthy pit staring at me like a million shiny glowing spider orbs, his slobber nothing but a stinky, sticky cobweb ready to be thrown at us, he said something else. He said: "*I know their secret!* They found eternal life! They found it in spider blood! They found the secret and they shot it straight into their veins! *Spider blood!*"

I thought: Spider blood? Is there even such a thing?

M. and I ran upstairs and went to bed, trying to ignore the sickening sub-bass sounds of some '90s Netherlandish dancehall classic that the man was now playing to smooth out the effects of drug abuse and heavy drinking. I forgot about our conversation, more or less.

I can live without clothes inside my home, to be honest, but as me and my gal had just moved in together I consented to buy a robe, a little bit like the one Steve Martin wears in *The Jerk*. That way she could leave the shades open and the glass door ajar.

One morning I woke up and put the robe on. I found it itchy at the neck, and assumed it was the tag.

I went to make some coffee—still itchy. I crushed a couple of avocados to spread on some baguette, and it continued to be itchy. I hate tags, I thought.

When M. woke up, we had a lovely breakfast. She says it's her favorite part of the day; M. wakes up smiling, with the happiest look on her face, and her eyes, instead of displaying the usual puffiness you'd expect, seem bigger and bluer than at any other time. She's a beauty when she just wakes up. I wouldn't miss the moment she opens her eyes for anything.

Anyway, at breakfast, our custom is that she'll tell me about her night dreams and visions. That night she'd dreamed of sea monsters, of running away with her twin sister, of me and her on an ice block somewhere in the ocean. At some point we were in a giant's abandoned house and I threw a shoe at Angelica Huston's face. I loved that part. I love Miss Huston.

I never remember my dreams well, really, and when I do, it's always the ones where everything happening is just exactly like it might have happened during the day. Like, I dream I'm walking to the train station, and then I take the train, or I dream I'm running to catch a bus, and I catch it. But that morning I couldn't even remember that much—I was having trouble concentrating, as my robe was still very itchy at the neck.

That's when I said "Damn this label!" and took the whole thing off, throwing it on the tiled floor in the kitchen. It turned out that what I thought was a tag was a big old spider. It seemed gigantic. I still had to behave, though, as I didn't want to be the weaker half of our recently moved-in couple.

So instead of shrieking, I said: "Baby, she got me! She got me, all right. But I might live forever now, through laughter and rains. They knew the

secret! Do you want a bite? Try the robe on and we'll meet all those other suckers in a century."
DAVID-IVAR HERMAN DÜNE
PARIS, FRANCE

DEAR MCSWEENEY'S,
I am writing to request that you publish a large-print edition. I have many older relatives who would enjoy reading your magazine, but their eyes are not so good, so they have trouble with reasonably sized fonts. Also they are often depressed.

My aunt, for example, is generally bedridden; a larger font will allow her to read your quarterly while resting her arms and reclining. And although she can no longer travel safely, after her stroke, I'm sure she'll be pleased that many of your stories are set in other parts of the world. Most of her friends and much of her family still lives abroad. There is also a nodule in her brain that she refuses to have checked—maybe she'd reconsider after reading some exciting new fiction with her tired old eyes. (Please note that this assumes that you will also be translating your publication into Chinese.)

I'm sure there are others like her, poised to discover the satisfaction of a well-crafted short story. Please let me know what you can do. Sincerely,

AVERY LEE
CHICAGO, IL

P.S. The other day my grandfather wandered the streets alone for several hours, disoriented. I think he would have stayed inside if it had been one of the four delightful days of the year when his large-print edition of *McSweeney's* arrives.

DEAR McSWEENEY'S,
I'm in Los Angeles editing a movie. At night I meet with three women and we play board games, specifically Settlers of Catan. More specifically Cities and Knights. The women are beautiful and the streets here are like the films you see in theaters full of crushed blacks, and deep redst every bulb round and colorful. There's always a soundtrack in my head.

The movie I'm editing is my directorial debut. I'm not actually editing it; I'm more like an assistant editor. I've moved into an apartment with the editor and we work here. There are large oak tables and French curtains. In the kitchen there is a half bottle of red wine and two hard oranges. It's like living in a still-life. I feel as if I'm waiting to be painted.

Sometimes the editor's boyfriend gets jealous that she is living with me, but he is far away, and he is not part of our film. Sometimes I look at the three women I play board games with and my intentions skew. My vision narrows and the sound of the world is like the sound on the outside of a car. It's quite possible I'm in love with one of the girls, but I lean against the other. I touch her leg with my foot. I say, "Think of me as your gay friend."

I thought you might have some insight into my dilemma, which is the same dilemma I suppose everyone faces from time to time. What would you say if I was David Lynch? How would you respond to a circus clown? Imagine me as a lonely mime, placing settlements and cities across a game board that in no way mimics real life and yet is the only life I know.

McSweeney's, my cities are burning. I gather sheep. I build roads of brick and wood. During the day I hide behind a computer screen and think about the women, but they don't think about me back. I'm safe, the only man allowed to play, like a baby in a coven. All I'm asking is, What would you do? What would anyone do? Sincerely,

STEPHEN ELLIOTT
LOS ANGELES, CA

The author wearing a Marimekko dress, sometime in the 1980s. Nantucket, Massachusetts.

THEY ALL
STAND UP AND SING

by JULIE HECHT

I WAS SOMEWHERE in a big room in an old apartment in New York. The room was in a brownstone, or limestone, and had what appeared to be twenty-foot-high ceilings. There were baroque moldings around the ceilings, around the tops of the radiator covers and on the mantelpiece. The apartment was on the fifth floor and there was no elevator, but it was near Gramercy Park.

This was during the era when very young women could afford such places with a roommate or two. The roommates in this apartment were happy that they'd found this great deal. I was so young that I lived in a much-worse situation, which I didn't notice at the time but now look back upon with horror and disbelief. I accepted the fact that graduate students lived in better circumstances than high school or college students did. This was before the arrival of the yuppie generation who thought they could have everything they wanted immediately, and proceeded to get it.

We all wore Marimekko cotton dresses—not by plan, or necessarily at the same time. I myself had at least five or six, or seven or ten. What does it matter now? Who cares about our Marimekko dresses? Sleeveless for summer, long-sleeved for winter, short-sleeved for spring. They were the only clothes that were desperately wanted by artistic, intellectual, highbrow or hip girls and young women. We were called girls at the time. One of the highbrow girls in the apartment happened to have an actual low brow—a monkey's low brow, even though she was highly intelligent.

Each dress was a work of art. Some were Op Art. We knew the fabric had originally been painted by Finnish women artists—we knew some story like that. We were too crazed by the dresses to care much how they came to be. One design was striped, thin stripes, as if painted with a watercolor paintbrush so that the lines were all in uneven waves. One line was the blue the sky sometimes turns right before the sunset, the other was green, the color of lichen growing on a tree. This was one of the best. The style of the dresses was almost completely plain—as plain and simple as a dress a child would draw. Just two lines like a capital A. The neckline would be round and high, or maybe a small V-neck, or thin, silver-looking buttons going up to a little stand-up collar.

The Marimekko design came right after the completely opposite kinds of designs, designs of the neat and perfect fifties. No one's form was visible under the loose A of the dress—so unlike today's tramp-ware—all that was seen was a face, a head of hair, and the personality and brain behind the face. Then the dress, and the legs. The legs didn't have to be perfect legs. The person counted.

People met, went out, fell in love, or not; some got married and lived happily ever after, or not. All the girls looked like adorable girls from a child's book. Even those who were not that adorable. How much fun were the end of the sixties and part of the seventies, when girls and women were people. Most men were still what were later called sexist pigs, but they didn't need to know exactly what was under the dress at first glance. In present times we know this is a must—seeing everything on everyone all the time.

In a documentary about Bob Dylan, Joan Baez can be seen singing at the Newport Film Festival. She's wearing a plain white sleeveless dress with a high, round neck. The dress has no shape, but her shape is visible when she moves. Her long dark hair is hanging down and around her shoulders, just natural and plain—she could have been anyone. A college student, or a teacher, or even a librarian. Only her arms are bare and the hem of her dress is just below her knees, not much different from a dress Jacqueline Kennedy might have worn.

I recently read that Jacqueline Kennedy owned eight Marimekkos, which she wore during the summer of the 1960 presidential campaign. Since I read it on Wikipedia the information was suspect. She would have had many more than eight. Maybe eighteen or eighty.

The mania and fascination with Marimekkos began with student-girls at Radcliffe. In the beginning, Cambridge was the only place to get the dresses. Design Research on Brattle Street was a holy shrine. Next there was Design Research on East Fifty-seventh Street in New York, but that was less holy. We'd been told that some architect, Ben Thompson, was the store's founder, and that he was responsible for bringing all this stuff here—Finnish dresses, Scandinavian furniture, glasses, everything from these superior-design countries. We didn't wonder about him, we cared only about the dresses. We didn't understand that all the designs were part of a revolution. We were so young we didn't have the experience of buying things. We didn't know how ugly things had been before.

Every day, the song "Get Off of My Cloud" was played on speakers throughout the store in New York. It got us all high—all of us who were lucky enough to be working there instead of Max's Kansas City. We were too high to have been working in this shrine. The Rolling Stones–induced madness wasn't right for staring at fabric in the fabric-bolt area—a short, wide, light-wood stairway open to the space of the whole store, going up to a small second floor of a wall of shelves and floor-to-ceiling bolts of too many colors to take in. A special, beautiful, light-wood rolling ladder was used to reach the bolts on the top shelves.

The dresses were not short enough, so we shortened them. My bad-mannered, good-looking boyfriend directed mine to be shortened even more. We stood in front of a mirror in his apartment and he kept pulling the hem up two more inches. He didn't appreciate the subtlety of the dresses. When he'd first seen the Marimekkos, he had told me in his crude way, "It's what my old lady would have called a 'shmata.'"

"No, like this," he'd say, turning the work of art into a minidress. "I want to see legs." I was surprised—this after my mother had always found fault with my legs, saying, "I won prizes for my legs in college." The boyfriend didn't know about perfect legs. I'd heard that his former girlfriend's legs were thick and clunky.

Later on, those of us in the fabric department were told that many male customers would ask for the bolts high on the wall so that when we climbed the ladder they could view our legs and underpants—modestly cut bikinis. At that time, that thing, the t_ _ _g, had not yet been invented. One must remember to be grateful for this.

I recall hearing an older woman, "older," in her forties, complain that the music was too loud. "And the same music every day," she said. She always came in at exactly 10 a.m., I assumed right after her

THEY ALL STAND UP AND SING

psychoanalyst appointment, which apparently was not helping her. So
angry at the Rolling Stones.

The music certainly wasn't loud like the loud music of today.
People could hear each other speak. In present times many people can't
go to stores because of all the so-called music and the loudness of it.

The frenzy about these Marimekko dresses was such that when describing a fellow student, one might say, "She has ten Marimekko dresses,"
or "She has seventeen Marimekkos." One student was reputed to have
all of them.

The world was small. There was New York. There was Cambridge.
There was Out West, but I didn't know about that.

It was a few years after the Marimekko era had begun, in the apartment near Gramercy Park, that the film student was discussing
movies, or "films," as they were beginning to be called. She and an
intellectual roommate were talking about *Casablanca*. They were
friends and roommates of one of my older siblings. Without this crew
I wouldn't have known anything. I was a young idiot still thinking about Elvis Presley and the Beatles. Sometimes Nietzsche and
Pirandello. But ever since I'd heard Elvis Presley sing "Heartbreak
Hotel," I'd been hooked for life. I was a rock-and-roll fanatic but this
was a secret, even to me.

The *Casablanca* talk continued.

"Is that the one where they all stand up and sing?" I asked.

The roommates knew that I was not a complete ignoramus, as
evidenced by the fact that my favorite movie was *The Red Shoes*, which
I had first seen at age five. The film student laughed. She repeated my

question while shaking her head in disbelief. She had a large, thick puff-head of long brown hair that she set on giant pink plastic rollers every day or night to make it even straighter and bigger, as was the way of the time. Not "big" like the hair of the Ronettes or the Supremes—just thicker and more "bouffant," a word from the sixties, used over and over to describe Jacqueline Kennedy's hair, the describing starting with the inauguration. It's no fun to think about that day.

The film student would sit and read, or take a nap—needed from overwork—while her head was under the hood of the kind of portable home hair dryer almost every female person owned, except for me. I still had long, straight blond hair down to my waist the way I'd had during my whole life of being a girl.

I remember the film student's head of hair bobbing and floating all around as she shook her head and laughed when I asked the *Casablanca* question. Is naïveté funny or stupid? I couldn't be sure what she was thinking. The others laughed, too. Maybe they just kept me around for entertainment. They couldn't stop smiling. The film student later went on to win many awards and rose to the top of her profession, whatever that is.

It may be this: I was told at some point, maybe fifteen years later, that she had to go to the original Henri Bendel on West Fifty-seventh Street to buy a dress to wear to the Oscars.

"Why?" I asked. "Why does she have to go to that Hollywood thing?"

"She's nominated for one," was the answer.

After another few years, I heard that she'd won the award. I wouldn't have known since I never watched the dastardly proceedings.

By then, as a grown-up idiot, I was acquiring an understanding of misery, tragedy, and history. I became one of the many *Casablanca* fanatics and believed I had seen it more times than the writer-director whose first movie was *Take the Money and Run*. Unlike that person, I would never besmirch the film by using it for my own purposes.

I believed I understood every other part of *Casablanca*, too—the love story, the writing, the directing, the length and beauty of Ingrid Bergman's white gloves. And then there was her white sun hat. I always wondered how she kept her clothes so well pressed and clean and perfect looking, in her circumstances—in hot, hot Casablanca. This is never shown.

More time passed. A decade or two.

One night, when desperately flipping around the TV channels, I saw that *Casablanca* was on. It had started twenty minutes before. I said to my husband, "Oh, *Casablanca* is on. We missed the beginning." He ignored that and went into the kitchen to slice vegetables, his only job for dinner. I called him a couple of times and said, "What are you doing?" How long does it take to slice a few vegetables for two people? Even for a dinner of all vegetables. I didn't want to sit alone with the PAUSE button. One of the times I called, he said he was washing lettuce. He was not supposed to be washing lettuce. He doesn't know how.

But the third time he said, "What do you care what I'm doing?"

Then I became suspicious that he was doing something bad, like drinking cheap wine, alone, before dinner.

"Come in," I said. "You can't miss this part."

He walked a few steps and was standing in the doorway.

"Is it the part when they sing the Marseillaise?" he said.

"Yes, yes!" I said. I hit the PLAY button.

"I'm tired of that," he said in his coldhearted way. "Aren't you?"

"I'll never get tired of it," I said.

"Do you cry?" he asked without interest.

"Almost," I said as a lie. Because I was already crying. With him it was a case of: "Cry and you cry alone."

I thought about the fact that this movie and the history that inspired it—this all happened before we were born. It's then that I always realize that we're not very important. Especially when I hear Humphrey Bogart say, "What of it? I'm going to die in Casablanca. It's a good spot for it." The use of the word "spot"—the two words, "good spot"—I'm just no one compared with that sentence. Our parents were more clever before we existed. This leads to other dreadful thoughts.

I watched the rest of the movie while my husband went back into the kitchen to drink his wine.

After a while he brought out the vegetables and offered me some. I said, "No thanks."

"Just because I'm having a glass of wine you're mad at me?" he asked.

"It's just that you're drinking alone in the kitchen while they're singing the Marseillaise."

He ate his vegetables and brought his dishes back into the kitchen. Then he came out and sat down in the antique, upholstered man-chair. I looked over there a few times. His eyes were closed and he was falling asleep. He kept trying to wake himself and eventually succeeded. He got up and sat next to me on the couch where I was lying down and thinking about life on this planet. Especially the times of life shown in that movie.

The second part of the double feature was starting. It was *The African Queen*. He was pretending that he could stay awake and watch it.

*   *   *

I remembered something that happened before we were married. It had to do with the filmmaker from the apartment in Gramercy Park. It was a Sunday in November a few months after I met this pre-husband. He was watching football in my apartment—I never watched TV after childhood until I found out that there were old movies on Channel Thirteen. My former roommate had temporarily left her TV in the living room when she moved out.

The apartment was in a brownstone on the third floor. It was the back half of one floor and had a view of other backs of other brownstones—trees and little backyards. I no longer worked at Design Research. In a productive mania, I had started my real work on my first book of photographs.

I wanted to go out for a walk in the park. He said, "When the game is over at four." But at four, that thing happened where more minutes get added to the game. He said, "Ten more minutes." When I went back he said, "That was game-minutes, not regular minutes."

"How much in human time?" I asked.

Later on in our life together he told some friends that I referred to these sports-minutes as not being human time. They all laughed. Ha, ha, for the waste of those minutes of life.

He said he didn't know how much time.

I fell into a wretched state. I saw that I was with a twenty-four-year-old man who wanted to watch sports on TV all the time—it wasn't even baseball.

The weather was the damp, gray kind—not hot, humid, and sunny like the new Novembers of this century. I called the number of the next apartment where the film students and my sibling were living. The apartment had a few gigantic rooms with a view of the Hudson

River. The formerly laughing, serious filmmaker answered. I described my plight. She offered to go for a walk in Riverside Park. I said I'd see about the minutes and call her back.

I waited, but by the time the unreal-minutes were over, it was getting dark. I'd lost the desire to go walk with the football-watching man. In a hopeless state, I forgot about calling the filmmaker.

If I had called her, maybe we would have gone for the walk. Sometimes I'd meet her on the street, then, out on ugly upper Broadway. She was often with one filmmaker or another. Later, they'd ask if I wanted to be in this or that film they were putting together. I always declined, assuming the film would be serious and spooky, not funny or absurd. That was their preferred, intellectual inclination.

Maybe on that walk she would have said just one illuminating thing, like every psychiatrist-psychoanalyst I'd ever seen, but it would have made an impression, because she was a real person, and we knew each other as humans, not the way psychiatrists know you only when you're in their offices and are part of a game invented for their own interest and business. I'd have seen that the TV-watching was not just a phase of youth. I would have returned to the slew of arty, film-y, musician-men I used to know as boyfriend material.

Somewhere along the line I had unconsciously started a list in my head of the one true thing each psychiatrist had said.

One: This concerned some plants. In the early years of our marriage, every summer we left the hot and filthy city of Manhattan, which for some reason is still called the "greatest city in the world"— if it's so great, why are there gigantic black plastic bags of garbage piled high on every corner? Why doesn't David Letterman ask that question of the mayor when he appears on the show? We left the greatest city for Nantucket Island before Nantucket was ruined. My mother, at my parents' beach house, not that far from New York, had offered to take care of my plants.

When we arrived with the small collection of maidenhair ferns, my mother started her comments. I was on the screen porch when I heard her say about me: "She's putting her plants to bed." Then she laughed in a mean way. Although I later forgave my mother for everything she ever said, and felt only sadness and grief for her tragic life, I became enraged at the time. She meant that she wanted her three daughters to produce babies when they were only in their twenties and barely formed beings themselves. She wanted them to be putting these imagined babies to bed.

She'd often said "Children are overrated," and "Children ruin your life—you lose everything—your youth, your looks, your figure, your soul." We'd heard this all our lives, and she wanted us to join right in.

The next week when I told the psychiatrist about the plants, he said, "But then, why did you go there?"

I said, "To have the plants taken care of."

He said, "Some people care more about themselves than their plants."

I didn't think much of that at the time as he was as stupid and dangerous as are most in his profession. As Thomas Bernhard, the great Austrian writer and truth-teller, wrote: "Psychiatrists are the real demons of our age... constrained by neither law nor conscience."

In recent years, when I have had no mother and more and more plants and I have lived in a little house where the plants can stay outside in my absence and be watered by a plant-watering person, I have still been compelled to pack two gigantic pots of four-foot, pale peach-pink dahlias rather than be parted from them for the whole summer.

One summer, the local nursery-man helped me pack a five-foot, tree-form lavender heliotrope. It smelled like vanilla and the blossoms, made up of many tiny petals, were hanging from the little branches like bunches of grapes. As we filled the carton and stuffed it with paper and bubble wrap and plastic air-pillows, wasting an hour or two, the sentence of the psychiatrist popped into my mind, but I went on packing. All this, on the globally warmed-up, hot June days—and at night— ordering extra-large triple-walled cartons, spending hours looking at the bubble wrap from the Uline company's bubble-wrap choices on the Mac-whichever. This Mac-thing would be heating up and burning the tops of my thighs, leaving red burn marks, but I kept going.

There were large bubbles and small bubbles. There was stick-bubble with large bubbles, and stick-bubble with small bubbles. There was a patient customer-service person to discuss these bubble choices with. I heard myself saying, "Two rolls of small stick-bubbles, two rolls of regular large bubbles, one roll of large stick-bubbles." A lot of thinking had gone into the decision. This was before I'd read in a PETA magazine that glue is an animal by-product. And there is no eco–bubble wrap. The whole bubble-wrap thing is a vast eco-crime.

There was one other thing this psychiatrist had told me when I couldn't stop thinking about a number of minor incidents: "You remind me of the myth of '…'"—a name I couldn't ever remember.

It was about a boy who got stuck to anything he touched and couldn't get unstuck. Later, when I told other psychiatrists—and this is what psychotherapy is, you tell the same things over and over until you go mad and would be institutionalized if there were any good institutions left—they didn't know what the myth was, either. They are an even more ignorant crew now. I guess I could google the myth, but life is short.

*　　*　　*

Next on my list there was the great German psychoanalyst who saw patients for consultation and then sent them on to someone way beneath him in every way. He asked me, "Are you happily married?" I said, "Yes, but it's not too exciting."

He said, "Well, you had enough excitement with your mother." I guessed he meant a bad kind of excitement. In the frenzy of youth, or manic depression, I'd never thought of that myself. There was no time to explain about the football-watching. Basketball, too. Even hockey was watched.

The third of the one true things was the one concerning the shirt of the German woman-psychoanalyst-psychiatrist.

These were the days when my husband would ask me to buy wedding presents and such for people he worked with—people I'd never met and about whom I knew nothing. But trying to buy this one present seemed to be an easy task. There was a French store on Madison Avenue and Sixty-something Street, when Madison Avenue was still normal and wasn't that expensive. The store was a branch of a store in France for the middle and upper-middle classes.

The towels they sold were white, or light pink, the color of a certain rose—there was even a middle-aged American saleswoman whose name was Rose—or they were dusty blue, or moss green. The loops of the towels were long and sewn wide apart so that the towels were soft and floppy like nothing I'd seen before or after. I see them now in the linen closet and they look the same.

I thought of going to this store to buy some special pillowcases for the wedding gift. The cases were white Euro-squares. I'd seen them in a catalog sent by the store. This was in the era when people received one or two catalogs per week. The cases were plain with cotton lace appliquéd onto the border. When I asked the very young French sales-clerk for them, she said there was no such thing. I insisted that they were in a picture in the catalog. I asked to see the catalog. The pillow-cases were right there, on the cover.

She became more and more infuriated. I could see her mental temperature rising. She was in her twenties. There was no reason for this behavior. She wasn't at the hysterical stage of life but her almost-pretty face was getting redder and redder and soon she was shrieking at me in her French accent, "We don't have these!" This was before the condition, now called PMS, had been named, but in retrospect it could have been that, or the rage part of manic-depressive psychosis.

At last she went to look in the basement stockroom—it might have been Rose, the older, sensible American saleswoman, who prompted her to do so—and after a lot of barely muffled screaming and the sound of boxes crashing around, she stomped up the stairs and threw the requested white European square pillowcases in my direc-tion. Perhaps Rose took over the task of the white monogram, neces-sary for the newlyweds—I never remember that part—but by the time I left I had only a small fragment of my former self remaining.

Later I learned that the young couple for whom I'd purchased the pillowcases were divorced. The bride was a privileged, crazy bitch. The groom—a hapless nerd. When I heard about the matter of the divorce, I wondered about the fate of the white monogrammed cases because of the monogram. At which thrift shop might they be sitting on a shelf or thrown into a bin?

A year passed. When I dared to enter the store again, the French psycho-girl was still there. It was winter and people in the store were discussing the weather.

"So what of it?" the girl was screaming. "So it snowed a lot of feet in Buffalo!"—pronouncing the name of that city, "Boofalo"—"I am so sick of hearing this—nine feet of snow in Boofalo, fifteen feet in Boofalo—Boofalo! Who cares!"

These two incidents were what I described to the German doctor. "This has happened to me, too," she said. "I saw in a catalog from Saks Fifth Avenue a plain white shirt that was just what I needed." This was before the internet. People had to go all over the place to hunt for things. The places we went—the things we did. At least people burned a lot of calories walking miles all over, up and down, from top to bottom and around New York, even down to Canal Street. We wore regular shoes, too, sometimes heels, or, the irony is, shoes called buffalo sandals. They had three-inch wedges. I found some with vegan, non-leather straps, but the cork wedges were hard as cement. Kork-Ease, they were dishonestly named. No ease involved.

That same uncouth, good-looking boyfriend who didn't understand the Marimekko dresses once told me as part of his screwed-up life story that he'd spent his first year in college going downtown every day to every department store, searching for a maroon corduroy suit. He did this instead of studying. Sometimes he'd cut classes. His "therapist" had cured him of the behavior and "helped him put things into perspective."

I thought this suit-searching was an interesting and good thing, not something to be cured of. It was one of his only admirable qualities. The other was his love for the Beatles.

About fifteen years later, sometime in the eighties, he came to New York from the other coast, where he had become, of course, a psychotherapist. His therapist from the corduroy-suit era had been his "role model," he'd once said.

We arranged to meet on some unpleasant corner in Greenwich

Village. I immediately detected the odor of garlic. When he mentioned he'd had lunch at a Chinese restaurant and the dish he'd chosen was pork with garlic sauce, I figured: Well, he must not care about me anymore—I certainly almost gagged when he said the word "pork."

"So I went down there," the psychiatrist-analyst continued, "on Saturday morning—you know how little free time I have—and this stupid little salesclerk made no effort to find out where the shirt was located in the store. I had brought the catalog, and she refused to look for it, and argued that she couldn't find out if they had it at all."

I pictured the German doctor, in her mid- or late sixties, with her gray hair cut in long bangs in a modified, less-severe Buster Brown style—plain, but not at all ridiculous or undignified. She was an obviously educated woman from a European culture. I imagined her trudging down to Saks Fifth Avenue from her simple yet perfectly situated apartment building in the upper East Sixties between Central Park and Madison Avenue. She probably walked—in sensible shoes, not sneakers. This was still before sneakers for walking. Or maybe she took the Fifth Avenue bus—or even a taxi down to Forty-eighth Street, if she was in a hurry. And then to encounter this attitude, as she put it, this rudeness and stupidity. To say nothing of going into any department store on Saturday.

I felt badly for her because at the time I was so young that most salesclerks were relatively nice to me, but she was at that age where clerks like that one didn't bother with her. As she told the story I could see she was still angry. She was looking at me as if she were talking to a friend, not a patient.

"I knew she was just a rude, ignorant clerk and it was no reflection on me. I was annoyed, but why should you feel so badly if a neurotic clerk behaves this way to you about some pillowcases?"

The answer was a long story, the telling of which had never helped with the increasingly uncivilized behavior in our society.

The last on the list of psychiatrists was a colleague of the German woman's—possibly more eminent. Kind and even-tempered, and even a friend of Anne Freud's. She also did consultations and the visit was one of those. This consulting-thing later became just a racket for others—to help younger, incompetent trainees in the field—those who needed patients.

I was leaving her spartan but pleasant-enough office, the kind with an ordinary plant here and there. She was older than the other woman—maybe eighty, her hair was white, and she wore a plain skirt and blouse. The wood floors weren't well finished—I made a note, mental or psychological, to tell our friend, the artist floor-man, about them. "Probably old cheap oak with polyurethane," I figured he'd guess. That was another thing to figure out years later—your work is more important than your floors. Maybe floors didn't need to be tung-oiled by hand-rubbing, over and over, time after time with a cloth. Or maybe the floors really are important.

A UPS man with a heavy box was standing outside when the doctor opened the door to let me go out. This doctor was a tiny German analyst and she asked in her kind, polite way: "Could you please put it inside the door?" He did so, while shooting an angry, disrespectful glance in her direction—this was before crystal meth, before people were murdered for asking a serviceman to do something—but she didn't even notice his face.

I believed I'd once come close to being killed by a Verizon man in Nantucket. They had missed three appointments and he was a few hours late when he finally appeared. When I questioned him about this situation, he flew into a wild rage, even growled out the sound of the rage, and made two fists in the air—almost screaming the way I have done, not the fists-in-the-air part but the scream—until I felt a pressure in my chest and thought of the book *Anger Kills*, kills the person who feels it, and thought that this kind of anger might bring on a heart attack or stroke, even though I was young and my vegan-powered blood pressure was low and my lipid panel just perfect.

At one time, when we first went to Nantucket, I used to go to the all-night supermarket searching for Ball Jelly Jars. This was during the era when I still had the desire and psychic energy to pick beach plums and make jelly—hours of picking and separating and cleaning—hanging a cheesecloth bag of berries from the faucet to get every last drop of juice to drip out into a pot, and then boiling the juice for hours with apple juice and no sugar.

It was a late-night visit to the supermarket then called Finast, the spelling of which my cousin's precocious little boy misunderstood and laughed at with great fun every time he heard the name. "Fine Ass, how could that be the name? Like, 'She's sure got a fine ass!'" No matter how it was explained to the five-year-old boy he couldn't get it, or pretended he couldn't. My cousin later proudly told me that the child had not invented the commentary himself, but had learned it from the master, his father.

In any case, on this night a most cheerful and helpful customer-service woman told me where the jars were—high up above the shelves, where they couldn't be reached. She said she knew the shelf so well because her husband made beach-plum jelly. Then she said he made every kind of jelly—wild grape, rosehip, even low-bush blueberry, a notoriously difficult find. He knew the blueberry patches all over the island. It turned out that he knew where every kind of berry and all the beach plums were hidden. One thing he didn't do was cut open each rosehip and remove the seeds with a demitasse spoon, as I did after reading an old recipe: "Scoop out all the seeds."

"He just boils them whole," she said. "He's a man."

When I asked how he knew where all the secret berries were, she said, "He works for the cable company. He sees them on the way to his jobs." I asked when he had time to pick them. She said, "Then. Whenever he sees them on the way to a job."

So now you know why you wait all day for the Cablevision man.

One year, recently, I was driving in the blazing heat past Finast— now a Stop & Shop, on Nantucket—on the way to the health-food store. A pedestrian crosswalk had been painted onto the road after the population and development boom of the eighties and nineties. A stocky woman with short red hair—she was wearing blue jeans and a plaid shirt in this heat, and no sunglasses—this woman dashed out into the crosswalk. I used my vegan-mesh-clog-shoed foot to hit the brakes, and she stood there and raised her fists while yelling and pointing at the small, four-foot, faded-outline area. This area does not mean that people should rush out into it without first looking to see whether cars are right there. As we both tried to recover, I saw that she was the formerly calm and pleasant customer-service clerk and wife of the jelly-making Cablevision man.

The tiny psychiatrist-analyst was looking at the box and still smiling as the UPS man left. That is when I realized, it's not me, it's them— the angry people are angry before they even meet you. I learned this from watching the doctor—she didn't have to say a word. The UPS man had acted as if she was just some old lady. I bet he'd never heard of the members of the Freud family or the history of all that. Of course not, why would he?

There was another thing I'd learned from this doctor, although she wasn't a cognitive therapist—this therapy probably hadn't been named yet—she'd said to me, "I wouldn't think you were twenty-seven—you look younger." And I said, "Oh, no, I look older. Some days I think I look forty." As if that was really old. A cruel joke, when I review it.

"Well, on certain days we all look older or younger," she said.

Now, that had never occurred to me.

Last year we were in a restaurant with a couple. They were both artists and the woman-artist and I were discussing the tight Lycra clothing available and worn in present times. She said she'd seen a mourner wearing a tight Lycra miniskirt at a memorial service. I myself had seen on the news that one of Caroline Kennedy's daughters had worn a very short, pleated miniskirt to the funeral service of Jacqueline Kennedy at Arlington National Cemetery.

At the time I was too grief-stricken to dwell on the subject. But at least it shocked me out of the reality of the moment, and distracted me from the memory of all those films and photographs of the many tragedies, and from all the photographs of Jacqueline Kennedy burned into my mind forever. Especially the one on the plane, when they got her to stand there, still in her blood-drenched, Chanel-pink suit while the other guy was sworn in. The look on her face—if only I could get it out of my mind.

*   *   *

We quickly remembered our Marimekko dresses.

We asked each other whether we still had them. We both said, "Of course."

I thought I saw some form of despair as I was looking at her. She'd been brought up by *Mayflower*-descended parents and wasn't about to burst into tears. I'd been crying since 1963 and much more so in the last decades.

We discussed what to do with the Marimekkos. She said she was thinking of cutting them up and using the fabric for some of her work.

"Oh, don't cut them up," I said. "They're already art."

"They are," she said, as if she'd never thought of that before. Or as if she had, but didn't care.

After trying to figure out what we could do, I said, "I think we should frame them. They're small enough."

She looked into my eyes and I looked into hers. They were a beautiful blue color but I could see beyond them into what she was thinking: What will become of our Marimekkos?

A psychiatrist once asked me, "Are you a mind reader?" Because I could tell what people were thinking.

"No, I'm a face reader," I said. "And a voice reader."

Most people are, in varying degrees. Why didn't he know that?

Somehow we got onto the subject of the conspiracy theories. The husband was a ferocious, left-wing artist. His paintings had such extreme social content that he was not as well known as he deserved to be. He and his wife lived near Canal Street. As a young man, he'd had stationery printed with a picture of his face and the caption: *Robert Cenedella, Unknown Artist*. He was on my list of the three funniest men in the world.

But as for the Three Conspiracies, they were:

1. The attack on the World Trade Center—did Bush and his gang of four, or five, or however many evil ones he had around him— did they know and even collude with the terrorists?

2. The moon landing—was it fake or real?

3. Last—but really first, just further back in time—the assassination of President Kennedy.

We asked each other which conspiracy theories we believed were real conspiracies. The artist believed they were all conspiracies. His wife and I agreed on the first and third. My husband believed only Kennedy.

Then, as a form of comic relief, the artist-husband reminded us about the letter he'd received in the sixties from Nixon's secretary, Rose Mary Woods. The artist had created a wooden dartboard with Nixon's face on it and sent this to Nixon at his campaign office. In return he received a form thank-you letter with a signature from Rose Mary Woods.

He opened his art-messenger bag and took out a copy of the letter. The original had been framed and hung in his studio. Here's the copy:

N

NIXON FOR PRESIDENT COMMITTEE,
P. O. BOX 1968, TIMES SQUARE STATION,
NEW YORK, NEW YORK 10036
PHONE (212) 661-6400

May 2, 1968

Mr. Robert Cenedella
Oggi Products, Inc.
61 E. 11th Street
New York, N. Y. 10003

Dear Mr. Cenedella:

Your letter of April 17 has arrived in Mr.
Nixon's absence from New York. I know he will
appreciate your courtesy in requesting a better
picture of him for use in your dart board project.

I am enclosing a picture which I believe
compares more favorably with the picture of Mayor
Lindsay which you forwarded.

Mr. Nixon, I know, would want me to extend
his best wishes to you.

Sincerely,

Rose Mary Woods
Executive Secretary
to Mr. Nixon

We passed the letter around and we laughed. We laughed hard. We laughed more. But it was a different kind of laughter—laughter with sadness behind it. It was a new kind of laughing and not that much fun.

We started talking about the clothes of former and present White House secretaries and presidents' wives. We don't want to say one bad thing about Michelle Obama, but why did she wear a diamond necklace in broad daylight on Inauguration Day? Why this, why that— many questions about her advisers. Hillary's, too, but her case was not as urgent anymore.

Then we moved on—to my favorite attire, the kind of clothes worn in *The Best Years of Our Lives* by Wilma, the fiancée of Homer Parrish, who was played by Harold Russell, a real soldier in World War II whose wounds really had caused the amputation of both his hands and forearms, leaving him with metal hooks for replacements. Not an actor, but as most everyone knows, he played himself in this part.

In the movie, Wilma wore pleated skirts, plain shirts, and little sweaters from the 1945 era, from before I was born, but the kind I still have. Because her part was acted with such heart-wrenching purity, goodness, and inner beauty radiating from every expression, I immediately looked, I'm ashamed to say, on IMDb, to find out who the actress was and what had become of her.

This is what: in spite of William Wyler's objections, she'd married his brother, Robert Wyler, disappeared from movies, and had a long happy marriage until the cruel and early end to her life at age forty-six. Her name was listed in the credits as Cathy O'Donnell, but her real, and better, name was Ann Steely. It probably sounded too film-noir for her pure inner light and beauty.

Other than this actress, only Teresa Wright had qualities of such purity and goodness. I read on IMDb that *The Best Years of Our Lives* was a big-cry movie, even though it had been unrealistically cheered up in scenes here and there.

Eventually we got around to talking about clothes in other old movies from the 1940s. We got to Ingrid Bergman's clothes. Then we got to *Casablanca*. We agreed about those, too. We didn't like a few wardrobe items from *Notorious*.

I started thinking about *Casablanca* again. Then I started thinking about the big room in that apartment near Gramercy Park and the laughing that went on there. And I was remembering the moment when I saw that *The African Queen* was better than I'd first realized. I was thinking about being very young and not knowing much about anything. And I thought that was a better time, when I had no understanding of *Casablanca*.

BENJAMIN BUCKS

nonfiction by JENNIE ERIN SMITH

BENJAMIN BUCKS'S FATHER was a lapsed Mormon from Lehi, Utah, who moved to Zurich in the 1970s along with a small collection of milk snakes and king snakes that he tucked into rolled-up socks in his luggage. The senior Bucks was a biochemist, and it seemed natural that Benjamin, a pretty, precocious, fluffy-haired youth who loved reptiles as much as his father did, would endeavor to become a man of science himself.* But just a few months after penning his first and only scientific article—"Further contributions to the knowledge of *Bradypodion uthmoelleri* (Müller, 1938) from Tanzania," for the German herpetology journal *Salamandra*—Benjamin bought a plane ticket and took off for Uganda, his parents unable or unwilling to stop him. It was 1994, and Bucks was sixteen.

---

* Bucks's name, and the names of some of his associates, have been changed.

This was not Bucks's first African trip; he'd gone on safari almost annually with one parent or another since the age of seven, and had once smuggled a chameleon—the same *Bradypodion uthmoelleri* he'd written about—back to Zurich using the sock-stuffing technique his father had taught him. He arrived at Entebbe airport in the fall of '94 with a vague idea that he would make a living exporting reptiles. At his hostel outside Kampala, though, he wound up in conversation with a former Tutsi rebel in the Rwandan Patriotic Front, and he decided on the spot to visit Rwanda.

Bucks took a bus across the border, not thinking anything could go wrong until he saw the shot-up walls and burnt, abandoned houses of Kigali. He hid in a hotel until the next day, when he managed to make it to the American embassy. "I'd like to go see some gorillas," he told the staff, and they told him to leave immediately. After that he ran into an Austrian relief worker who told him, with more patience, that he couldn't go see the gorillas because the forests were mined and he would be blown up.

Two years later American reptile dealers started receiving mysterious, crude price lists hand-scribbled on stationery from Kenyan hotels. They didn't know Bucks was a teenager; they didn't know anything about him except that he was selling such rare and seldom-offered snakes as *Atheris ceratophora*, a little horned viper from a small range in Tanzania. Bucks's snakes made it out thanks to an arrangement he'd struck with the Kenyan agricultural ministry. That ministry didn't have the authority to approve snake exports—only the wildlife service did—but American and European customs inspectors didn't necessarily know that.

Bucks, by then a tall, blond young man with a nicely chiseled jaw, slept in an apartment behind a Mombasa nightclub where in the wee hours the bouncers tied petty thieves to chairs and beat them for stealing empty beer bottles. After losing his virginity to a Kenyan woman ten years his senior who refereed boxing matches, he began keeping a computer spreadsheet of the names, ages, and "habitats" of his partners, making sure to list what he paid in exchange for sex— two eggs and a tomato in one case, a can of coke in another. He built and lost three businesses, including a doomed venture to smuggle hippopotamus teeth to Hong Kong. Just as his sex diary was getting epic, Kenyan officials confiscated Bucks's computer and put him on a plane to Switzerland.

Bucks returned to Kenya in short order. He met a barmaid who became pregnant and left with him for Uganda, where they were soon estranged. For a while afterward he moved between that country and Kenya, once again attracting scrutiny for exporting protected snakes: his new specialties were *Bitis worthingtoni* and *Bitis parviocula*, highland adders from Kenya and Ethiopia. On New Year's Eve 2005, Bucks was arrested and thrown into a Kenyan jail. The official charge was something about illegal frogs in one of his terrariums, but Kenya now had a long list of grievances against him, as did Uganda and Ethiopia.

Bucks slept on the concrete floor of his cell for four nights before they let him out. This wouldn't have been so terrible except for the fact that two weeks earlier, Bucks's night bus from Kampala had crashed, breaking several of his vertebrae. But nine of his fellow passengers had died, so Bucks felt relatively lucky.

He was thinking about giving up Africa for good when, that March, he visited his brother in Zurich. When he tried to return, Kenya blocked his reentry.

Bucks managed to return to East Africa a few months later. I met him on the tarmac at Entebbe airport in the fall of 2006, while working on a book about reptile smugglers; it was the second time I'd seen him in three years. His hair was cropped and he wore camouflage pants, and he looked very handsome except for one long, chipped canine that extended from his mouth like a lateral fang. It was the type of thing, he said, that would have caused him enough embarrassment in Switzerland that he wouldn't have ventured out; in Uganda he barely gave it any thought.

It was Bucks's dual citizenship that had helped him slide back in. In previous years, Bucks had used his passports interchangeably—it seemed that it was his E.U. passport that had set off the most recent alarm. Thus, during his sojourn in Switzerland, Bucks had claimed to have lost his American passport, and received a clean one—no stamps—from the American embassy. Now it bore a fresh Ugandan visa.

At Bucks's side, at the airport, stood a good friend of his whom he called Captain. Captain was three decades older and a foot shorter than Bucks; he looked like the late King Hussein of Jordan, smelled very boozy, and held a plastic flask of Ugandan *waragi*, a local rotgut made from bananas. Captain smiled steadily, like a friendly demon. His teeth were black and decayed, with some shards of incisor bound together with gold.

The two were very close. It was Captain who'd pulled an unconscious Bucks out of the wrecked bus the previous winter, and Captain who, Bucks said, had gotten him started in a new business after the reptile-smuggling flamed out. Kenyan and Ethiopian wildlife officials were still on the lookout for him; if he was to stay in Africa, he needed a new line of work.

Bucks had written me months before about Captain, so that I would know what to expect.

There is this Captain as we all call him. He is a Pakistani who was trained under Ghadaffi in Libya in the early 1980s. He came to Uganda as a pilot supplying the NRM (National Resistance Movement) which is Pres. Museveni's party with weaponry to oust Milton Obote. Anyhow he has been on death row for conspiracy in the later 80s and managed to escape only by unfortunately needing to kill his warden who was a very friendly young guy who even brought him food from home. He was in for murder 2 years ago again. He was cheated by an Italian in Uganda for like $10,000 and a couple days later the Italian was found on the side of the road with his dick cut off and in his mouth and his eyes pierced out. The police checked his phone and checked the last received calls. Second last was Captain. So prime suspect. The facts are that 3 months later he was out and the Italian officially committed suicide ;-) In Uganda THE SHIT happens. Anyways he is a really good guy...

It was a Monday night, and when we left the airport we headed for a club. "The kind of place with loud music and a lot of whores," Bucks explained on the way.

The club comprised a giant courtyard with a dance floor and a tiki island in the middle. It was the kind of place that attracted foreign men, mostly white and up to no good: A white man in Africa was up to a lot of good or absolutely no good, Bucks said. You were Médecins Sans Frontières or you were a Russian cocaine smuggler with tattoos all over your forearms and your own plane.

"Captain!" a woman yelled when we walked in, beckoning with one long, manicured finger. Her dress was sheer black gauze, her bare breasts visible beneath. Captain grabbed one, then grumbled.

"He's been fucking her a few weeks," Bucks said, and ordered himself a warm beer, a habit he'd developed over the years.

Behind Bucks stood a girl of about twenty in a tracksuit, eyeing

Captain and looking very mad. When the woman in the gauze dress noticed this she squatted, for some reason, and turned up two middle fingers at her challenger. The girl in the tracksuit lunged. Bucks tried, unsuccessfully, to direct the fight away from us. Captain leaned back and laughed, arms wide, half ecstatic from all the attention. Then he hunched over to cough up a lung.

By the time Bucks settled on a girl for himself, a third seething woman had come to the bar to stare Captain down. "I have a baby with him," she said. "And he won't even buy me a beer!"

"Does she really?" Bucks asked Captain.

Captain shrugged. "Maybe," he conceded.

Bucks shook his head. Nobody bought her a beer.

Outside the bar, the earthen pockmarked streets of Kampala were dark—scheduled blackouts limited power to alternate days, since the whole country faced electricity shortages. Only gas stations were consistently lit at night, and grasshoppers swarmed the lamps. Women swung large nets over their heads, catching all that they could. They would tear off the insects' legs, fry them, and sell them in little grease-stained paper bags the next morning. Bucks sometimes ate the bugs for breakfast.

For the last few months he'd been living with the sister of the Ugandan woman he'd had a child with a few years earlier. She was fourteen years old and hadn't been in school for some time. They had a half-furnished apartment on a street clogged with ducks, chickens, and burning garbage. The girl cared for Bucks's daughter there; her other duties included scratching Bucks's head on demand and washing his shirts. In exchange for these services, he fed her.

Bucks's building alone sustained a small village of laundry boys and housemaids, young women who hacked their hair short and wore ill-fitting dresses and had the inscrutable faces of the impossibly poor. In a tiny shack by the door lived a middle-aged security guard and his teenage companion, whom I'd find nursing their baby in the building's dark stairwell. The lock on Bucks's apartment would have befitted a bank.

Inside, the place was devoid of animals save for a scorpion in a tank and two frogs in a jar by the window. Bucks was trying to ease reptiles and amphibians out of his life, but he could not completely do it. His new business, he said, helped keep his mind off them.

The morning after my arrival, Bucks and I collected Captain from an apartment down the hall, where we found him sitting at his dining-room table having his morning waragi. This time it came in a little plastic packet, which he cut with scissors and emptied into a glass. Bucks had under his arm a copy of *National Geographic*. He didn't want to wait for Captain to finish his drink. They were late for a meeting.

Bucks and Captain did not travel far for meetings; this one was at a grocery-cum-outdoor-café a hundred feet from their apartment building. From its aluminum roof came the sound of scurrying animals, and seated in plastic chairs were three men—two in suits, and one in a tracksuit.

Bucks began. "All right," he said. "I'm going to show you the samples." He pulled from his *National Geographic* a sheet of uncut fifty-dollar bills and another sheet of fives. Bucks passed them around. Flies gathered in my glass of juice while the men rubbed and regarded the money. Then Bucks demanded it back.

The currency came from Switzerland and was available in blocks of $1 million, he said, for 40 percent of face value. A long discussion on bank transfers ensued. One of the suits, who spoke with a refined English accent, turned out to be a banker. The other was a lawyer.

I sat next to Captain, who wasn't paying attention. He stared alternately at the waitress and at me. "This is all bullshit," he would slur in my ear, before making a gurgling, semi-obscene outburst to the table. Captain had been deteriorating, mentally and physically, Bucks had told me, and was becoming something of a hindrance.

When the suits departed twenty minutes later—looking happy— Bucks and Captain remained, as did the tracksuit man, a very big and very fit Nigerian. The Nigerian had quietly deferred to Bucks during the meeting, but now took over, speaking in a theatrically deliberate baritone. From mid-morning he drank waragi from those same little plastic packets Captain used. Unlike Captain, he never seemed drunk. People called him the Lion, since he liked to remind them that he ate like a lion, hunting ruthlessly but sharing the kill. His body gave off an aroma detectable for yards. It was his natural smell, but it was sort of like incense, and it suited so lordly a man to have a trailing scent.

Bucks and the Lion conferred briefly about laser-cutting machinery. The machines would have to come from South Africa, the Lion explained, and would cost three hundred thousand dollars. Bucks listened attentively, then countered by insisting that the machines would come from Germany.

It took me a while to figure out that the machines were a fiction, part of the narrative with which they would further their con. It was all a con. Bucks's currency sheets were merely uncut legal tender, readily available as souvenirs from the U.S. Bureau of Engraving and Printing; he was passing them off as splendid counterfeits. The bankers who had been with us a moment ago were the *mugus*, the name that Nigerians called their marks. The Lion specialized in currency scams like this one—baroque, multinational, executed by a team of Europeans and Africans in concert. Some of the scams the Lion ran were already getting worn out, like the black-dollars trick; the UN, according to this story, dyed currency black for security in transit, and the mugu would be persuaded to invest in a chemical that removed the pigment. The Lion still ran the black dollars once in a while, if a mugu seemed ripe for it, but he was eager for newer things.

The Lion was a very good scammer, famous for stringing mugus along. Once a man was invested by even just a few hundred dollars, he said, that man would be overcome by a kind of tunnel vision, and after that he could be picked clean in stages. "It is better for the hungry man never to have tasted food, than to have a little taste," was a Lion maxim. The Lion was full of maxims and pronouncements. He was also, Bucks said, a born-again Christian who did not do business or even answer his phone on Sundays.

Bucks had only recently joined the company, by introduction of Captain—Captain and the Lion had known each other for years. But I could see that the Lion favored Bucks: Bucks had ideas. This real-fake-currency scam was Bucks's. The Lion now talked about taking it to Dubai.

Bucks believed that his luck as a scammer would be as dispropor-tionately good as his luck as a reptile smuggler had been bad. "The reptiles I did out of passion," he said, and passion had its pitfalls. He was firmly on the Kenyan government's radar now, blacklisted among the ivory and rhino-horn and hippo-tooth poachers, which irked him, since he didn't feel he deserved to be classed with such scum. At this point his days mostly consisted of meetings with Captain and fellow members of the Lion's organization.

One afternoon Bucks and Captain met with a middle-aged German who smoked menthol cigarettes constantly without inhal-ing. "I do it for the pleasure," the German said. He was gently spoken, with eyes that scanned about like a nervous rodent's, and his teeth were almost as bad as Captain's. The German, named Burkhard, was an old friend of Bucks's, a trained electrician who had moved to Kenya for reasons that had more to do with his sexual tastes than anything else. Burkhard liked his girlfriends young, no older than fourteen or fifteen. When he couldn't find work as an electrician, he smuggled drugs from Brazil to Africa and then sometimes on to Europe. For years Burkhard had lived in Mombasa without incident, but Kenya, as Bucks had recently learned, was purging itself of white opportunists. Burkhard had found himself suddenly among the purged.

He'd crossed the Kenya-Uganda border by bicycle, finding employment with Bucks and Captain and the Lion, supplying them with the foreign SIM cards they needed to appear to be calling from Switzerland or Germany, as their scams sometimes required. Burkhard also acted as company bookkeeper, tracking everyone's activities—the clean phone numbers, the dirty phone numbers, who'd been seen with whom—in a logbook. For this he employed German words written with Cyrillic letters. The Cyrillic-German was a code that a junior FBI clerk would have cracked over half a cup of coffee, but Burkhard was quite confident that the Ugandan authorities would be too daunted to bother.

Burkhard's first African girlfriend had died of AIDS. His neighbors accused him of sorcery when he kept her coffin aboveground, right next to his house, for days—he was waiting for her mother to arrive from the countryside before burying her, he told them, but they refused to believe it. Eventually he buried the girlfriend and took up with a series of ever-younger girls, until he was imprisoned in Kenya, Bucks said, for "defilement." Now he was broke and stuck in Uganda, where he slept in a seven-dollar-a-night hotel with no hot water. Impressively, he had already managed to get himself a Ugandan girlfriend, a fifteen-year-old who ate only chicken and chips, the national fast food. She looked, with her matted hair and glum expression, like she'd arrived on a slow bus from a very remote village. She'd had sex with Captain once, but everyone kept that a secret from Burkhard. For now, while Burkhard scratched up some money, it was Bucks who kept her in chicken and chips.

During one of their interminable daily meetings, Burkhard and Bucks sent the girl, along with Bucks's child and her fourteen-year-old aunt, to an amusement park. Once they were gone, Burkhard sifted through his SIM cards and smoked while Bucks wandered over to an internet café across the street. Captain disappeared into a seamstress's shop. The seamstress, it turned out, was a part-time prostitute. Half an hour later, when Captain sat back down, I noticed that his right shoulder protruded strangely.

Captain explained. Once upon a time, he had flown for a major American carrier, but he'd been dismissed. "We need caring pilots, not daring pilots," his bosses told him. So Captain bought two planes in the Gambia and started a business flying charters. On an early-morning flight from Dakar to a Club Med resort on the coast, Captain crashed. Thirty-one of Captain's passengers, all of them French tourists, were killed. He severed a shoulder muscle in that accident, and had to have a steel plate put in his chest. Sometimes the plate still bothered him, he said.

The story, as Captain told it, was much longer, sadder, and rigorous in a way that suggested he'd perfected it over the years. He emphasized certain mitigating details, such as weather information that had failed to arrive, and a mistake made by the tower. When he was done talking he stared soberly out at the street.

After the crash Captain returned to flying around weapons and killing people, a better job for daring pilots.

*   *   *

I came down with malaria. Captain, the daring pilot and murderer, was the only one who noticed my symptoms—he pitied me enough to take me to the hospital, where I paid five dollars for tests and another five dollars for medicine. Bucks was by then deeply involved in the planning of a con involving the Lion, Burkhard, and a mugu from Dubai, scouted for the Lion by his contacts in London. "You thought you would have to go to Dubai," the Lion told Bucks, "but I have brought Dubai to you."

Since Bucks was preoccupied, and his hospitality had been a little lacking all along anyway, I checked into a lakeside resort to recover.

Lake Victoria had sunk by more than six feet in the previous eight years, turning the lakefront half of the resort—with its boat slips and careful landscaping—into an amorphous swamp. It gave off an overwhelming stench in the sun and burst into a deafening concert of frog calls at night. Bucks showed up there the second morning of my stay, dressed as a "legitimate Swiss businessman," as he described himself, in an Oxford shirt, khakis, and a wedding ring. His plan was to sell the mugu from Dubai some black dollars. Coincidentally, the mugu had just checked in to my hotel, so the control center of the operation would, it seemed, be my sick room.

The setup was decided: Burkhard would play a courier from Germany, newly arrived with the black dollars. He would check in to the hotel himself as part of the setup, and meet with the mugu first, over drinks at the bar. After Burkhard collected the money, the scam would be turned over to Bucks, the legitimate Swiss businessman and vendor of the magic pigment-removing chemicals. The Lion would supervise things from a distance.

It was 6 p.m. now. The scam would commence in an hour.

The Lion went home for dinner, promising to check in later. I was feeling a little better, so Bucks and I went for a walk. Bucks wanted to hunt some of the reed frogs that were making such a racket in the hotel swamp, and for a while we did so, with a flashlight Bucks had brought along, but by 8 p.m. a terrible nervousness had overcome him. He suddenly felt he could not trust Burkhard. Burkhard was desperate and broke—he would take the mugu's down payment and escape with it, Bucks just knew it. He might be tempted to do the same thing himself, he realized.

"First the German, then the frogs," Bucks said.

Bucks called Burkhard's cell phone, but it was turned off. He cursed himself. Why hadn't he thought to spy on Burkhard at the restaurant? We stopped by the restaurant—no Burkhard, no mugu. Bucks was too scared to call the Lion with his suspicions. The Lion, he was sure, would blame him.

At 10 p.m., Burkhard called back. The mugu had been tired when he arrived, so Burkhard had met with him in his room. The mugu could only manage two thousand dollars for a down payment, it turned out, and that wouldn't be until the next morning.

By then the mugu had disappeared.

The Lion wasn't all that mad about the lost mugu; it happened. Within a week he had produced at least four new marks for his team, including a high-ranking bureaucrat in Uganda's water ministry.

The company converged at an Ethiopian restaurant in Kampala to discuss their progress with the water minister. It was the Lion; Burkhard; two Somalians; a good-looking Englishman named Andy; Bucks and his little daughter, whose caretaker had briefly run off after Bucks whacked her across the face; and me. I had gotten over my malaria. Captain was home feeling wheezy and sick, which was happening a lot lately.

The Lion was not feeling well, either. He had on the table a little box of medicine called Vermex.

"Worms," he explained.

The scam currently under way was referred to as the "ball-bearings scam." It required three con artists—two white men, to pose as foreign businessmen, and one African. The first white guy poses as the buyer of a special type of ball bearing needed, supposedly, for an oil-exploration project in the Sudan. His local accomplice approaches the mugu and says, "I know a guy who wants these special bearings—he'll pay seventeen hundred dollars apiece for them. I think I know where to get some for three hundred." He introduces the mugu to the buyer. The buyer agrees to buy as many ball bearings as the mugu can get, at seventeen hundred dollars apiece.

The local then puts the mugu in touch with the seller of the bearings, who is played by the other white guy. The bearings, the white seller confirms, are three hundred dollars apiece. He produces them. The mugu-middleman buys as many of the three-hundred-dollar bearings as he can afford, thinking he's about to make a fourteen-hundred-dollar profit on each one. Then the buyer and seller disappear.

This time the buyer was being played by the Englishman, Andy. Burkhard was playing the seller. The "local" was one of the two Somalians at the table, Isaac, who had just come from a meeting with Andy and the mugu. Isaac was protesting that he would have to move now, because the mugu had seen where he lived. The Lion, he was hinting, should give him extra money because of this.

Andy, on the other hand, was exuberant. He'd picked a fight with Isaac at the meeting, he told us, just to make things look less conspiratorial. When he recounted how he'd called the Somalian a "fucking Dinka," the whole table erupted with laughter, the Lion the hardest.

Andy told me he'd never been a criminal until now. In the late

1970s he'd married a Ugandan fashion model, and they'd moved to Kampala from London. Now their kids were about to enter college, and money had become a little tight. He loved this work. "I was an actor in college—a poor one," he said. The con artistry brought back the thrill of the stage.

The Lion returned to his agenda—the state of the mugu. "Can he buy eight but only pay for four today?" he started in. "No, okay. Can he buy six and pay for four?"

While the Lion talked, Burkhard hoisted Bucks's young daughter onto his knee. Bucks gave him a hard look.

Just then a stream of young men in white shirts and black pants entered the restaurant. All but a few were white; a disproportionate number were blond. More followed, dozens of them, all milling around seeking seats.

Mormons! The rest of the table looked mildly annoyed at this invasion, but Bucks was excited. He stood.

"Any of you guys from Lehi?" he called out.

The Lion and his teammates looked up, incredulous. They did not know, and could not bring themselves to believe, that Benjamin Bucks was a Mormon.

Captain died two weeks after I left. The morning it happened, Bucks ran into Captain and Burkhard eating breakfast at the café near their apartment building; all three planned to go elsewhere that afternoon, for another meeting, but Captain said he needed to lie down first, so Bucks ran an errand. When he returned, Captain's roommates told him that Captain had begun to have trouble breathing, and that they had taken him to the hospital. Captain was dead by the time Bucks found him there, his body still warm.

Bucks emailed to say how sad he was. *Captain was like a father and a brother to me,* he wrote. He wanted to know if I could look up Captain's crash in Senegal, back in 1992. He had always been curious about it.

I did find a brief report. There was no mention of weather, or any message from the tower. The pilot had simply mistaken the lights of a hotel for the airstrip. Survivors remembered him announcing that they would be landing in five minutes; seconds later, they crashed.

This scenario made more sense to Bucks than Captain's own tortured account. *I pretty much can imagine him aiming for the hotel thinking it's the runway. He used to get really confused on waragi even in Kampala,* Bucks wrote. Club Med's owners were charged with criminal negligence in the affair, but Captain, somehow, was not.

On the fourth day after his death, Captain's autopsy results came back. Bucks, Burkhard, and the Lion went to look at them, and to collect his body for burial. They thought they knew Captain's real name—it was Sajjad Heider Soorie, he'd told them, or perhaps Sorie—but none of them had been able to find his family. His body was a painful sight, having decomposed rapidly in the unrefrigerated morgue.

The autopsy stated that Captain had died of a massive brain aneurysm. It made no mention of any steel plate in Captain's chest. Bucks asked about it. It didn't exist, he was told.

Captain's neighbors in the building, meanwhile, decided that Bucks had poisoned Captain, and reported as much to the police. Bucks managed to persuade them that he had done no such thing, but the neighbors persisted in their talk.

The police wouldn't leave Bucks alone. Even the Lion, whom the police relied on for bribes, couldn't keep them at bay. Officers kept coming by, often when Bucks wasn't home, alleging that they were continuing to investigate the poisoning rumors. *I can only think that they are some fucking asshole Cops who think they can lock me up claiming that I am a suspect of having murdered Captain in order to extort money from me,* Bucks wrote to me. He wasn't hanging around Kampala to find out.

The Lion sent Bucks to Hong Kong, to embark on a black-dollars scam there; then on to Dubai, and the Philippines. Within months he was back in Switzerland, living at his brother's. His daughter and her aunt were still in Kampala, subsisting on whatever money Bucks could send—an arrangement that would persist indefinitely.

Bucks's older brother, an upright Zurich entrepreneur, was both proud of and embarrassed by Benjamin. He wanted to arrange some sort of job for him in Zurich, but Bucks wasn't having it. Instead he began receiving government subsidies, claiming mental illness. His father and brother had paid into the Swiss social system all their lives, he said—it was only right that a family member should benefit.

Swiss welfare merely covered the basics, though. If he wanted luxuries, he would have to smuggle reptiles.

A year after my visit to Uganda, I flew from Florida to Germany to see Bucks again. He made me fill half my suitcase with boxes of Jell-O, which, like many Mormons, he was addicted to.

It had been a few months since he'd left Africa, and his whole life had changed. He was back in the reptile business, making trips to Mexico and Mauritius. He had a new girlfriend, a seventeen-year-old Mauritian who now lived with Bucks in the government-subsidized apartment his mental illness had earned him. His snaggletooth had been fixed.

I asked him what had happened to his old associates. The Lion was still running scams in Kampala, he said; the irrepressible Burkhard, meanwhile, had recently accompanied Bucks to Mauritius, where Bucks had outfitted him with what looked like an exoskeleton of small, lizard-stuffed PVC pipes. Once Burkhard had thrown some clothes over that, he'd flown to Europe.

A few weeks later, after returning to Africa, Burkhard had received an offer from a group of Nigerians to fly to Europe again with a rather sizable amount of cocaine. Burkhard had elected to divert the shipment and sell it himself.

Unfortunately, aside from the cocaine's intended recipient, the German had no real drug connections in Europe. He had been living near Bucks while he attempted to figure out what to do, and he was wearing out his welcome. Knowing nobody with the wherewithal to buy the shipment, Burkhard had been trying to sell it bit by tiny bit. He was broke again, as usual.

Bucks, meanwhile, had been cultivating his Mexican operation. He was interested in a few species of lizards that sold as cheap pets there—because Mexico banned wildlife exports, the lizards were worth substantial sums overseas. A new friend of Bucks's named Guillermo, a Mexican living in Spain, had arranged for his mother to accrue them on Bucks's behalf. When Bucks flew in, every month or so, he mailed the lizards from Mexico to Switzerland himself, choosing to save his suitcase space for Jell-O.

During Bucks's last Mexican foray, Burkhard had shown up at Bucks's apartment. Bucks had flown his girlfriend's even-younger teenage cousin up from Mauritius to keep her company during his absence; now Burkhard was demanding that Bucks's girlfriend "arrange" for him a sexual encounter with the cousin, and getting increasingly angry when she wouldn't. Bucks's horrified girlfriend had called him in a panic.

Bucks was furious. "He thinks he's still in Africa!" he told me later. It made Bucks wish that Captain were still alive—Captain would have taken care of Burkhard, and with flair.

Instead, when Bucks returned from Mexico, he bought Burkhard a round-trip ticket to Africa for an errand that would have him back in Switzerland within days. Burkhard would not be there long enough for the Nigerians to notice, Bucks assured him. But then, after the German had left, Bucks canceled Burkhard's return flight.

This was still going on at the time of my visit, with Burkhard calling frantically from somewhere in Africa and Bucks looking at his cell phone and laughing. We were en route to Hamm, Germany, to the Terraristika reptile show, where Bucks hadn't shown his face in four years. He had become, in the interim, something of a legend.

Some fifty thousand people had come in for Terraristika—smugglers, pet-store owners, private collectors, industrial-quantity snake breeders, Asian and African exporters. Bucks drove to the fairgrounds in the early-morning darkness, the highway exits clogged with reptile people, his girlfriend beside him. I sat in the back with a duffel bag full of Mexican alligator lizards and Bucks's friend Guillermo, a very boyish twenty-five-year-old with a funny, loping gait who smiled a lot and wore a backpack everywhere.

When we arrived in Hamm, the fairground complex was cold and smelled faintly of farm animals; by 10 a.m. it was overheated and stinking of human sweat. Guests stood five or six deep at each tiny vendor table, elbowing for a glimpse of the merchandise. Many species that were highly controlled in the United States, thanks to the Endangered Species Act, could be sold openly in Europe. At lunch, in the fairground's cafeteria, Bucks entertained a pitch from a middle-aged Swiss gentleman in a safari vest, a collector who knew Bucks by reputation and had a smuggling assignment for him. "This dead-butterfly type wants me to go to Australia!" said Bucks, who was having none of it. He had better ideas. He was at the stage now, he said, where he didn't want to smuggle anymore—he wanted someone to do his smuggling for him.

Bucks was grooming Guillermo for that. The young Mexican certainly seemed ripe for such assignments. While Bucks was selling lizards surreptitiously out of a soft-sided cooler, Guillermo paced the tables in the venomous-snake rooms, bug-eyed with excitement. He spoke very little English, but mustered together enough of it to tell me that this day, the day of the Terraristika Hamm reptile show, had been the best day of his entire life.

At the end of it, Bucks paid him two thousand euros. It was Guillermo's share of the proceeds from the Mexican lizards, and Guillermo immediately blew the whole sum. He bought deli cups full of baby cobras, which he stacked in his backpack. He bought big, heavy coffee-table books on rattlesnakes and Asian vipers, some of them in German.

As we headed back toward Zurich on the autobahn, Guillermo ate beef jerky and ogled his snake books in joyful silence.

Guillermo turned out to be smarter than Bucks had thought. Not only did he not become Bucks's mule, but within a year he had cut Bucks out of his lucrative Mexican connection entirely—he was making tens if not hundreds of thousands of dollars mailing his lizards from Mexico to Spain, sometimes with the help of his mother, and Bucks was seeing none of it. Lately Guillermo was wearing a Breitling watch, a thing that looked like a dinner plate on his skinny wrist. He emerged from the next Hamm show thirty thousand dollars richer, though he tended to blow at least half of what he made on snakes for himself.

Bucks had no choice but to let Mexico go. He focused instead on an extraordinary reptile from Oman, *Uromastyx thomasi*, a stout, flat desert lizard with an alert dinosaur face and a fantastic dappling of orange down its back. It was rumored that the sultan of Oman was so personally fond of the colorful *Uromastyx thomasi* that he had imposed the death penalty on anyone caught stealing them. That rumor had apparently been a very clever marketing strategy by the one German who had so far managed to get the species out of Oman, but Bucks, who soon found his own way in, saw fit to perpetuate it.

Soon afterward Bucks reconciled with Burkhard, which surprised me, as did the fact that Burkhard was still alive, after what Bucks had done to him. But that was how people like Bucks and Burkhard were. Burkhard, a veteran smuggler always in need of work, was too useful for Bucks to stay mad at forever, though he would lose his patience when the German made slurping noises at young girls in the grocery store.

Reunited, Burkhard and Bucks made a quick, very successful run to South Africa. Bucks collected armadillo lizards, which curl into tight balls when they are scared, and taped them to Burkhard's legs for the ride home. This worked beautifully, but when they did it again with the fleshier, squirmier *Uromastyx thomasi*, Burkhard was stopped in the Dubai airport. "Had it been Oman, we really would have been fucked," Bucks told me. Instead, when he saw Burkhard being led away by airport police—"so relaxed, smiling and talking to them," Bucks said admiringly—he changed plans and got on another plane.

Burkhard was detained for a week in Dubai, insisting to officials that the lizards had been so plentiful on the roads in Oman that he'd collected them for fear of running them over, and then decided to bring some home for his daughter. As for taping them to his legs, he did that because the air conditioning in the airport was so cold. "All this he thought up on the spot," Bucks told me later. He had wired all the money he could to a sheikh friendly with the Lion once he'd made it back to Switzerland, and after two more days Burkhard was released. The lizards stayed behind.

A few weeks later Bucks returned to Oman alone, rented a car, and drove into the desert to collect *Uromastyx thomasi* himself. He showed up with four of the lizards in time for the next Hamm show, where he unloaded them for ten thousand euros.

Bucks had always been cocky, but he was getting cockier. He had recently discovered Facebook, and was now keeping his religious relatives in Lehi up to date on his Emirates Airlines upgrades, his hot chicks, his rare lizards. His American passport, so fresh and blank in Uganda, had extra pages in it now. The slender, fawn-like young man I'd met years before had become muscular and imposing, and had covered himself with tattoos. On the way to the Hamm shows from Zurich he'd drive 120 miles an hour in a cheap rental Skoda. While there he'd sleep two or three hours a night, and chide anyone who couldn't keep up. He was acting invincible again, which never befits a smuggler.

Two months before another Terraristika show, in 2010, a German man was arrested at the airport in Christchurch, New Zealand, with jeweled geckos sewn into an undergarment. The little green-and-white geckos were released back into the park from which they'd come, with much fanfare; not long afterward the German was sentenced and jailed. A month later, another German—Burkhard—was arrested walking around Christchurch with sixteen of the same creatures in his backpack, arranged in protective plastic pipes. A day after that, the police found Bucks and Guillermo and arrested them, too.

Guillermo and Bucks—who had reconciled in the interim—had

arrived first in New Zealand and quickly plucked the geckos off trees. In Christchurch they'd waited for Burkhard, who had lingered in Fiji in an aborted attempt, orchestrated by Bucks and some Austrians, to steal some of that island's famous blue-and-green iguanas. Bucks and Guillermo had sent Burkhard a wire transfer that would allow him to fly to New Zealand and meet them; once he was in country, they communicated by cell phone, but only in Swahili. None of their precautions did any good, because Burkhard, exhausted and overwhelmed by what the police already seemed to know about him, told his interrogators the rest. The New Zealand newspapers identified Bucks as a "Swiss stockbroker" and Guillermo as a "Mexican chef" until it became clear that neither was employed in either capacity, or at all.

Bucks, Burkhard, and Guillermo spent the spring of 2010 in the well-appointed Manawatu prison, where Burkhard played cards with the other lizard-smuggling German, who was finishing out his term. Sometimes the incarcerated Maoris danced at night while everyone else circled around and watched. One tattooed Maori chastised Bucks and Guillermo for stealing lizards that his culture considered sacred; Bucks explained that they weren't the same lizards the Maori was thinking of, and that seemed to satisfy the man. Guillermo stole cigarettes and cookies from the other prisoners, and fell back on his near-total lack of English when confronted. Bucks let him get beat up. The younger man was first to be released, and soon turned up online under a new identity, "Joaquim," with more Mexican lizards for sale.

Burkhard, after his own release, decided that he needed to be back in Uganda. Africa pulled at him, always.

When I talked to Bucks again, just after his return to Europe, he seemed uncharacteristically maudlin and self-pitying, announcing that he would "probably end up working at McDonald's." Feeling mistrustful, he deleted most of his Facebook friends and braced himself for the numbing boredom of the normal-citizen world. This plan, however, did not last long. A month later he was bringing reptiles back from Egypt; within a year he would extend his reach to the Galapagos, Somalia, and Zanzibar, with Interpol having him stopped now and then to check for animals in his bags. They never found any.

At the first Hamm show after his release from prison, Bucks made the rounds in a New Zealand Department of Conservation T-shirt, earning himself laughs and a few high-fives. There, he told me what had happened with the jeweled geckos after he, Guillermo, and Burkhard had been arrested. His Austrian friends had flown to New Zealand and stolen themselves yet another batch, he said, this time with more success. The jeweled geckos that had put him in jail—perhaps even the same individual animals—were here in this fairgrounds, somewhere.

THE NEOCHILEANS

by ROBERTO BOLAÑO

THE TRIP BEGAN one happy day in November,
But in a sense the trip was over
When we started.
All times coexist, said Pancho Ferri,
The lead singer. Or they converge,
Who knows.
The prologue, however,
Was simple:
With a resigned gesture we boarded
The van our manager
Had given us in a fit
Of madness
And set off for the North,
The North which magnetizes dreams
And the seemingly

Meaningless songs of the Neochileans,
A North, how should I put it?
Foretold in the white kerchief
Sometimes covering
My face
Like a shroud.
A white kerchief unsullied
Or not
On which were projected
My nomadic nightmares
And my sedentary nightmares.
And Pancho Ferri
Asked
If we knew the story
Of Caraculo
And Jetachancho
Grasping the steering wheel
With both hands and
Making the van tremble
As we looked for the exit
From Santiago,
Making it tremble as if it were
Caraculo's
Chest
Carrying a weight unbearable
For any human.
And I remembered then that on the day
Before our departure
We'd been
In the *Parque Forestal*

Visiting the monument
To Rubén Darío.
Goodbye, Rubén, we said, drunk
And stoned.
Now those trivial acts
Get confused
With screams heralding
Real dreams.
But that's how we Neochileans were,
Pure inspiration
And no method at all.
And the next day we rolled
On to Pilpilco and Llay Llay
And shot through
La Ligua and Los Vilos
Without stopping
And crossed the Petorca River
And the Quilimarí
River
And the Choapa until we arrived
At La Serena
And the Elqui River
And finally Copiapó
And the Copiapó River
Where we stopped
To eat cold
Empanadas.
And Pancho Ferri
Returned to the intercontinental
Adventures

Of Caraculo and Jetachancho,
Two musicians from Valparaíso
Lost
In Barcelona's Chinatown.
And poor Caraculo,
The lead singer said,
Was married and needed
To get money
For his wife and children
Of the Caraculo lineage
So badly he started dealing
Heroin
And a little cocaine
And on Fridays a little ecstasy
For the subjects of Venus.
And bit by bit, stubbornly,
He was moving up,
And while Jetachancho
Hung out with Aldo Di Pietro,
Remember him?
In Café Puerto Rico,
Caraculo saw his checking account
And his self-esteem grow.
And what lesson can we
Neochileans learn
From the criminal lives
Of those two South American
Pilgrims?
None, except that limits
Are tenuous, limits

Are relative: reeded edges
Of a reality forged
In the void.
Pascal's horror
Precisely.
That geometric horror
So dark
And cold,
Said Pancho Ferri
At the wheel of our race car,
Always heading
North, till we reached
Toco
Where we unloaded
The amp
And two hours later
Were ready to go on:
Pancho Relámpago
And the Neochileans.
A tiny
Pea-sized failure,
Though some teens
Did help us
Load the instruments back
In the van: kids
From Toco
Transparent like
The geometric figures
Of Blaise Pascal.
And after Toco, Quillagua,

Hilaricos, Soledad, Ramaditas,
Pintados, and Humberstone,
Playing in empty banquet halls
And brothels converted
Into Lilliputian hospitals,
A really rare sight, rare they even had
Electricity, really
Rare that the walls
Were semi-solid, in short,
Places that kind of
Scared us a little
And where the clients
Took a liking to
Fist-fucking and
Feet-fucking,
And the screams that came
Through the windows and
Echoed through the cement courtyard
Through outhouses
Between stores full
Of rusted tools
And sheds that seemed
To collect all the moon's light,
Made our hair
Stand on end.
How can so much evil exist
In a country so new,
So minuscule?
Might this be
The Prostitutes' Hell?

Pancho Ferri
Pondered aloud.
And we Neochileans didn't know
What to answer.
I just sat wondering
How those New York variants of sex
Could go on
In these godforsaken
Provinces.
And with our pockets emptied
We continued north:
Mapocho, Negreiros, Santa
Catalina, Tana,
Cuya, and
Arica,
Where we found
Some rest—and indignities.
And three nights of work
In the *Camafeo*, owned by
Don Luis Sánchez Morales, retired
Official.
A place filled with little round tables
And potbellied lamps
Hand-painted
By don Luis's mom,
I suppose.
And the only really
Amusing thing
We saw in Arica
Was the sun of Arica:

A sun like a trail
Of dust.
A sun like sand
Or like lime
Tossed artfully
Into the motionless air.
The rest: routine.
Assassins and converts
Chitchatting
With the deaf and mute,
With imbeciles turned loose
From Purgatory.
And Vivanco the lawyer,
A friend of don Luis Sánchez,
Asked what the fuck we were trying to say
With all that Neochilean shit.
New patriots, said Pancho,
As he got up
From the table
And locked himself in the bathroom.
And Vivanco the lawyer
Tucked his pistol back
In its holster
Of Italian leather,
A fine repoussé of the boys
Of Ordine Nuovo,
Detailed with delicacy and skill.
White as the moon
That night we had to tuck
Pancho Ferri in bed

Between all of us.
With a forty-degree fever
He was growing delirious:
He didn't want our band
To be called *Pancho Relámpago*
And the Neochileans anymore,
But instead *Pancho Misterio*
And the Neochileans:
Pascal's terror.
The terror of lead singers,
The terror of travelers,
But never the terror
Of children.
And one morning at dawn,
Like a band of thieves,
We left Arica
And crossed the border
Of the Republic.
By our expressions
You'd have thought we were crossing
The border of Reason.
And the Peru of legend
Opened up in front of our van
Covered in dust
And filth,
Like a piece of fruit without a peel,
Like a chimeric fruit
Exposed to inclemency
And insults.
A fruit without a rind

Like a cocky teenager.
And Pancho Ferri, from
Then on called Pancho
Misterio, didn't break
His fever,
Murmuring like a priest
In the back part
Of the van
The ups and downs,
The avatars—Indian word—
Of Caraculo and Jetachancho.
A life thin and hard
As the soup and noose of a hanged man,
That of Jetachancho and his
Lucky Siamese twin:
A life or a study
Of the wind's caprices.
And the Neochileans
Played in Tacna,
In Mollendo and Arequipa,
Sponsored by the Society
For the Promotion of Art
And Youth.
Without a lead singer, humming
The songs to ourselves
Or going *mmm*, *mmm*, *mmmmh*,
While Pancho was melting away
In the back of the van,
Devoured by chimeras
And cocky teenagers.

Nadir and zenith of a longing
That Caraculo learned to sense
In the moons
Of the drug dealers
Of Barcelona: a deceptive
Glow,
A minute empty space
That means nothing,
That's worth nothing, and that
Nevertheless exposes itself to you
Free of charge.
And if we weren't
In Peru? we
Neochileans
Asked ourselves one night.
And if this immense
Space
That instructs
And limits us
Were an intergalactic ship,
An unidentified
Flying object?
And if Pancho Misterio's
Fever
Were our fuel
Or our navigational device?
And after working
We went out walking
Through the streets of Peru:
With military patrols,

Peddlers, and the unemployed,
Scanning
The hills
For Shining Path's bonfires,
But we saw nothing.
The darkness surrounding the
Urban centers
Was total.
This is like a vapor trail
Straight out of
World War II
Said Pancho lying down
In the back of the van.
He said: Filaments
Of Nazi generals like
Reichenau or Model
Escaping in spirit
Involuntarily
To the Virgin Lands
Of Latin America:
A hinterland of specters
And ghosts.
Our home
Positioned within the geometry
Of impossible crimes.
And at night we would
Go out to the clubs:
The sweet-sixteen-year-old whores
Descendants of those brave men
Of the Pacific War

Loved hearing us talk
Like machine guns.
But above all
They loved seeing Pancho,
Wrapped in piles of colored blankets
With his wool cap
From the altiplano
Pulled down to his eyebrows,
Appear and disappear
Like the gentleman
He always was,
A lucky guy,
The great ailing lover from southern Chile,
The father of the Neochileans.
And the mother of Caraculo and Jetachancho,
Two poor musicians from Valparaíso,
As everyone knows.
And dawn would find us
At a table in the back
Discussing the kilo and a half of gray matter
In the adult
Brain.
Chemical messages, said
Pancho Misterio burning with fever,
Neurons activating themselves
And neurons inhibiting themselves
In the vast expanses of longing.
And the little whores said
A kilo and a half of gray
Matter

Was enough, was sufficient, why
Ask for more.
And Pancho started to
Weep when he heard them.
And then came the flood
And the rain brought silence
Over the streets of Mollendo,
And over the hills,
And over the streets in the barrio
Of the whores,
And the rain was the only
One talking.
A strange phenomenon: we Neochileans
Shut our mouths
And went our separate ways
Visiting the dumps of
Philosophy, the safes, the
American colors, the unmistakable manner
Of being born and reborn.
And one night our van
Made for Lima, with Pancho
Ferri at the wheel, like in
The old days,
Except now a whore
Was with him.
A thin young whore,
Whose name was Margarita,
An unrivaled teen,
Resident of the permanent
Storm.

You might have also
Called her Agile
Shadow,
The dark ramada
Where Pancho
Might heal his wounds.
And in Lima we read
Peruvian poets:
Vallejo, Martín Adán, and Jorge Pimentel.
And Pancho Misterio went out
Onstage and was convincing
And versatile.
And later, still trembling
And sweaty,
He told us the plot
Of a novel
By an old Chilean writer.
One swallowed by oblivion.
A *nec spe nec metu*
We Neochileans said.
And Margarita added:
A novelist.
And the ghost,
The mournful hole
Where all endeavors
End,
Wrote—it seems—
A novel called *Kundalini*,
And Pancho could hardly remember it.
He really tried, his words

Poking around in a dreadful infancy
Full of amnesia, gymnastic
Trials and lies,
And he was telling it to us like that,
Fragmented,
The Kundalini scream,
The name of a race-loving mare
And the shared death on the racetrack.
A racetrack that no longer exists.
A hole anchored
In a nonexistent Chile
That's happy.
And the story had
The virtue to illuminate
Like an English landscape painter
Our fear and our dreams
Which were marching east to west
And west to east,
While we, the real
Neochileans
Traveled from south
To north.
And so slowly
It seemed we weren't moving.
And Lima was an instant
Of happiness.
Brief but effective.
And what is the relationship, asked Pancho,
Between Morpheus, god
Of Sleep,

And *morfar*, slang for
To eat?
Yes, that's what he said,
Hugged around the waist
By the lovely Margarita,
Skinny and almost naked
In a bar in Lince, one night
Glimpsed and fractured and
Possessed
By the lightning bolts
Of the chimera.
Our necessity.
Our open mouth
Where bread
Goes in
And dreams
Come out: vapor trails
Fossils
Colored with the palette
Of the apocalypse.
Survivors, said Pancho
Ferri.
Lucky Latin Americans.
That's it.
And one night before leaving
We saw Pancho
And Margarita
Standing in the middle of an infinite
Quagmire.
And then we realized

The Neochileans
Would be forever
Governed
By chance.
The coin
Leapt like a metallic
Insect
From between his fingers:
Heads, to the south,
Tails, to the north,
And we all piled into
The van
And the city
Of legends
And fear
Stayed behind.
One happy day in January
We crossed
Like children of the Cold,
Of the Unstable Cold
Or of the Ecce Homo,
The border of Ecuador.
At the time Pancho was
Twenty-eight or twenty-nine years old
And soon he would die.
And Margarita was seventeen.
And none of the Neochileans
Was over twenty-two.

—*Blanes, 1993*
Translated by Laura Healy

THE SHAH'S MAN

nonfiction by TOM BARBASH

O N MARCH 22, 1980, fourteen months after he was driven from the Peacock Throne and on the eve of his flight from Panama to Egypt, the Shah of Iran turned to Bobby Armao. Armao, who had met the shah as a twenty-nine-year-old lawyer and PR man, had through attrition and then loyalty become the king's closest adviser. Except for an Iranian bodyguard cradling a submachine gun, the two men were alone.

If they're going to kill me, the shah said, tonight would be a good night.

For weeks they'd heard rumors that their hosts were bargaining with the Iranians on behalf of the U.S., attempting to arrange the shah's extradition or arrest. Fifty-two American diplomats had been taken hostage in Tehran four months earlier; the shah now faced the chance that he would be sent back against his will in exchange for their release. Then came the report that a Panamanian doctor assigned to treat the shah's worsening lymphoma had been offered a million dollars to botch the surgery. Some 230 Panamanian national guardsmen had been posted on Contadora Island, where the royal family had taken refuge, but with a bounty on the shah's head, the marksmen on the beach had lately seemed like small comfort.

During his reign the shah had survived several attempts on his life. Thirty years before his last night in Panama, a man posing as a photographer at an official ceremony in Tehran had fired five shots at him from a few yards away. One bullet entered the shah's right cheek and exited through his upper lip. Sixteen years after that, another would-be assassin killed two palace guards in an effort to reach the shah, only to be killed himself.

"It's very quiet in the house now," the shah said to Armao.

Armao took out a deck of cards and sat down facing the king. "Anyone wanting to get to you will have to get by him first," he said, nodding toward the guard. "And then me."

As was their routine, they played into the night.

Of all the improbable twists of fate that marked the last days in the life of the Shah of Iran, perhaps the most striking was that he put himself in the hands of a well-connected and impeccably dressed American he had only just met. Bobby Armao had been a close adviser to Vice President Nelson Rockefeller, and then served as New York City's official greeter under Ed Koch, meeting princes and foreign ministers at Kennedy Airport and shepherding them to the stores on Fifth Avenue or out to Studio 54. Rockefeller was a longtime friend of the shah's, and late in 1978, as demonstrations in Tehran reached their boiling point, he asked Armao to fly to Iran and help the shah salvage his regime. There was no one left in the shah's inner circle that he trusted, Rockefeller said. Armao, at the time, knew more about Italian suits than Iranian politics, but he had never said no to Rockefeller.

Armao traveled first class from Paris in a plane crowded with Ayatollah Khomeini supporters and DEATH TO THE SHAH signs. He spent a few days observing the chaos: banks and movie theaters vandalized and set on fire, cars and liquor stores destroyed. Government strikes had left the city paralyzed.

The Iranian ambassador to the U.S., Ardeshir Zahedi, arranged a grand dinner for Armao, but the mood was grim. "It was like the last meal on the *Titanic*," Armao remembers. He had been directed by Rockefeller to help the shah reshape his image, but it was clearly too late for that. Less than a week after Armao's abortive visit, the shah would leave Iran forever.

When I meet Armao, it's been more than thirty years since his walk-on role in the drama. He is now a white-haired sixty-two, and his career has become a strange mix of lucrative and unlikely consulting projects—a Venezuelan election here, a private-equity expansion there. We meet at a bar in Greenwich Village, an NYU hangout, Pete's Tavern. Armao is dressed in a blue suit with a three-point handkerchief in the jacket pocket; with his narrow build and expressive eyebrows, he looks like Jerry Orbach.

"On some chemical level, we clicked," he says, referring to the shah. "I understood him, and right away he trusted me."

Rockefeller had told Armao "to serve the shah as you would serve me"; having failed to prevent the revolution, Armao had planned to spend a few additional weeks with the king, to "help get him back on his feet." Instead, the job quickly took over his life. Ten days after the shah left Iran, Rockefeller succumbed to a heart attack—Armao suddenly had no one to tell him that his assignment was over. The shah, in turn, having lost the governmental apparatus that had once advised him along with his throne, had found someone eager to take on any task, and well versed in how to treat royalty. To this day Armao refers to the shah as "His Imperial Majesty," as in, "I said, 'Your Imperial Majesty, what *I* would recommend...'"

With no hope of returning to their former stations, the two men fell back on the kind of protocol that they'd relied on for much of their lives. The immediate circumstances—the revolution, Tehran's new regime—faded into the background. Armao acknowledges that in those early months, he never spent much time wondering what the shah had done to invite the wrath of his countrymen.

"It's like a doctor with a patient," he says. "I had a very specific job to do."

For nearly four decades, and through eight U.S. presidencies, Mohammad Reza Shah Pahlavi was among America's closest allies in the Middle East. Pahlavi had been educated in Swiss boarding schools; he went on to become a friend of celebrities like Frank Sinatra and Grace Kelly and a mainstay on the slopes of Saint Moritz. In 1962, when he visited New York City with his glamorous young wife (his third), he was given a ticker-tape parade up Broadway.

The shah's White Revolution, a brazen and culture-shaping modernization program begun in 1963, was modeled largely on what he'd admired in America. Under his rule, Iran's oil profits exploded, a prosperous middle class emerged, and women were given the right to vote. The shah and his family, meanwhile, grew unimaginably rich.

As the years passed, though, his regime became increasingly autocratic. Delegitimized by corruption, the shah came to rely on SAVAK, the Iranian secret police, in order to silence his political opponents. An untold number of civilians were tortured or put to death. It wasn't until early 1978 that the Ayatollah Khomeini, long an opponent of the shah, managed to catalyze a full-fledged opposition movement, but the kindling for an Iranian revolution had been building up throughout the decade. Within months of the first demonstration, the marchers in the streets numbered in the millions. The government responded clumsily, and then brutally,[1] and then not at all.

On January 16, 1979, the shah fled to Egypt. He called it a vacation, but no one was fooled; two weeks later, Khomeini ended his own fifteen-year exile and swept back into Tehran, where he was greeted by the largest crowd the country had ever seen.[2] The shah, still hoping the tide could be turned back, made plans to regroup in Southern California, where a home awaited him on the desert estate of billionaire publishing magnate Walter Annenberg. But within days of his departure from Iran, Washington sent word that it wasn't the right time to come. The White House, it turned out, wanted to keep its options open with the emerging Iranian regime. Other rejections arrived from Switzerland, where the shah still owned a home; France;

---

[1] On September 6, the shah implemented martial law, but word of this decision had yet to spread throughout Tehran when thousands of protesters turned out the next day. The shah's troops opened fire after the demonstrators began throwing brickbats; an estimated three hundred people were killed. (Some reports put the number in the thousands.) Soon afterward the shah ordered his troops to hold their fire even as the protests raged around them, and the country fell into chaos.

[2] In his book *The Crisis*, David Harris puts the turnout at as high as 10 million, suggesting that it "might well have been the largest assemblage in one place for a single event in the history not only of Iran, but of the entire planet."

and England, where just weeks before Margaret Thatcher had pledged to help him in whatever way she could. Nearly overnight, one of the richest and most internationally established leaders in the world had become radioactive.

Within a week, the shah left Egypt for Morocco. Working in concert with the shah's twin sister, Princess Ashraf Pahlavi, as well as with steadfast Pahlavi supporter Henry Kissinger, Armao began to canvass the globe for a more permanent destination. Paradise Island, in the Bahamas, emerged in short order as more or less their only option.[3]

When the royal family arrived on Paradise, with Armao there to greet them, they discovered that the beach house that the Bahamian government had provided wasn't big enough for all their luggage. The shah's four children (ages nine, thirteen, sixteen, and eighteen) were moved to guest suites at a nearby resort, along with the rest of the family's entourage; the suitcases were kept in the courtyard. Outside the house, nearly two hundred reporters gathered to witness the shah's arrival—Armao managed to chase them away after arranging a quick family photo.

And then, with little else to do, the shah and his queen ventured out for a swim. Tennis became a daily preoccupation for them as well, drawing swarms of onlookers to the courts. With funds provided for the family's upkeep by Princess Ashraf, Armao brought in several dozen security contractors from a firm in Miami; these men, meant

---

[3] South Africa had also offered to take the shah, but the shah's father had passed away there during his own exile. The shah's sense of the country, as a result, was too bleak.

to supplement the Bahamian soldiers that the shah's new hosts had insisted he employ, dotted the beach whenever the royals emerged. The island's less-exalted guests suddenly found themselves sharing the shoreline with clusters of foreign bodyguards carrying machine guns hidden in briefcases. A report in *Paris Match* emphasized the dissonance: it featured a photo of the shah walking out of the ocean, tanned and toned, above another photo of three of his army officers lying dead in an Iranian prison yard.

It didn't help that such coverage included nothing from the shah himself—as a condition of their asylum, the Pahlavis were prohibited from speaking publicly about the revolution. Still, the king spent his mornings glued to the radio, and followed the reports of his regime's decimation in a dozen newspapers. Armao, meanwhile, seamlessly slipped into the roles of personal assistant, press secretary, government liaison, and arms provider.[4] He found schools for the shah's children, travel documents and permanent housing for the family pediatrician, and additional accommodations for their two valets, a governess, and seven colonels from the Iranian Revolutionary Guard who were now acting as the family's adjutants. (All seven had death warrants out on them in Iran. They could never go home again.)

To the press, Armao was a charismatic "mystery man," oddly omnipresent during the Iranians' time on Paradise; to the shah, he was the one person outside of the royal family's inner circle who had taken the fallen ruler's side. It was Armao who fought off the Bahamians'

---

[4] "I gave him a .357 Magnum," Armao told me. "I said, 'Your Majesty, I'm told you're a very good marksman. I think you should keep this in your bedroom.' He said, 'You think so?' and I said, 'I do. I sleep with a gun next to my pillow.'" Armao's weapon of choice at the time was a Smith and Wesson .38.

demands for additional payments, as the shah's stay dragged on—the security guards were already sleeping in luxury suites costing $250 a night, and subsisting on salmon and lobster tails from room service. At the end of ten weeks on the island, the bill had reached $1.2 million. The sum must have seemed reasonable to the king's hosts, who'd been reading accounts that suggested he'd made off with $50 billion, but both the shah and Armao called such estimates "ridiculous."[5]

According to Armao, the Bahamians ultimately tried to get the shah to buy an island or two, and wouldn't extend his visa when he declined. At that point, Armao turned once again to Kissinger. The shah's old friend, in turn, secured an invitation from the government of Mexico.

In early June, the royal road show moved on to Cuernavaca. Armao found a quiet, spacious house at the end of a cul-de-sac, surrounded by a tropical garden; the king and queen were pleased, though the queen complained about the mildew and the scorpions. Richard Nixon flew down for a visit,[6] as did Kissinger and David Rockefeller. The shah's eldest son, a capable pilot, found an opportunity to rent a helicopter; when he buzzed the house unannounced to show off his skills, the

---

[5] In the shah's only interview during his exile, with the journalist David Frost, the shah insisted that he had less than "many, many American millionaires." Armao told me he didn't know the exact figure, but put it closer to one billion than to ten.

[6] Nixon's visit, coming just a few years after his resignation, offered the shah the company of someone who'd faced a similar reversal of fortune. The two men took long walks together in the afternoon, and stayed up talking into the night.

Mexican security guards opened fire with submachine guns. It took the queen running out and shouting "That's my son! That's my son!" to get the men to stand down.

Armao sent the helicopter to Italy for repairs. As for the shah himself, he spent his time picking up steam on his memoirs (published posthumously as *Answer to History*), and decided to get his first driver's license—the State of Morales DMV came to the house with cameras and a laminating machine.[7]

It was a few months later, in October of 1979, that the shah suddenly became very sick. Unbeknownst to Armao, the shah had been struggling with lymphoma for at least five years; now, as his deterioration became increasingly undeniable, the truth came out. Armao, who had permitted himself to begin envisioning a permanent residence for the shah, somewhere in the world, and a resumption of a more normal life for himself, threw himself into the question of finding his employer a way into a hospital in the U.S.

President Carter, despite concerns that the new Iranian regime might retaliate against American citizens in Iran, ultimately gave the go-ahead for the shah to come to New York. The shah, the queen, and Armao left Mexico City on the night of October 22, 1979. Mexican president José López Portillo had assured Armao that the shah could return to Mexico whenever he wanted; "He told us, 'This is your *home*,'" Armao says. "And then of course they slammed the door after we left."

The private plane they'd arranged for the trip stopped first in Fort Lauderdale, their point of entry. The pilot landed at the city airport, rather than at the private airfield where they were expected,

---

[7] Armao says the shah loved to drive. That kings weren't likely to be asked for their driver's license didn't stop him from enjoying his ownership of one.

which meant that no one was there to greet them. After an hour of confusion, the plane continued on. As they flew over the farmland of the Carolinas, Armao remembers, the shah gazed down in wonder. "He said, 'What I would have *given* to have land like that back in Iran.'"

In New York, on October 24, doctors removed the shah's gall bladder. When word of his presence in the city got out, the shah acknowledged his cancer publicly for the first time, setting off speculation in Iran (and in the *New York Post*) that it was all a ruse to get the king in closer contact with Washington before an attempted return to power. The rumors had a precedent: the shah had gone into exile before, in 1953, only to be placed back on his throne within the week by the CIA.[8] Angry protesters began to gather outside the hospital, denouncing the U.S. government for harboring him. Two weeks later, Iranian students overran the American embassy in Tehran.

For those who came of age after 1980, it may be hard to imagine a time when the notion of mobs of young men on television chanting "Death to America" was close to unknown. Equally implausible might be the fact that the U.S. and Iran were ever so close as they were in the 1960s and early '70s, when the shah was viewed as an appealing, progressive leader, and the brightest Iranians flocked to American universities. From the shah's perspective, it was as though he'd fallen asleep one night a generational hero and awoken as a murderous villain. His countrymen wanted to kill him; his old allies now blamed his faulty gall bladder for putting their diplomats' lives at risk. What especially distressed the shah, Armao says, was watching people he'd

---

[8] The shah insisted afterward that the CIA had played only a tangential role, and that it was the Iranian people who had demanded his return. Few experts share this perspective.

known and trusted suddenly cozying up to Khomeini.

"I remember he saw Kurt Waldheim"—the UN's secretary general—"with microphones in front of him, saying, 'The Iranians have a right to their revolution,'" Armao said. "The shah turned to me and said, 'Can you believe this? That man used to lick my boots.'"

In Armao, by contrast, the king found a young American not only willing to hear his version of history, but to repeat it as though it were God's truth itself.

I once asked Armao if he's returned to Iran in the decades since the shah passed away. He looked amazed at my question.

"They sent me letters asking me to appear in Evin Prison for my execution," he said. "No, I've never been back."

Unable to speak directly to the shah about the crisis or his condition, the media threw questions at Bobby Armao. He talked to David Hartman on *Good Morning America*, to Ted Koppel, to every newspaper that called. (He had been the shah's semiofficial spokesman for some time, at this point: in May, he'd compared the shah to Ed Koch and Nelson Rockefeller in an interview with *New York* magazine, explaining that all three men "can relate to the plight of the working man"; in August, he'd told the *New York Times* that "I can't put my finger on why [the shah] got the image he did," and switched the comparison to Harry Truman.) When Barbara Walters or Frank Sinatra wanted to see the shah at the hospital, they called Armao.[9]

---

[9] Sinatra was livid at the way the U.S. was treating the shah, Armao says, and called from Las Vegas to say he was coming to New York to see his old friend in his hospital room. Armao brought him in through a service entrance.

Armao also began to take on the Carter administration, "blasting them every chance I got" for failing to find a permanent sanctuary for the shah even as they struggled to contend with the hostage crisis. Gary Sick, a Carter aide, wrote afterward that Armao's combativeness toward the White House "severely complicated relations" between Washington and the king. Armao, of course, was speaking not only for the shah but for his allies—Kissinger and the Rockefellers, who believed the U.S. should never have let Khomeini emerge from exile in the first place. The argument spread to the presidential primaries, where Teddy Kennedy took up the other extreme, criticizing Carter for allowing the shah into the States at all.

By the end of November, as their tentatively scheduled return to Mexico drew near, it was clear that the shah needed to leave New York very soon. But less than forty-eight hours before their return flight to Cuernavaca, Armao was called to a meeting with the Mexican consul general at Mr. Chow's restaurant, in midtown Manhattan. The consul told him that Mexico was retracting its welcome. In the following days, South Africa rescinded its original invitation as well.

With nowhere to turn, Armao held a press conference. The world's most powerful nation was ducking its obligations to its longtime ally, he said, and effectively placing his fate in the hands of a small group of well-meaning American citizens. He berated the Carter administration for what he termed disloyalty and cowardice.

The White House, faced with the possibility of the shah maintaining a high-profile presence in New York, responded by finding a home for the royals at Lackland Air Force Base, in San Antonio, Texas. The king left New York a few days later; fifty heavily armed FBI men guarded the hospital as he made his way out. After touching down in San Antonio, a van sped the shah and his queen to a psychiatric ward at Lackland—for their security, they were told. The windows were barred, and the doors, once they entered their room, were closed and locked.

Eventually the couple was moved into a small apartment in the officers' quarters. Hamilton Jordan, Carter's young chief of staff, described the suite as small and dreary in his memoir (everyone besides Armao seems to have written one)—like "a seventy-five-dollar-a-day Holiday Inn suite in Peoria." The shah, he said, greeted him in a blue bathrobe with USA stitched on the back when Jordan came to check in.

Nevertheless, the royals were happy to have left New York behind them. The base commander found tennis partners for the queen, and the shah took up dinners and bridge games with the air force colonels, some of whom had gotten their hands on T-shirts mocking the ayatollah. Dozens of Iranian pilots had trained at the base, in earlier years, and the sense of friendship was still there.

They were playing cards late one night when the phone rang. "It was the air-force switchboard operator with a heavy drawl," Armao remembers. "She said, 'It's the Ay-a-to-llah Kho-*mein*i on the line for the *Shaw*.'"

It might have been one of Khomeini's underlings, Armao thought, but wouldn't he have identified himself a little more explicitly? Could the world actually work this way?

Armao turned to the shah and said it was Khomeini on the line.

"See what he wants," the shah said.

And of course, what was it? Some San Antonio kids playing a prank. When Armao picked up the phone, all he heard was laughter, and then a click as they hung up.

The U.S. still believed that, for the sake of the hostage negotiations, the shah needed to be moved to a new refuge. The Carter administration proposed Panama, and promised the shah that he could return to the U.S. if it became medically necessary; Armao argued against the idea, unhappy with what he'd heard about General Omar Torrijos, Panama's de facto leader, and suspicious of Carter's assurances. By this point, a year into his employment, Armao didn't put much stock in promises.

Hamilton Jordan dismissed Armao's concerns. He held a higher view of Torrijos, based in part on long nights of drinking with the man. Torrijos also had his own incentives—his hospitality had less to do with any empathy for the shah and more to do with helping Jimmy Carter get reelected. Ronald Reagan had been vocally critical of the Panama Canal Treaty, the 1977 agreement that had offered Panama a path toward controlling the waterway the country depended on, and Torrijos believed that helping to defuse the hostage crisis would help Carter beat Reagan. The situation didn't have the makings of the sanctuary Armao was searching for, but it was the only option on the table. Armao told the shah to take it.

When Armao and Jordan arrived at the Panamanian president's residence to hammer out the details, "Torrijos was peeling off a few hundred-dollar bills to a lady of the evening," Armao says. "He didn't even say hello to us until she left. Then he and Jordan hug and kiss. 'Hello, Papi,' that kind of thing. They're drinking like crazy. Beers. Torrijos is telling me how the night he first met Jordan to talk about Panama, he was in bed with a woman, and he told Hamilton to jump in bed with them. They were party boys."

It was one of those historical pivot points when the world spins off its axis, like 1968, or 2001, or 2011. In Tehran, militants were battling the leftists for control of the revolution; in France, secret meetings were being held in sequestered hotel suites about the shah and the hostages, and the shah's nephew had been assassinated in front of his apartment on the rue Pergolèse by a gunman wearing a motorcycle helmet. The Russians had invaded Afghanistan, something the shah would later claim would never have happened under his rule.

I asked Armao what he thought thirty years later, when Hosni Mubarak (an acquaintance of Armao's) appeared in a cage before an Egyptian court.

"*Terrible*. And sad. I was thinking of how lucky the shah was that he never went through something like that."

On the day we spoke, Libyan rebels had just seized control of an oil refinery outside Tripoli, and a chorus of world leaders had demanded that Syrian president Bashar al-Assad step down. The same week, an Iranian court sentenced two American hikers who'd crossed the border from Iraq to eight years in jail. After Yemen, and Tunisia, and Egypt, a few of the old leaders were still clinging to power in the face of inexorable opposition. And Assad and Qaddafi had both chosen to allow their countries to be torn through with violence rather than relinquishing control.

"You know, I'd always believed—and I told him this—that the shah should have used his military to put down the insurgency," Armao says. "But when I see what's happening now, all the bloodshed, I think he was very smart to get out the way he did."

Nothing about Panama sat well with Armao—not the roach he saw climbing up Torrijos's drapes ("I kept thinking of Woody Allen's *Bananas*," he said), nor the plane he rode in with Jordan and Manuel Noriega, Torrijos's head of military intelligence, to scout out potential homes. Armao remembers the plane as "a flying whorehouse," shaking like hell and decorated in red velvet.

Nevertheless, shortly after that preliminary visit, the shah made his way to Panama's Isla Contadora, and took up residence in the vacation home of Gabriel Lewis, Panama's ambassador to the U.S. From day one, Armao began bumping heads with Noriega, whom he viewed as an unrepentant thug bent on shaking down the shah for money. (Jordan, in his memoir, calls Armao's claims a fiction, and says the shah cost the Panamanians a fortune in tourism dollars.) The shah and his family, meanwhile, determined to hold their heads high in the face of international exasperation with their continued existence, spent the winter playing tennis, swimming, and reviving the public resentment they'd inspired during their time in the Bahamas. The queen and their children knew their time with the shah was limited, Armao remembers, and they were making the most of it.

But faced with unrelenting media speculation about the shah's culpability for the hostage crisis, Armao thought it was time for the king to speak out. Over Kissinger's objections, he invited David Frost to come to Panama and conduct an interview. Frost had been tough on Kissinger, as well as on Nixon, but Armao believed that, having grown up in a monarchy (Frost was British), the man "would know how to treat a king."

The eventual broadcast was edited down from ten hours of discussions. (Armao lent me a homemade DVD recording, which included an ad for the 1980 Winter Olympics featuring Sammy Davis Jr. on a sled.) The two men sit across from each other in a well-lit room, with a view of palm trees outside. It looks sometimes like the air conditioning has given out, as both men's faces glisten. Frost asks early on if the shah would consider returning to Iran to face trial.

The shah, wearing a dark blue suit, his face somewhat drawn, responds, "First of all, who are they to try me? They should be tried first!"

The shah with his second wife, Soraya, sometime in the 1950s.
The two divorced in 1958, after Soraya failed to produce an heir for the king.

The shah with a group of ayatollahs, in happier times. The ayatollahs supported the king during the overthrow of Iran's prime minister in 1953, in the course of which the shah was briefly forced to flee the country.

A 1962 Saturday Evening Post *profile called the shah "our stanchest ally in the Middle East." The end of the article touched on the possibility of revolution, but quoted an American official arguing that "The Persians need a strong hand guiding them for a while."*

Il s'est cru l'héritier de Cyrus le roi des rois

Dans le palais
du Golestan, sur le trône
aux 26 733 pierreries, l'empereur
en majesté. A ses côtés,
l'impératrice Farah et le prince
héritier en grand
uniforme de l'Académie militaire.
Au cours d'une cérémonie
grandiose, le Shah vient de se
couronner lui-même
comme l'avait fait son père vingt-cinq

The shah at his coronation ceremony, in October 1967, twenty-six years into his rule, flanked by his queen and heir. The throne on which he's seated contains 26,733 gems.

The shah issuing orders to one of his generals from the deck of his Caspian villa, in 1978.

A soldier kisses the hand of the shah on his final day in Iran—January 16, 1979. Command of the army would soon pass to the new regime.

The shah on Paradise Island, in the Bahamas, accompanied by his bodyguards.

The shah on Contadora Island, in Panama, listening to the news from Iran.

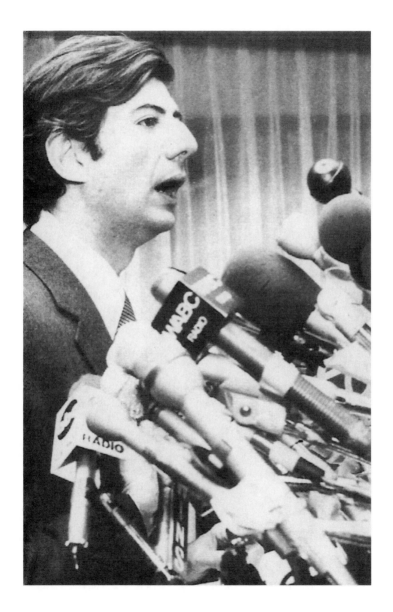

Armao, in mid–press conference.

Armao, the shah, and the queen, debarking in Mexico City in June 1979.

*Armao with New York City Mayor Ed Koch at the John Jay School
of Criminal Justice, Armao's alma mater.*

Surprise Award

. . . President Joseph P. Tonelli, right, accepts the 1976 Columbus Citizens Committee Award from Special Assistant for Labor Affairs to the Vice President Nelson Rockefeller, Robert Armao. The Award was given for outstanding leadership in the field of Labor.

A clipping from Armao's personal collection.

Frost cites a pro-Khomeini ad in the *New York Times* accusing the shah of killing more than a hundred thousand people.

"Who? My regime? Where? At what occasion?"

Frost says that he hasn't substantiated the charge, but asks what the shah's reaction is to the number.

"Preposterous. It's *ridiculous.* I wouldn't even use the word *disgusting.* I would say, they don't know how to count."

He goes on to claim that torture in Iran had not occurred since 1976. The two men talk back and forth about numbers for a while longer—how many killed in the initial uprising, how many victims of SAVAK, the shah insisting that the figures Khomeini has put out are grossly exaggerated. Finally, referring to torture and government-sanctioned killing, Frost asks, "In all of these areas, would you say one is too many?"

The shah looks away. And then he says, "Yes, yes. For our code of principles, and approach to civilization, that is quite true."

It's a subject the shah avoided in his memoirs, and in his conversations with Armao. But whatever the final tally may have been, it's indisputable that his regime had a brutal history of interrogations: shock treatment, prisoners' fingernails pulled out with pliers, beatings to the point of broken bones. In addition, tens of thousands of secret agents operated within Tehran's neighborhoods and workplaces, and even inside families. The shah relentlessly spied on his own people, and the effect was chilling.

The shah, of course, had counterarguments. At one point Frost suggests that the shah was responding to legitimate threats to his regime, from "the communists" and others, by designating anyone who opposed him an enemy of the state. The shah adds that Khomeini's new government had done away with trials altogether, opting instead for immediate executions.

At the end, Frost asks the shah whether there was a moment in his last months in power when he realized he might have to leave.

"Not exactly," he says. "But I had many sleepless nights wondering, What is happening? Because I still don't understand what has happened."

It's often hard to tell when Armao's being candid, or when, thirty years later, he's *still* talking on behalf of the shah. He acknowledges, in retrospect, that the shah lost touch with what was occurring under his rule, and that he should have acted sooner against SAVAK.

But his criticism is focused more on the wisdom of ruling from such a distance than on the morality of the regime's conduct. Of the two narratives he had to choose from at the time, Armao picked the Abandoned Dying King Whose Nation Was Stolen By Madmen over the one about the brutal despot chased out by his own people. He still repeats the shah's claim that Western human-rights standards "don't always work in the developing world," and says that it was only after 9/11 that Americans began to understand what the shah was up against during his final years in power.

He also told me stories of comedians and singers being thrown in jail for offhand comments about the shah, as if to prove that SAVAK was more bumbling than sinister. And he relayed a joke that the shah liked to tell, as well:

As Armao explains it, it seems the shah was called to a ribbon-cutting ceremony at the aquarium. The aquarium director asked if His Imperial Majesty would favor them by feeding the porpoises. The shah goes to the pool, and is handed a basket of fish. He throws them in, one by one, until someone asks, "Your Imperial Majesty, how do you know when you've given the porpoises too much to eat?" Which is when the shah says, "When they jump from the water and yell Death to the Shah, you'll know I've fed them too much."

Of course, these anecdotes only reinforced my sense of how repressive life was for ordinary Iranians in the years before the revolution, and how uninterested in their suffering the shah was. What's certain is how much Armao genuinely *liked* the king and his family, regardless of what they did, and saw them as victims of international inconstancy rather than as architects of an oppressive police state. He saw himself, in turn, as their last line of defense against assassination, extradition, or both.

By March of 1980, the shah's condition was deteriorating once again. Armao, in response, grew more belligerent and volatile. "The shah used to say to me, 'Calm down; what's happened to you? You're like a hot pepper.'"

Armao argued with Torrijos and Noriega; with Hamilton Jordan; sometimes even with the shah's bodyguards, who had become his close friends. One often-repeated story revolves around a day Armao believed the shah had been kidnapped, and called up Ambler Moss, the American ambassador to Panama, to threaten to make it into an international incident. As it turned out, the shah was out with a woman, Moss says—"a Canadian tourist he'd met on the beach."

Over the following weeks, things only got worse. Noriega's guards battled daily with Armao and his assistant, Mark Morse, at one point carting Morse off to jail for several hours. They bugged the shah's house, ineptly (Morse found one of Noriega's men hiding in a supply closet, holding a recording device, with a set of fuzzy headphones on his ears), and billed the shah for the cost.

White House officials, meanwhile, were becoming increasingly impatient with the shah. The hostages had been held captive for four months by now, and the shah was unwilling to take responsibility for their fate. When Armao presented the Carter administration with a plan for the shah to return to Egypt, White House Counsel Lloyd Cutler and Arnie Rafael, the State Department's Middle East envoy, decided to fly down to Contadora. They feared the King's presence in Egypt would incite outrage in the Arab street; and, privately, the White House had been edging toward a desire to see their old friend formally admit that he was no longer king at all. Abdication, they thought, might be enough to entice the ayatollah to release his imprisoned Americans.

Two days before the shah's planned departure, Cutler and Rafael arrived at the royal family's lodgings and asked to speak to the king. They also asked Armao to leave the room, something he at first refused to do. Cutler scolded him, claiming he didn't have the necessary security clearance to listen in, and forced him out.

Outside, Armao fumed. Then he found the queen and told her what was happening. She, in turn, quickly forced her way in.

"She talked directly to the shah in Farsi," Armao says, "calling the two Americans sons of bitches, saying Don't listen to them, and this and that, not knowing until I told her later that Arnie Rafael spoke Farsi perfectly. They backtracked, then, and started inviting him back to Houston, saying 'Of course you're welcome in the United States.'"

It was the last thing the Americans wanted. They wanted the hostages back, and without the shah in Panama, at the mercy of Torrijos and Noriega, they couldn't see a clear way to get them. At the time, Torrijos was closing in on a deal with the Iranians, with the king's abdication as a key concession. But the moment the Americans broached this, having abandoned their attempts to convince the shah to steer clear of Egypt or America, Armao knew they'd played the wrong hand. To abdicate would mean legitimizing the Khomeini regime, something the shah would never be willing to do.

"When they brought that up, the shah looked at them and said, 'Gentlemen, thank you very much, but we've made the decision to leave, and abdication is *not* in the *vocabulary* of a monarch,'" Armao told me. "Then he added, 'The luggage assembled outside is ours.'"

At midday on March 23, 1980, the royals took a small plane off of Contadora. They boarded an old DC-8 in Panama City ("Terrible, six seats across, the smallest coach seats you could imagine," Armao remembers) to take them to Egypt. The children's pediatrician and their ailing Great Dane, Beno, went with them. Noriega bid them a chilly farewell.

The pilots were CIA, Armao said, which neither alarmed the shah's entourage nor made them feel secure. If worse came to worse, the shah knew how to fly the plane, as did Colonel Nevissi, the queen's bodyguard.

"I said, 'Colonel, sit in the cockpit. If they turn the plane the wrong way, you know what to do,'" Armao tells me. "So he said, 'All right, but what do I do if they're flying to Tehran?' I said, 'Shoot them.'"

Armao's paranoia was well founded. The plane had been scheduled to stop in the Azores for refueling, but when they'd been waiting there for more than an hour, the queen began to panic. The temperature inside the plane had dropped, and the shah's fever was getting worse.

Armao asked around to find out what was going on. An air force officer informed him that they'd been told to hold the plane.

"By *whom?*" Armao asked.

After four hours, he got his answer. There had indeed been a last-ditch plan to fly the shah back to Panama and arrest him. In exchange, the Iranians would transfer the hostages from the student militants' custody to the government's, a first step toward their release.

But the deal, unbelievably, fell apart on a clerical error. The extradition papers were filed too late, meaning the arrest would have to be postponed.

The Iranians, who had been negotiating with Hamilton Jordan, suggested that Jordan hold the shah in the Azores for twenty-four hours, calling it a medical emergency. But even Jordan had had enough by then, and told them to forget it.

Armao was in an airport in Frankfurt, en route back to Egypt from New York, when the shah died of non-Hodgkin's lymphoma on July 27, 1980. Armao had been looking for new doctors for the king, and trying to talk school directors into letting the shah's kids in for the next academic year. More than a few declined, saying they feared terrorist repercussions, but a few had come through. Ali Reza ended up at St. David's in Manhattan, Leila went to Marymount, Farahnaz went to Ethel Walker in Connecticut, and Reza went to Williams College.

The shah was buried near his father, in the Al Rifa'i Mosque in Cairo. The hostage crisis, despite the constant efforts of the Carter administration, dragged on for another six months. (In April 1980, a month after the shah left Panama, a covert rescue attempt had been hobbled by equipment malfunctions; one helicopter crashed, killing eight Americans.) The failure to secure the hostages' release became a unprecedented national humiliation—the most powerful nation in the world was, by all appearances, impotent in the face of an aged and fanatic mullah. Exactly a year from the start of the crisis, with the hostages still barricaded in the embassy, Ronald Reagan won the presidency in a landslide.[10]

Armao never quite had the career he seemed destined for in his early years with Rockefeller. When I ask why, he says, "The shah." While some doors closed for him, though, just as many opened up. And besides, he's sort of a family member by now. In the years after the shah's death, Armao's name often appeared (sympathetically) in the New York tabloids, in items about him escorting one or another of the shah's kids to a nightclub or out to dinner. Armao was especially close to the shah's younger son, Ali Reza, who worked for him.

It was thus particularly difficult for Armao to hear, early in 2011, that Ali Reza had taken his own life. He was the second of the shah's five children to do so; the youngest, Leila, killed herself at thirty-one, having suffered for years from depression.

Armao liked to joke with Ali Reza about how he'd saved the family's lives. "I used to tell him," he says, "that without me you would have ended up like the Romanovs." He chaperoned Ali Reza on his first dates, and took him to his first day of school in the U.S. More than money, or any political belief, Armao was driven by a desire to fill the void left by those who had betrayed the shah. "Friends who'd known them their whole lives" abandoned them, he says. "Seeing that hardened me."

---

[10] In his book *October Surprise*, Gary Sick asserts that William Casey, head of the Reagan campaign team, arranged a deal with the Iranian government to delay the release of the hostages until after the election. The intention, of course, was to humiliate Carter and tilt the election to Reagan.

Over the years, he's had to endure accusations that he betrayed his country by becoming the shah's errand boy, or that he was angling for millions from the shah's family. It's all bullshit, he says.

I ask him if he felt that he was the shah's last friend, whether it felt that way at the funeral.

He answered, "If you're drowning, you grab a life raft, and there was nobody around in the end. I was the one who was around, so he grabbed on to me. I was the life raft."

POLITICS
AND CONSCIENCE

by VÁCLAV HAVEL

with an introducution by
FLAGG TAYLOR

THE FIRST INSPIRATION for *The Great Lie*, the anthology of anti-totalitarian writing from which this essay is taken, came after I began teaching a class called "Dissident Political Thought" that focused on three great anti-communist dissidents—Aleksandr Solzhenitsyn, Czeslaw Milosz, and Václav Havel. In the course of the class, I realized that, in addition to being such keen analysts of twentieth-century communist regimes, these thinkers addressed the same questions that political philosophers had been struggling with for centuries—questions about the nature of tyranny and the ground of human freedom. What enabled men to carry out such horrific crimes against their fellows? What did the endurance of communist regimes reveal about human liberty? Why did so many suffer rule by ideological lies for so long, and what kept them open to the truth? And, perhaps most disconcertingly, what is the relationship between the totalitarian enterprise and the principles of democratic modernity?

They also all had something important to say about the utter strangeness, the novelty of totalitarian tyranny. Whatever the prevalence or scarcity of the phenomenon of ideocratic or totalitarian tyranny today, there are strong arguments to be made that we have yet to see the last of it. As Jean-Francois Revel has put it, "As long as we have not really understood the genesis of this phenomenon, who can say we are safe and immunized against new outbreaks of madness?" Revel's is a crucial question, and one that many thinkers have shied away from. Perhaps we were too confident that 1989–91 put ideocratic tyranny to rest, too tempted by the idea of an end to history. We think we have been liberated from the totalitarian temptation because the ideological contents of Nazism and Communism have been rejected. But the contributors to *The Great Lie* argue that real liberation will only come through a rejection of their *form*—their mode of thought. "The authentic subject is neither a fanatic nor a nihilist, but a witness," wrote Chantal Delsol. The dignity of the human person, she argues, will not be restored through cool detachment but through the recognition of truths outside oneself. *The Great Lie*'s writers are still relevant precisely because of their unyielding reflections on the philosophic conditions for the emergence of now-fallen regimes: their work compels us to reflect on the present status of those conditions. That is the first step in our immunization against new outbreaks of madness.

This brings us to a prominent theme in *The Great Lie*, one that belies the common criticism of the use of totalitarianism as a category—that it allows for a simplistic division between the evil, totalitarian East and the good, liberal West. Both Solzhenitsyn and Havel suggest that a broad civilizational crisis infects the whole world, both East and West—as Solzhenitsyn puts in his famous Harvard Address, "The split in the world is less terrifying than the similarity of the disease afflicting its main sections." He roots the crisis in what he variously terms rationalistic humanism or anthropocentric humanism; technological civilization has brought us many material comforts, he says, but it has exacted a price on our spirits. There are a number of key elements to this sort of humanism: (1) the denial of intrinsic evil in human beings; (2) the denial of any higher task than the attainment of happiness on earth (happiness understood as material well-being); and (3) the claim that material progress automatically entails moral progress, and that this process will make us kinder, gentler creatures—replacing a world dominated by conflict and war with a world dominated by cooperation and commerce. All these elements depend on a common premise: the strict separation of politics from morality.

Havel, in the essay presented here, has a complementary account of the human personality under the dominance of technological civilization. According to Havel, totalitarian systems are "a convex mirror of all modern civilization"; "the avant-garde of a global crisis." Havel argues that modern, technological civilization has allowed us to turn away from our natural longing for meaning and responsibility. As a result, we might succumb to mere "existence-in-the-world" by enveloping ourselves in everyday desires, in consumption, and investing our efforts in ever-more-efficient strategies to fulfill these desires. Or we might even sign on to an ideological project to remake human beings and their world—the totalitarian temptation. In either case, we turn away from the work required to resist "the irrational momentum of anonymous, impersonal, and inhuman power."

Havel's "Politics and Conscience" is his most concise and compelling statement on the limits and dangers of what we might recognize as a distinctly modern rationalism, and on that rationalism's concomitant understanding of politics as the mere technology of power. He reminds us of the inescapable moral dimensions of political life by recalling those two pre-modern traditions whose dialogue constitutes the vitality of Western civilization: Athens and Jerusalem. Havel's striking though unstated premise seems to be this: the philosophic wonder of Athens and the awe and obedient love of our Creator of Jerusalem have more in common with one another than either have with the modern rationalism still ascendant today. Havel—and each of our pre-modern traditions—compel us to confront the question of man's place in the whole and the nature of that whole. It is our lived experience, where we encounter categories like good and evil, beauty and ugliness, duty and rights, that points us back to a natural order that grounds and limits our freedom. Whether a civilization that turns away from these matters can endure is no less of an urgent question now than when Havel put it to us in 1984.

Havel wrote this speech for the occasion of his acceptance of an honorary degree from the University of Toulouse. He was denied travel privileges, and was represented at the university by the English playwright Tom Stoppard. The footnotes are by Flagg Taylor.

I

A S A BOY, I lived for some time in the country and I clearly remember an experience from those days: I used to walk to school in a nearby village along a cart track through the fields and, on the way, see on the horizon a huge smokestack of some hurriedly built factory, in all likelihood in the service of war. It spewed dense brown smoke and scattered it across the sky. Each time I saw it, I had an intense sense of something profoundly wrong, of humans soiling the heavens. I have no idea whether there was something like a science of ecology in those days; if there was, I certainly knew nothing of it. Still that "soiling of the heavens" offended me spontaneously. It seemed to me that, in it, humans are guilty of something, that they destroy something important, arbitrarily disrupting the natural order of things; and that such things cannot go unpunished. To be sure, my revulsion was largely aesthetic; I knew nothing then of the noxious emissions which would one day devastate our forests, exterminate game, and endanger the health of people.

If a medieval man were to see something like that suddenly on the horizon—say, while out hunting—he would probably think it the work of the Devil and would fall on his knees and pray that he and his kin be saved.

What is it, actually, that the world of the medieval peasant and that of a small boy have in common? Something substantive, I think. Both the boy and the peasant are far more intensely rooted in what some philosophers call "the natural world," or *Lebenswelt*, than most modern adults. They have not yet grown alienated from the world of their actual personal experience, the world which has its morning and its evening, its *down* (the earth) and its *up* (the heavens), where the sun rises daily in the east, traverses the sky and sets in the west, and where concepts like "at home" and "in foreign parts," good and evil, beauty and ugliness, near and far, duty and rights, still mean something living and definite. They are still rooted in a world which knows the dividing line between all that is intimately familiar and appropriately a subject of our concern, and that which lies beyond its horizon, that before which we should bow down humbly because of the mystery about it. Our "I" primordially attests to that world and personally certifies it; that is the world of our lived experience, a world not yet indifferent since we are personally bound to it in our love, hatred, respect, contempt, tradition, in our interests and in that pre-reflective meaningfulness from which culture is born. That is the realm of our inimitable, inalienable, and nontransferable joy and pain, a world in which, through which, and for which we are somehow answerable, a world of personal responsibility. In this world, categories like justice, honor, treason, friendship, infidelity, courage, or empathy have a wholly tangible content, relating to actual persons and important for actual life. At the basis of this world are values which are simply there, perennially, before we ever speak of them, before we reflect upon them and inquire about them. It owes its internal coherence to something like a "prespeculative" assumption that the world functions and is generally possible at all only because there is something beyond its horizon, something beyond or above it that might escape our understanding and our grasp but, for just that reason, firmly grounds this world, bestows upon it its order and measure, and is the hidden source of all the rules, customs, commandments, prohibitions, and norms that hold within it. The natural world, in virtue of its very being, bears within it the presupposition of the absolute that grounds, delimits, animates, and directs it, without which it would be unthinkable, absurd, and superfluous, and which we can only quietly respect. Any attempt to spurn it, master it, or replace it with something else, appears, within the framework of the natural world, as an expression of hubris for which humans must pay a heavy price, as did Don Juan and Faust.

To me, personally, the smokestack soiling the heavens is not just a regrettable lapse of a technology that failed to include "the ecological factor" in its calculation, one which can be easily corrected with the appropriate filter. To me it is more the symbol of an age which seeks to transcend the boundaries of the natural world and its norms and to make it into a merely private concern, a matter of subjective preference and private feeling, of the illusions, prejudices, and whims of a "mere" individual. It is a symbol of an epoch which denies the binding importance of personal experience—including the experience of mystery and of the absolute—and displaces the personally experienced absolute as the measure of the world with a new, man-made absolute, devoid of mystery, free of the "whims" of subjectivity and, as such, impersonal and inhuman. It is the absolute of so-called objectivity: the objective, rational cognition of the scientific model of the world.

Modern science, constructing its universally valid image of the world, thus crashes through the bounds of the natural world, which it can understand only as a prison of prejudices from which we must break out into the light of objectively verified truth. The natural world appears to it as no more than an unfortunate leftover from our backward ancestors, a fantasy of their childish immaturity. With that, of course, it abolishes as mere fiction even the innermost foundation of our natural world; it kills God and takes his place on the vacant throne so that henceforth it would be science which would hold the order of being in its hand as its sole legitimate guardian and be the sole legitimate arbiter of all relevant truth. For, after all, it is only science that rises above all individual subjective truths and replaces them with a superior, suprasubjective, suprapersonal truth, which is truly objective and universal.

Modern rationalism and modern science, though the work of people that, as all human works, developed within our natural world, now systematically leave it behind, deny it, degrade and defame it—and, of course, at the same time colonize it. A modern man, whose natural world has been properly conquered by science and technology, objects to the smoke from the smokestack only if the stench penetrates his apartment. In no case, though, does he take offense at it metaphysically since he knows that the factory to which the smokestack belongs manufactures things that he needs. As a man of the technological era, he can conceive of a remedy only within the limits of technology—say, a catalytic scrubber fitted to the chimney.

Lest you misunderstand: I am not proposing that humans abolish smokestacks or prohibit science or generally return to the Middle Ages. Besides, it is not by accident that some of the most profound discoveries of modern science render the myth of objectivity surprisingly problematic and, via a remarkable detour, return us to the human subject and his world. I wish no more than to consider, in a most general and admittedly schematic outline, the spiritual framework of modern civilization and the source of its present crisis. And though the primary focus of these reflections will be the political rather than ecological aspect of this crisis, I might, perhaps, clarify my starting point with one more ecological example.

For centuries, the basic component of European agriculture had been the family farm. In Czech, the older term for it was *grunt*—which itself is not without its etymological interest. The word, taken from the German *Grund*, actually means ground or foundation and, in Czech, acquired a peculiar semantic coloring. As the colloquial synonym for "foundation," it points out the "groundedness" of the ground, its indubitable, traditional and prespeculatively given authenticity and credibility. Certainly, the family farm was a source of endless and intensifying social conflict of all kinds. Still, we cannot deny it one thing: it was rooted in the nature of its place, appropriate, harmonious, personally tested by generations of farmers and certified by the results of their husbandry. It also displayed a kind of optimal mutual proportionality in extent and kind of all that belonged to it; fields, meadows, boundaries, woods, cattle, domestic animals, water, roads, and so on. For centuries no farmer made it the topic of a scientific study. Nevertheless, it constituted a generally satisfactory economic and ecological system, within which everything was bound together by a thousand threads of mutual and meaningful connection, guaranteeing its stability as well as the stability of the product of the farmer's husbandry. Unlike present-day "agribusiness," the traditional family farm was energetically self-sufficient. Though it was subject to common calamities, it was not guilty of them—unfavorable weather, cattle disease, wars, and other catastrophes lay outside the farmer's province. Certainly, modern agricultural and social science could also improve agriculture in a thousand ways, increasing its productivity, reducing the amount of sheer drudgery, and eliminating the worst social inequities. But this is possible only on the assumption that modernization, too, will be guided by a certain humility and respect for the mysterious order of nature and for the appropriateness which derives from it and which is intrinsic to the natural world of personal experience and responsibility. Modernization must not be simply an arrogant, megalomaniac, and brutal invasion by an impersonally objective science, represented by a newly graduated agronomist or a bureaucrat in the service of the "scientific world view."

That, however, is just what happened to our country: our word for it was "collectivization." Like a tornado, it raged through the Czechoslovakian countryside thirty years ago, leaving not a stone in place. Among its consequences were, on the one hand, tens of thousands of lives devastated by prison, sacrificed on the altar of a scientific utopia offering brighter tomorrows. On the other hand, the level of social conflict and the amount of drudgery in the countryside did in fact decrease while agricultural productivity rose quantitatively. That, though, is not why I mention it. My reason is something else: thirty years after the tornado swept the traditional family farm off the face of the earth, scientists are amazed to discover what even a semiliterate farmer previously knew— that human beings must pay a heavy price for every attempt to abolish, radically, once for all and without trace, that humbly respected boundary of the natural world, with its tradition of scrupulous personal acknowledgment. They must pay for the attempt to seize nature, to leave not a remnant of it in human hands, to ridicule its mystery; they must pay for the attempt to abolish God and to play at being God. This is what in fact happened. With hedges plowed under and woods cut down, wild birds have died out and, with them, a natural, unpaid protector of the crops against harmful insects. Huge unified fields have led to the inevitable annual loss of millions of cubic yards of topsoil that have taken centuries to accumulate; chemical fertilizers and pesticides have catastrophically poisoned all vegetable products, the earth, and the waters. Heavy machinery systematically presses down the soil, making it impenetrable to air and thus infertile; cows in gigantic dairy farms suffer neuroses and lose their milk while agriculture siphons off ever more energy from industry—manufacture of machines, artificial fertilizers, rising transportation costs in an age of growing local specialization, and so on. In short, the prognoses are terrifying and no one knows what surprises coming years and decades may bring.

It is paradoxical: people in the age of science and technology live in the conviction that they can improve their lives because they are able to grasp and exploit the complexity of nature and the general laws of its functioning. Yet it is precisely these laws which, in the end, tragically catch up with them and get the better of them. People thought they could explain and conquer nature—yet the outcome is that they destroyed it and disinherited themselves from it. But what are the prospects for man "outside nature"? It is, after all, precisely the sciences that are most recently discovering that the human body is actually only a particularly busy intersection of billions of organic microbodies, of their complex mutual contacts and influences, together forming that incredible mega-organism we call the "biosphere" in which our planet is blanketed. The fault is not one of science as such but of the arrogance of man in the age of science. Man simply is not God, and playing God has cruel consequences. Man has abolished the absolute horizon of his relations, denied his personal "pre-objective" experience of the lived world, while relegating personal conscience and consciousness to the bathroom, as something so private that it is no one's business. Man rejected his responsibility as a "subjective illusion"—and in place of it installed what is now proving to be the most dangerous illusion of all: the fiction of objectivity stripped of all that is concretely human, of a rational understanding of the cosmos, and of an abstract schema of a putative "historical necessity." As the apex of it all, man has constructed a vision of a scientifically calculable and technologically achievable "universal welfare," that need only be invented by experimental institutes while industrial and bureaucratic factories turn it into reality. That millions of people will be sacrificed to this illusion in scientifically run concentration camps is not something that concerns our modern man unless by chance he himself lands behind barbed wire and is thrown drastically back upon his natural world. The phenomenon of empathy, after all, belongs with that abolished realm of personal prejudice which had to yield to science, objectivity, historical necessity, technology, system, and the apparat—and those, being impersonal, cannot worry. They are abstract and anonymous, ever utilitarian, and thus ever a priori innocent.

And as for the future, who, personally, would care about it or even worry about it when the perspective of eternity is one of the things locked away in the bathroom, if not expelled outright into the realm of fairy tales? If a contemporary scientist thinks at all of what will be in two hundred years, he does so solely as a disinterested observer who, basically, could not care less whether he is doing research on the metabolism of the flea, on the radio signals of pulsars, or on the global reserves of natural gas. And a modern politician? He has absolutely no reason to care, especially if it might interfere with his chances in an election, as long as he lives in a country where there are elections.

II

The Czech philosopher Václav Belohradsky has persuasively developed the thought that the rationalistic spirit of modern science, founded on abstract reason and on the presumption of impersonal objectivity, has its father not only in the natural sciences—Galileo, but also a father in politics—Machiavelli, who first formulated (albeit with an undertone of malicious irony) a theory of politics as a rational technology of power. We could say that, for all the complex historical detours, the origin of the modern state and of modern political power may be sought precisely here, that is, once again in a moment when human reason begins to "liberate" itself from the human being as such, from his personal experience, personal conscience, and personal responsibility and so also from that to which, within the framework of the natural world, all responsibility is uniquely related, his absolute horizon. Just as the modern scientists set apart the actual human being as the subject of the lived experience of the world, so, ever more evidently, do both the modern state and modern politics. To be sure, this process by which power becomes anonymous and depersonalized, and reduced to a mere technology of rule and manipulation, has a thousand masks, variants, and expressions. In one case it is covert and inconspicuous, while in another case it is entirely overt; in one case it sneaks up on us along subtle and devious paths, in another case it is brutally direct. Essentially, though, it is the same universal trend. It is the essential trait of all modern civilization, growing directly from its spiritual structure, rooted in it by a thousand tangled tendrils and inseparable even in thought from its technological nature, its mass characteristics, and its consumer orientation. Rulers and leaders were once personalities in their own right, with particular human faces, still in some sense personally responsible for their deeds, good and ill, whether they had been installed by dynastic tradition, by the will of the people, by a victorious battle, or by intrigue. But they have been replaced in modern times by the manager, the bureaucrat, the apparatchik—a professional ruler, manipulator, and expert in the techniques of management, manipulation, and obfuscation, filling a depersonalized intersection of functional relations, a cog in the machinery of state caught up in a predetermined role. This professional ruler is an "innocent" tool of an "innocent" anonymous power, legitimized by science, cybernetics, ideology, law, abstraction, and objectivity—that is, by everything except personal responsibility to human beings as persons and neighbors. A modern politician is transparent: behind his judicious mask and affected diction there is not a trace of a human being rooted in the order of the natural world by his loves, passions, interests, personal opinions, hatred, courage, or cruelty. All that he, too, locks away in his private bathroom. If we glimpse anything at all behind the mask, it will be only a more or less competent technician of power. System, ideology, and apparat have deprived us—rulers as well as the ruled—of our conscience, of our common sense and natural speech and thereby, of our actual humanity. States grow ever more machinelike; people are transformed into statistical choruses of voters, producers, consumers, patients, tourists, or soldiers. In politics, good and evil, categories of the natural world and therefore obsolete remnants of the past, lose all absolute meaning; the sole method of politics is quantifiable success. Power is a priori innocent because it does not grow from a world in which words like "guilt" and "innocence" retain their meaning.

This impersonal power has achieved what is its most complete expression so far in the totalitarian systems. As Belohradsky points out, the depersonalization of power and its conquest of human conscience and human speech have been successfully linked to an extra-European tradition of a "cosmological" conception of the empire (identifying the empire, as the sole true center of the world, with the world as such, and considering the human as its exclusive property). But, as the totalitarian systems clearly illustrate, this does not mean that modern impersonal power is itself an extra-European affair. The truth is the very opposite: it was precisely Europe, and the European West, that provided and frequently forced on the world all that today has become the basis of such power: natural science, rationalism, scientism, the

Industrial Revolution, and also revolution as such, as a fanatical abstraction, through the displacement of the natural world to the bathroom down to the cult of consumption, the atomic bomb, and Marxism. And it is Europe—democratic western Europe—which today stands bewildered in the face of this ambiguous export. The contemporary dilemma, whether to resist this reverse expansionism of its erstwhile export or to yield to it, attests to this. Should rockets, now aimed at Europe thanks to its export of spiritual and technological potential, be countered by similar and better rockets, thereby demonstrating a determination to defend such values as Europe has left, at the cost of entering into an utterly immoral game being forced upon it? Or should Europe retreat, hoping that the responsibility for the fate of the planet demonstrated thereby will infect, by its miraculous power, the rest of the world?

I think that, with respect to the relation of western Europe to the totalitarian systems, no error could be greater than the one looming largest: that of a failure to understand the totalitarian systems for what they ultimately are—a convex mirror of all modern civilization and a harsh, perhaps final call for a global recasting of how that civilization understands itself. If we ignore that, then it does not make any essential difference which form Europe's efforts will take. It might be the form of taking the totalitarian systems, in the spirit of Europe's own rationalistic tradition, for a locally idiosyncratic attempt at achieving general welfare, to which only men of ill-will attribute expansionist tendencies. Or, in the spirit of the same rationalistic tradition, though this time in the Machiavellian conception of politics as the technology of power, one might perceive the totalitarian regimes as a purely external threat by expansionist neighbors who can be driven back within acceptable bounds by an appropriate demonstration of power, without having to be thought about more deeply. The first alternative is that of the person who reconciles himself to the chimney belching smoke, even though that smoke is ugly and smelly, because in the end it serves a good purpose, the production of commonly needed goods. The second alternative is that of the man who thinks that it is simply a matter of a technological flaw, which can be eliminated by technological means, such as a filter or a scrubber. The reality, I believe, is unfortunately more serious. The chimney "soiling the heavens" is not just a technologically corrigible flaw of design, or a tax paid for a better consumerist tomorrow, but a symbol of a civilization which has renounced the absolute, which ignores the natural world and disdains its imperatives. So, too, the totalitarian systems warn of something far more serious than Western rationalism is willing to admit. They are, most of all, a convex mirror of the inevitable consequences of rationalism, a grotesquely magnified image of its own deep tendencies, an extreme offshoot of its own development and an ominous product of its own expansion. They are a deeply informative reflection of its own crisis. Totalitarian regimes are not merely dangerous neighbors and even less some kind of an avant-garde of world progress. Alas, just the opposite: they are the avant-garde of a global crisis of this civilization, first European, then Euro-American, and ultimately global. They are one of the possible futurological studies of the Western world, not in the sense that one day they will attack and conquer it, but in a far deeper sense—that they illustrate graphically the consequences of what Belohradsky calls the "eschatology of the impersonal."

It is the total rule of a bloated, anonymously bureaucratic power, not yet irresponsible but already operating outside all conscience, a power grounded in an omnipresent ideological fiction which can rationalize anything without ever having to come in contact with the truth. Power as the omnipresent monopoly of control, repression, and fear; power which makes thought, morality, and privacy a state monopoly and so dehumanizes them; power which long since has ceased to be the matter of a group of arbitrary rulers but which, rather, occupies and swallows up everyone so that all should become integrated within it, at least through their silence. No one actually possesses such power, since it is the power itself which possesses everyone; it is a monstrosity which is not guided by humans but which, on the contrary, drags all persons along with its "objective" self-momentum—objective in the sense of being cut off from all human standards, including human reason, and hence entirely irrational—toward a terrifying, unknown future.

Let me repeat: totalitarian power is a great reminder to contemporary civilization. Perhaps somewhere there may be some generals who think it would be best to dispatch such systems from the face of the earth and then all would be well. But that is no different from an ugly woman trying to get rid of her ugliness by smashing the mirror that reminds her of it. Such a "final solution" is one of the typical dreams of impersonal reason—capable, as the term "final solution" graphically reminds us, of transforming its dreams into reality and thereby reality into a nightmare. It would not only fail to resolve the crisis of the present world but, assuming anyone survived at all, would only aggravate it. By burdening the already heavy account of this civilization with further millions of dead, it would not block its essential trend to totalitarianism but would rather accelerate it. It would be a Pyrrhic victory, because the victors would emerge from a conflict inevitably resembling their defeated opponents far more than anyone today is willing to admit or able to imagine. Just a minor example: imagine what a huge Gulag Archipelago would have to be built in the West, in the name of country, democracy, progress, and war discipline, to contain all who refuse to take part in the effort, whether from naïvete, principle, fear, or ill will!

No evil has ever been eliminated by suppressing its symptoms. We need to address the cause itself.

III

From time to time I have a chance to speak with Western intellectuals who visit our country and decide to include a visit to a dissident in their itinerary—some out of genuine interest, or a willingness to understand and to express solidarity, others simply out of curiosity. Beside the Gothic and Baroque monuments, dissidents are apparently the only thing of interest to a tourist in this uniformly dreary environment. Those conversations are usually instructive: I learn much and come to understand much. The questions most frequently asked are these: Do you think you can really change anything when you are so few and have no influence at all? Are you opposed to socialism or do you merely wish to improve it? Do you condemn or condone the deployment of the Pershing II and the Cruise missiles in western Europe?[1] What can we do for you? What drives you to do what you are doing when all it brings you is persecution, prison—and no visible results? Would you want to see capitalism restored in your country?

Those questions are well intentioned, growing out of a desire to understand and showing that those who ask do care about the world, what it is and what it will be.

Still, precisely these and similar questions reveal to me again and again how deeply many Western intellectuals do not understand—and in some respects, cannot understand—just what is taking place here, what it is that we, the so-called dissidents, are striving for and, most of all, what the overall meaning of it is. Take, for instance, the question: "What can we do for you?" A great deal, to be sure. The more support, interest, and solidarity of freethinking people in the world we enjoy, the

---

[1] The missiles placed by the United States and its allies in western Europe to counter the threat of the Soviet missiles deployed in eastern Europe.

less the danger of being arrested, and the greater the hope that ours will not be a voice crying in the wilderness. And yet, somewhere deep within the question there is built-in misunderstanding. After all, in the last instance the point is not to help us, a handful of "dissidents," to keep out of jail a bit more of the time. It is not even a question of helping these nations, Czechs and Slovaks, to live a bit better, a bit more freely. They need first and foremost to help themselves. They have waited for the help of others far too often, depended on it far too much, and far too many times came to grief: either the promised help was withdrawn at the last moment or it turned into the very opposite of their expectations. In the deepest sense, something else is at stake—the salvation of us all, of myself and my interlocutor equally. Or is it not something that concerns us all equally? Are not my dim prospects or, conversely, my hopes *his* dim prospects and hopes as well? Was not my arrest an attack on him and the deceptions to which he is subjected an attack on me as well? Is not the suppression of human beings in Prague a suppression of all human beings? Is not indifference to what is happening here or even illusions about it a preparation for the kind of misery elsewhere? Does not their misery presuppose ours? The point is not that some Czech dissident, as a person in distress, needs help. I could best help myself out of distress simply by ceasing to be a "dissident." The point is what that dissident's flawed efforts and his fate tell us and mean, what they attest about the condition, the destiny, the opportunities, and the problems of the world, the respects in which they are or could be food for thought for others as well, for the way they see their, and so our, shared destiny, in what ways they are a warning, a challenge, a danger, or a lesson for those who visit us.

Or the question about socialism and capitalism! I have to admit that it gives me a sense of emerging from the depths of the last century. It seems to me that these thoroughly ideological and often semantically confused categories have long since been beside the point. The question is wholly other, deeper and equally relevant to all: whether we shall, by whatever means, succeed in reconstituting the natural world as the true terrain of politics, rehabilitating the personal experience of human beings as the initial measure of things, placing morality above politics and responsibility above our desires, in making human community meaningful, in returning content to human speech, in reconstituting, as the focus of all social action, the autonomous, integral, and dignified human "I," responsible for ourselves because we are bound to something higher, and capable of sacrificing something, in extreme cases even everything, of his banal, prosperous private life—that "rule of everydayness," as Jan Patocka used to say—for the sake of that which gives life meaning. It really is not all that important whether, by accident of domicile, we confront a Western manager or an Eastern bureaucrat in this very modest and yet globally crucial struggle against the momentum of impersonal power. If we can defend our humanity, then perhaps there is a hope of sorts—though even then it is by no means automatic—that we shall also find some more meaningful ways of balancing our natural claims to shared economic decision-making and to dignified social status, with the tried-and-true driving force of all work: human enterprise realized in genuine market relations. As long, however, as our humanity remains defenseless, we will not be saved by any technical or organizational trick designed to produce better economic functioning, just as no filter on a factory smokestack will prevent a general dehumanization. To what purpose a system functions is, after all, more important than how it does so. Might it not function quite smoothly, after all, in the service of total destruction?

I speak of this because, looking at the world from the perspective which fate allotted me, I cannot avoid the impression that many people in the West still understand little of what is actually at stake in our time.

If, for instance, we take a second look at the two basic political alternatives between which Western intellectuals oscillate today, it becomes apparent that they are no more than two different ways of playing the same game, proffered by the anonymity of power. As such, they are no more than two diverse ways of moving toward the same global totalitarianism. One way of playing the game of anonymous reason is to keep on toying with the mystery of matter—"playing God"—inventing and deploying further weapons of mass destruction, all, of course, intended "for the defense of democracy" but in effect further degrading democracy to the "uninhabitable fiction" which socialism has long since become on our side of Europe. The other form of the game is the tempting vortex that draws so many good and sincere people into itself, the so-called struggle for peace. Certainly it need not always be so. Still, often I do have the impression that this vortex has been designed and deployed by that same treacherous, all-pervasive impersonal power as a more poetic means of colonizing human consciousness. Please note, I have in mind impersonal power as a principle, globally, in all its instances, not only Moscow—which, if the truth be told, lacks the capability of organizing something as widespread as the contemporary peace movement. Still, could there be a better way of rendering an honest, freethinking man (the chief threat to all anonymous power) ineffectual in the world of rationalism and ideology than by offering him the simplest thesis possible, with all the apparent characteristics of a noble goal? Could you imagine something that would more effectively fire a just mind—preoccupying it, then occupying it, and ultimately rendering it intellectually harmless—than the possibility of "a struggle against war"? Is there a more clever means of deceiving men than with the illusion that they can prevent war if they interfere with the deployment of weapons (which will be deployed in any case)? It is hard to imagine an easier way to a totalitarianism of the human spirit. The more obvious it becomes that the weapons will indeed be deployed, the more rapidly does the mind of a person who has totally identified with the goal of preventing such deployment become radicalized, fanaticized and, in the end, alienated from itself. So a man sent off on his way by the noblest of intentions finds himself, at the journey's end, precisely where anonymous power needs to see him: in the rut of totalitarian thought, where he is not his own and where he surrenders his own reason and conscience for the sake of another "uninhabitable fiction"! As long as that goal is served, it is not important whether we call that fiction "human well-being," "socialism," or "peace."

Certainly, from the standpoint of the defense and the interests of the Western world, it is not very good when someone says "Better Red than dead." But from the viewpoint of the global, impersonal power, which transcends power blocs and, in its omnipresence, represents a truly diabolical temptation, there could be nothing better. That slogan is an infallible sign that the speaker has given up his humanity. For he has given up the ability personally to guarantee something that transcends him and so to sacrifice, *in extremis*, even life itself to that which makes life meaningful. Patocka once wrote that a life not willing to sacrifice itself to what makes it meaningful is not worth living. It is just in the world of such lives and of such a "peace"—that is, under the "rule of everydayness"—that wars happen most easily. In such a world, there is no moral barrier against them, no barrier guaranteed by the courage of supreme sacrifice. The door stands wide open for the irrational "securing of our interests." The absence of heroes who know what they are dying for is the first step on the way to the mounds of corpses of those who are slaughtered like cattle. The slogan "Better Red than dead" does not irritate me as an expression of surrender to the Soviet Union, but it terrifies me as an expression of the renunciation by Western people of any claim to a meaningful life and of their acceptance of impersonal power as such. For what the slogan really says is that nothing is worth giving one's life for. However, without the horizon of the highest sacrifice, all sacrifice becomes senseless. Then nothing is worth anything. Nothing means anything. The result is a philosophy of sheer negation of our humanity. In the case of Soviet totalitarianism, such a philosophy does no more than offer a little political assistance. With respect to Western totalitarianism, it is what constitutes it, directly and primordially.

In short, I cannot overcome the impression that Western culture is threatened far more by itself than by SS-20 rockets.[2] When a French leftist student told me with a sincere glow in his eyes that the Gulag was a tax paid for the ideals of socialism and that Solzhenitsyn is just a personally embittered man, he cast me into a deep gloom. Is Europe really incapable of learning from its own history? Can't that dear lad ever understand that even the most promising project of "general well-being" convicts itself of inhumanity the moment it demands a single involuntary death—that is, one which is not a conscious sacrifice of a life to its meaning? Is he really incapable of comprehending that until he finds himself incarcerated in some Soviet-style jail near Toulouse? Did the newspeak of our world so penetrate natural human speech that two people can no longer communicate even such a basic experience?

IV

I presume that after all these stringent criticisms, I am expected to say just what I consider to be a meaningful alternative for Western humanity today in the face of political dilemmas of the contemporary world.

---

[2] The missiles deployed by the Soviet Union in eastern Europe.

As all I have said suggests, it seems to me that all of us, East and West, face one fundamental task from which all else should follow. That task is one of resisting vigilantly, thoughtfully, and attentively, but at the same time with total dedication, at every step and everywhere, the irrational momentum of anonymous, impersonal, and inhuman power—the power of ideologies, systems, apparat, bureaucracy, artificial languages, and political slogans. We must resist its complex and wholly alienating pressure, whether it takes the form of consumption, advertising, repression, technology, or cliché—all of which are the blood brothers of fanaticism and the wellspring of totalitarian thought. We must draw our standards from our natural world, heedless of ridicule, and reaffirm its denied validity. We must honor with the humility of the wise the limits of that natural world and the mystery which lies beyond them, admitting that there is something in the order of being which evidently exceeds all our competence. We must relate to the absolute horizon of our existence which, if we but will, we shall constantly rediscover and experience. We must make values and imperatives the starting point of all our acts, of all our personally attested, openly contemplated, and ideologically uncensored lived experience. We must trust the voice of our conscience more than that of all abstract speculations and not invent responsibilities other than the one to which the voice calls us. We must not be ashamed that we are capable of love, friendship, solidarity, sympathy, and tolerance, but just the opposite: we must set these fundamental dimensions of our humanity free from their "private" exile and accept them as the only genuine starting point of meaningful human community. We must be guided by our own reason and serve the truth under all circumstances as our own essential experience.

I know all that sounds very general, very indefinite, and very unrealistic, but I assure you that these apparently naïve words stem from a very particular and not always easy experience with the world and that, if I may say so, I know what I am talking about.

The vanguard of impersonal power, which drags the world along its irrational path, lined with devastated nature and launching pads, is composed of the totalitarian regimes of our time. It is not possible to ignore them, to make excuses for them, to yield to them or to accept their way of playing the game, thereby becoming like them. I am convinced that we can face them best by studying them without prejudice, learning from them, and resisting them by being radically different, with a difference born of a continuous struggle against the evil which they may embody most clearly, but which dwells everywhere and so even within each of us. What is most dangerous to that evil are not the rockets aimed at this or that state but the fundamental negation of this evil in the very structure of contemporary humanity: a return of humans to themselves and to their responsibility for the world; a new understanding of human rights and their persistent reaffirmation, resistance against every manifestation of impersonal power that claims to be beyond good and evil, anywhere and everywhere, no matter how it disguises its tricks and machinations, even if it does so in the name of defense against totalitarian systems.

The best resistance to totalitarianism is simply to drive it out of our own souls, our own circumstances, our own land, to drive it out of contemporary humankind. The best help to all who suffer under totalitarian regimes is to confront the evil which a totalitarian system constitutes, from which it draws its strength and on which its "vanguard" is nourished. If there is no such vanguard, no extremist sprout from which it can grow, the system will have nothing to stand on. A reaffirmed human responsibility is the most natural barrier to all irresponsibility. If, for instance, the spiritual and technological potential of the advanced world is spread truly responsibly, not solely under the pressure of a selfish interest in profits, we can prevent its irresponsible transformation into weapons of destruction. It surely makes much more sense to operate in the sphere of causes than simply to respond to their effects. By then, as a rule, the only possible response is by equally immoral means. To follow that path means to continue spreading the evil of irresponsibility in the world, and so to produce precisely the poison on which totalitarianism feeds.

I favor "antipolitical politics," that is, politics not as the technology of power and manipulation, of cybernetic rule over humans or as the art of the utilitarian, but politics as one of the ways of seeking and achieving meaningful lives, of protecting them and serving them. I favor politics as practical morality, as service to the truth, as essentially human and humanly measured care for our fellow humans. It is, I presume, an approach which, in this world, is extremely impractical and difficult to apply in daily life. Still, I know no better alternative.

V

When I was tried and then serving my sentence, I experienced directly the importance and beneficial force of international solidarity. I shall never cease to be grateful for all its expressions. Still, I do not think that we who seek to proclaim the truth under our conditions find ourselves in an asymmetrical position, or that it should be we alone who ask for help and expect it, without being able to offer help in the direction from which it also comes.

I am convinced that what is called "dissent" in the Soviet bloc is a specific modern experience, the experience of life at the very ramparts of dehumanized power. As such, that "dissent" has the opportunity and even the duty to reflect on this experience, to testify to it and to pass it on to those fortunate enough not to have to undergo it. Thus we too have a certain opportunity to help in some ways those who help us, to help them in our deeply shared interest, in the interest of mankind.

One such fundamental experience, that which I called "antipoliti-cal politics," *is* possible and can be effective, even though by its very nature it cannot calculate its effect beforehand. That effect, to be sure, is of a wholly different nature from what the West considers political success. It is hidden, indirect, long-term, and hard to measure; often it exists only in the invisible realm of social consciousness, conscience, and subconsciousness, and it can be almost impossible to determine what value it assumed therein and to what extent, if any, it contributes to shaping social development. It is, however, becoming evident—and I think that is an experience of an essential and universal importance—that a single, seemingly powerless person who dares to cry out the word of truth and to stand behind it with all his person and all his life, ready to pay a high price, has, surprisingly, greater power, though formally disenfranchised, than do thousands of anonymous voters. It is becom-ing evident that even in today's world, and especially on this exposed rampart where the wind blows most sharply, it is possible to oppose personal experience and the natural world to the "innocent" power and to unmask its guilt, as the author of *The Gulag Archipelago* has done. It is becoming evident that truth and morality can provide a new start-ing point for politics and can, even today, have an undeniable political power. The warning voice of a single brave scientist, besieged some-where in the provinces and terrorized by a goaded community, can be heard over continents and addresses the conscience of the mighty of this world more clearly than entire brigades of hired propagandists can, though speaking to themselves. It is becoming evident that wholly personal categories like good and evil still have their unambiguous content and, under certain circumstances, are capable of shaking the seemingly unshakable power with all its army of soldiers, policemen, and bureaucrats. It is becoming evident that politics by no means need remain the affair of professionals and that one simple electrician with his heart in the right place, honoring something that transcends him and free of fear, can influence the history of his nation.

Yes, "antipolitical politics" is possible. Politics "from below." Politics of man, not of the apparatus. Politics growing from the heart, not from a thesis. It is not an accident that this hopeful experience has to be lived just here, on this grim battlement. Under the "rule of everydayness" we have to descend to the very bottom of a well before we can see the stars.

When Jan Patocka wrote about Charter 77, he used the term "solidarity of the shaken." He was thinking of those who dared resist impersonal power and to confront it with the only thing at their disposal, their own humanity. Does not the perspective of a better future depend on something like an international community of the shaken which, ignoring state boundaries, political systems, and power blocs, standing outside the high game of traditional politics, aspiring to no titles and appointments, will seek to make a real political force out of a phenomenon so ridiculed by the technicians of power—the phenomenon of human conscience?

Translated by Roger Scruton and Erazim Kohák

BUMSTERS

by E. C. OSONDU

T HEY WERE SITTING under one of the raffia huts when Mallama let out a hiss. Pat had become aware of the sound only since arriving in the Gambia. The hiss was an all-purpose sound. It could signify anger, exasperation, disgust.

"What do white women see in these men?" Mallama said. "They are layabouts. Drug addicts. Most of them have diseases."

Pat looked up. An older white lady was walking hand in hand with a twentysomething Gambian boy. They were laughing. The older lady seemed to be laughing very hard. They both looked happy and carefree. Pat turned to Mallama.

"Who are they?" she asked, nodding in the direction of the couple, who were apparently headed toward one of the more exclusive beach huts.

"The boy is a *bumster*," Mallama replied.

*   *   *

Two years later Pat returned to the Gambia. Her husband had died the year before. He had died of cancer, and his illness had not been easy on either of them. She needed a break from it all.

On her second day there, the young man who had helped take her luggage to her room from the lobby knocked on her door. He was dressed in the red and black uniform of the hotel, with its garish crest of a lion and a palm tree sewn into the pocket. He smiled at her and introduced himself as Usman.

"Madam lost someone very close to her and is unhappy," he said.

She could not tell if he was asking a question or making a statement. For some reason Pat always assumed that non-Westerners had a gift for divining. It was not something she had given much thought to. She merely assumed it, the same way she assumed that the blind had an acute sense of hearing.

"Why do you say that, Usman?" she asked.

She found the name pleasant on her lips. She thought the uncomplicated nature of it rather charming. Besides, the two syllables that made up the name were familiar—*Us-Man*.

"Usman can help madam be happy again," the young man said. He smiled as he said this, and bowed.

"Everyone wants to be happy, don't they?" Pat said. "Including you, I imagine."

"I will arrange introductions," Usman said. "If madam is happy, Usman would be happy." Then he bowed his head and left.

That evening, Usman returned with a tall dark man who seemed to be in his thirties. Usman introduced him as *my senior brother*. His name was Ahmed. Pat invited them in and asked Ahmed to take a seat on the sofa, but he made for the rug and quickly sat with both feet tucked underneath him. He smiled, and gestured for Pat to sit on the sofa herself. Usman disappeared for a moment, then returned with a tray of hot water, Lipton tea bags, and milk and sugar. He handed the tray to Ahmed, and then he left.

Ahmed sat at Pat's feet and began to brew her a cup of tea. He added a cube of sugar without asking her if she drank her tea with or without sugar. There was a certain serenity that he brought to the task. Pat had never had anybody brew her tea for her. She accepted the cup of tea thankfully. They had not exchanged many words. Ahmed made a cup for himself, took a sip, and smiled.

"My small brother Usman say madam travel from far and lose someone and is not happy. God bring madam happiness soon. Ahmed here to help madam be happy." He smiled again and took another sip from his teacup.

"I would be quite glad if you showed me the tree of happiness," Pat said. The phrase sounded to her like something from an African folktale. "We could both sit underneath it."

Ahmed smiled and said nothing for a while. Then he raised his index finger and said to her, "God give happiness. Me, I fear God. You believe in God, madam?"

From her previous travels she knew that to answer in anything but the affirmative would be deemed highly offensive.

"Yes, I believe in a kind and happy God," she said.

She went with Ahmed to the market. A large, open space with lots of color. She would remember the Gambia as the most colorful place she had ever been to. The women had colorful cotton wrappers and head ties—dazzling green, pink, yellow, red. They tied their babies to their backs with brightly colored pieces of cloth. Pat thought the babies looked contented, even carefree, sleeping in the warmth of their mothers' backs. She wondered why women in the West who didn't carry their babies in strollers carried them in front, like kangaroos.

She did not particularly want to buy anything, but Ahmed steered her in the direction of the men who sold carvings. She thought the carvings grotesque and not very well done. The masks scared her, bringing to mind a movie she'd once seen or more likely a story she'd once read, where a Western couple bought a carving from Africa that began to terrorize them back home in America. She recalled that the object had brought the couple lots of misfortune; then, when they were planning to throw it away, their house had caught fire and burned down along with the carving. An anthropologist had somewhere in the movie or story commented that the carving must have been an African god or goddess of some sort and properly belonged in a shrine.

She refused to buy anything. When Ahmed noticed this, he turned to her and said, "Maybe madam will like to drink some *ataya*? To clean her system and make blood pure?"

"What is ataya, Ahmed?"

"Come. We go try some ataya, you sure to like it."

He led her into a shed that offered some coolness away from the heat of the open market. Inside, on top of a large stove, was a giant black pot emitting a somewhat strong but not unpleasant herbal aroma. Ahmed asked the proprietor for two cups of ataya.

Pat watched as the man poured the liquid first into one cup, and then poured that cup into another, and then poured the second cup back into the first, back and forth. She asked Ahmed why the man did that, and Ahmed said it was to make the ataya cool enough to drink. Soon the first cup, full again, was handed to her. She took a cautious sip. It was not bad. It tasted good, as a matter of fact. Only it was too sugary. She drank and looked around her. There was another patron, a young man; he was taking huge gulps of the ataya. The proprietor took a rumpled stick of a cigarette out of his pocket and lit it. He took a few puffs and pinched out the cigarette and put the quarter-smoked stick behind his ear. Pat thought the act cute, and smiled to herself as she took a larger sip.

Turning to her, Ahmed said, "You see this ataya, it is good for everything—fever, pain, bellyache. And it cleans the blood very well. You take ataya every day, before long you see changes all over your body. You become a young girl."

Pat had not given a thought to the age difference between Ahmed and herself. He seemed to be not so young. He had a maturity that created an impression of a wise old man. For some reason an animal imagery came to her mind when she thought of Ahmed. He reminded her of a camel, an animal she had seen only in books and on TV. It was probably the way he folded his legs under him when he sat down.

As they left the ataya stall she felt sprightly. The warm wind cooled her face. She felt lighter on her feet. A feeling of freedom overcame her. All the faces she saw on the narrow street looked happy and satisfied. She almost wanted to hold Ahmed's hand, but stopped herself. She had not seen anybody holding hands on the street.

"Would you like to come back to the hotel with me?" she asked him.

"Oh yes, if madam want me to, I will be very happy to come," Ahmed said.

"Let's go, then," she said. She was feeling so good. Her intention was to walk to the hotel.

"Better to take taxi, too many people, too many eyes," Ahmed said, and hailed a passing cab.

When they got to her room she went to the bathroom and washed her face. Water had never felt the way it did then. There was a certain separateness between the water and her face, and then the two became one. When she stepped out of the bathroom, Ahmed came toward her with a cup of ice water.

"Cool your throat with this. Sometimes ataya make the throat very dry," he said.

She drank the water and a feeling of gratitude overwhelmed her. The thought that ran through her mind was—He knows exactly what I want. Nobody has ever known what I desire in this way. She gestured to Ahmed to hold her. She could smell the herbal smell of the ataya on him as she led him to the bedroom.

When Pat opened her door the next afternoon, she found Usman standing there. His face was sweating slightly, and he looked gloomy.

"What can I do for you, Usman?" she asked, smiling.

"Sorry, madam, but there is small trouble."

"Trouble? What kind of trouble?"

"Ahmed send me. There is trouble with Ahmed, madam. She want to cause trouble with you and Ahmed."

She found the talk of trouble and Ahmed a bit confusing. She took in a long breath and tried to be patient.

"What happened to Ahmed?"

"Nothing happen to Ahmed," Usman said. "It is Ahmed's wife that says she wants to come and make trouble here in the hotel. She say someone saw you and Ahmed in the market walking together like husband and wife. She lock the door against Ahmed and is threatening to come to this hotel and cause trouble for you. She is calling you a husband-snatcher. Ahmed say to tell you to send him money to give his wife so she stop threatening to cause trouble and embarrass you."

Now she understood. So Ahmed was married, and there was a poor little Mrs. Ahmed.

"So what does Ahmed want me to do?"

"Ahmed is requesting two hundred dollars to give the wife so she no cause trouble. She will use the money to start a little business. Have her own stall in the market. She want to be senior wife. No problem after that."

She let herself be led to the Bureau de Change in the lobby, where she changed some of her traveler's checks and handed the money to Usman. He thanked her profusely, and bowed twice to her as he pocketed the bills. She didn't smile. Usman seemed like he wanted to say something, but then he looked at her and kept quiet and walked away.

For the first time since she came to the Gambia, she walked to the hotel bar and ordered a stiff bourbon.

Pat had always thought about seeing her dead husband just one more time. She had toyed with the idea of consulting a medium. A few months before this latest trip, she had walked into a palm reader's booth at the state fair.

One look at the reader and she realized she had made a mistake. The woman had the odor of stale cigarette smoke clinging to her, and her hands were sweaty. The only thing she managed to discern, holding Pat's cringing hands in hers, was that Pat was unhappy. Of course Pat was unhappy. She did not need a palm reader to tell her that. When she had asked the woman if she could talk to her late husband, the woman had laughed out loud and asked—You mean like Whoopi in *Ghost?* Nah, the woman had said. Only the dead can speak with the dead.

The night after Usman's visit, Pat dreamed about her late husband. Their conversation was almost commonplace. He asked her about her hips. Were they still giving her pain? Were the pain medications working? Has she been able to consult the doctor in Florida about the noninvasive laser surgery?

She, in turn, asked him about his karate. He looked as sprightly as ever. He ignored her question, though, and changed the topic. They talked about the cat, Old Country. The cat had wandered in one day and stayed. He'd looked quite old, and they had given him the name Old Country. A joke they shared about America not being a country for old men and women. They talked and talked for what seemed like hours until her husband said he had to leave. When Pat opened her eyes, the sun was shining in through the window. Day had broken.

Ahmed came by later that day with a large thermos filled with ataya. Before she could ask him any questions, he poured out a cup for her. She drank it gratefully. After that she found herself suddenly becoming talkative.

"But you never told me you had a wife, Ahmed. Were you being sneaky?"

"Oh, madam, you know I am not a small boy," Ahmed replied.

"I know. But don't you think I deserve to know? She would have embarrassed me before the other guests here. That wouldn't have been nice."

"I would not have let her cause you embarrassment. She only make threats."

"Usman told me she was going to make trouble for me."

"She is a God-fearing woman. No cause trouble at all. Only make threaten because she need help. I tell her you are a kind woman and you fit to help us, that's all."

He offered her another drink of ataya. She took it. As if reading her mind, he went to the basin and got her a cold glass of water. She drank it. She felt a huge urge to laugh, and so she laughed out loud.

"Ahmed tell you that I will help you be happy," Ahmed said. "See, now you are happy. See how you are laughing like a child playing in the rain."

She found his comment even funnier and laughed out loud once more. Taking his large hands in hers, she led him to the bedroom.

"Ahmed in big, big, trouble," Usman said, stretching out both palms in the air to indicate the size of the trouble.

Pat smiled. "You do love to bring bad news, my dear Usman, don't you? Now tell me, what is this big, big trouble?"

"He was arrested by soldiers when he was leaving the hotel last night. He is not supposed to move around at that time. Soldiers patrol here at night to protect and give security. Too many bad things happening nowadays. Government put soldiers to guard the streets. The soldiers take Ahmed and lock him up in guardroom. They beat him small but not too much. Ahmed manage to send message through kind army corporal."

There was something in Usman's tone and manner that gave Pat pause. Could it have been the rush of the words? The way they came out almost as if they were practiced?

"Where is he being held?" she asked. "I'll go there and tell them he was with me. I can speak to whomever is in charge." This would be fine, she thought. She had noticed during her last visit that people deferred to her because of the color of her skin.

"No, no, you cause more trouble for him if you go there. Moving with foreign woman make his case worse. Give Usman money, Usman go bail him out. He come back to madam, no problem. He make madam happy once again."

"And where am I supposed to pluck this money from?" Pat asked. "From the money tree here in my room?"

"Money tree?"

"Look here, Usman, I am not rich. I want to see who is holding your brother. I can testify that he was with me last night. My word should count for something, even here in your country."

"Madam, Ahmed in big, big trouble. He said go tell her Ahmed in big, big trouble. Nobody to help him unless you, kind madam."

Pat looked at him. "How much are they asking for?"

"Five hundred, because this is big, big trouble," Usman said.

"I see," was all Pat could say.

"The more he stay in detention, the bigger the trouble become. You help him, madam. Only you can help him now, because he has nobody."

"I will think about this, okay?" She began to shut the door.

When Usman was gone Pat sat on the bed and thought. She recalled that Mallama's husband was a high-ranking military officer, though he had originally trained as a dentist. She picked up the phone and called Mallama.

They were at the beach. It was the day before Pat's departure; Mallama had suggested they go to the beach before she left. After Pat's call a few days earlier, Mallama had driven down to the hotel and taken Pat to her house. She had also called her husband, who had in turn gotten Usman and Ahmed arrested. Ahmed had not been in jail at all. Usman had led the police to him. He had been drinking ataya in the same stall he had gone to with Pat.

"The beach is almost empty. Where are the bumsters and their clients?" Pat asked.

"They have been swept off the beaches. The government launched a campaign called Operation Keep Our Beaches Clean, which got rid of them."

"And their patrons, have they been swept off as well?"

"We hear the economy is bad over there right now," Mallama said, laughing. "A few still come, but they stay in the hotels and the hotel boys link them up. Usman must have mistaken you for one of those women."

"I'd love to drink ataya one more time before I leave," Pat said.

"Ataya? How do you know ataya? We drink Tetley, PG Tips, and Lipton tea. Ataya is for *bush people*."

"But I loved it when Ahmed took me to an ataya shop in the market. He brought some in a thermos flask to the hotel, too. I found it a rather refreshing kind of tea."

Mallama glanced at her with her mouth wide open.

"No, you did not. Don't tell me you did. You did not."

"I did and I loved it, I must confess," Pat said.

"You know what these criminals do? They connive with the ataya sellers to add marijuana to the tea when they take foreign women to the stalls."

Pat laughed.

"So what happened after you drank it in the stall?" Mallama asked.

"I went back to the hotel and took a nap," Pat said.

Mallama exhaled slowly. "And that time you said he brought some for you in a thermos flask?"

"Oh, I took the thermos from him and thanked him. I had the drink later and then I went to sleep."

"Thank goodness. You were lucky."

"Oh, yes, I was indeed very lucky. My late husband used to call me Lucky Girl," Pat said, smiling as they both rose to leave. Now she had a story to tell her husband when next he came to her in a dream. In all their travels to different parts of the world, he had always complained that they had never been on any real adventures. This time she would have a real adventure story for him.

CHICK KILLER

by ELMORE LEONARD

KAREN SISCO WAS telling her dad, "This guy wearing cowboy boots walks into the bar..."

Her dad said, "I've heard it."

"I'm serious," Karen said. "Yesterday afternoon, my last day as a federal marshal after six and a half years. In less than an hour I'll hand in my star." She paused, watching her dad. "And Bob Ray Harris, high on our Five Most Wanted list, walks into the bar. O'Shea's on Clematis, up the street from the courthouse. I'm waiting for my supervisor. You met him, Milt Dancey, the one recruited me out of Florida Atlantic. Milt's coming up from Miami and called to say he was stuck in traffic, 95 bumper to bumper. He'd be in West Palm in about an hour. Milt's idea, talk me out of leaving the marshals."

"I can hear him," her dad said. "'You want to work for your old man? Take over his investigations? Work your tail off getting the stuff on some poor guy in divorce court?' He says, 'You should be ashamed of yourself.'"

Karen and her dad were sitting in the Florida room of his home in Coral Gables, comfortable in wicker chairs done in green and red hibiscus patterns, their drinks on the bamboo cocktail table.

"I told Milt I'd made up my mind and wasn't going to change it," she went on. "Three months on courtroom security's all I can take. Listen to lawyers nine to four. Take the defendant to a holding cell for baloney sandwiches. Milt said they were keeping an eye on me after socializing with the guy who broke out of Glades Correctional, Foley, the bank robber. I said, 'Socializing? I shot him, didn't I, and brought him back?'"

"You did tell me you spent time with him," her dad said, "but not what you were doing."

"I'm trying to tell you," Karen said, "about a wanted felon walking into O'Shea's while I'm waiting for Milt. You know why I recognized him? I'm cleaning out my desk yesterday and come across his wanted dodger, with mug shots. Bob Ray Harris, a forty-year-old white male born October the tenth."

"Columbus Day," her dad said.

"Wanted by Atlanta police for a double homicide. Two girls in a movie theater. I remembered that one," Karen said. "A witness described the girls talking out loud and laughing. The guy sitting right behind them told the girls to shut up. They said something he didn't like. The witness said he watched the guy grab each one by the hair, pull their heads back as they started to scream, and cut their throats ear to ear with a switchblade."

After a beat her dad said, "He got up and left?"

"Once he'd wiped the blade. One of the girls had long blond hair. That's what he used, her hair."

"What was the movie?"

"*Bridesmaids*. R-rated, the girls shouldn't've been there. The guy sitting behind Bob Ray almost asked him to remove his straw cowboy hat and was glad he didn't. Later, the girl at the candy counter—Bob Ray scared her to death asking for a box of popcorn—picked him out of mug shots as the guy in the hat. His dodger said he was wanted for stabbing his girlfriend. Also raping and stomping to death a sixteen-year-old girl in Orlando."

Her dad said, "Honey, you're working for Sisco Investigations, you won't run into anyone carries a switchblade."

"I saw him come into O'Shea's and hold the door open to look both ways down the street. Then he walked up to the bar, his shirttail hanging out, and ordered a Diet Pepsi."

"You were close enough to hear him?"

"I saw the can."

"I was testing your powers of observation."

Sometimes her dad was funny. At seventy-six he'd been running his private-investigations company in Miami for forty years; the only time he'd spent inactive was when his prostate was acting up and he'd gotten rid of it.

He said, "You wondered about his shirttail hanging out."

"The knife in his back pocket," Karen said. "He started staring at me. Finally he takes a swig of Pepsi and comes over to place the can on my table and lean over on his hands to tell me he was buying. 'What would you like?'"

"You said no thanks or a double Early Times over crushed ice?"

"I did, but didn't see myself drinking it right away. This guy with a record of violence against women pulled the chair out to sit down and there's my bag sitting on it. He picked it up and hefted it like he's gonna guess its weight and said, 'What you got in there?' as he's handing me the bag."

"Your Sig Sauer," her dad said, "and a pair of cuffs."

"Two," Karen said. "I always carry an extra pair. I laid the bag on my lap and worked the Velcro loose to slip my hand inside. I'm not gonna tell Bob Ray he's under arrest without a .38 pointing at him."

"Well, since you're telling me about it," her dad said, "I believe this turned out in your favor."

"Wasn't it in the paper?"

"Not the *Herald*. But you're sittin' here, you musta put him on the floor and cuffed him."

"You think he'd let me? This guy who killed at least four women we know of? He said, 'I'm at the bar, I see you lookin' me over, like you're not sure you know me. We ever met somewheres?' I told him he looked like Brad Pitt with long hair coming out of his cowboy hat. He goes, 'Yeah...?' grinning at me. He asked me how old I thought he was. I said, 'Forty, this past October.' He said, 'How'd you know that?'"

Her dad said, "You're givin' yourself away."

"I'm a girl in a bar he'd like to take to a motel and beat the shit out of, after he rapes me. I asked him what his sign was. He said, 'My sign?' I said, 'You're a Libra, aren't you? Born in October?' I said I was a Libra too."

"You're an Aries," her dad said. "Your mother knew all that stuff. I can see her with her tarot cards, doing a reading about me."

Karen said, "You want to hear what happened or keep interrupting? I said to Bob Ray, 'When a Libra meets another Libra they can know things about each other.' I made that up. I don't know anything about astrology. But this guy who stabs women, raped and stomped a girl to death, knows even less. I said, 'You know what I've got in my handbag?'"

"You're callin' him," her dad said.

"He's seated at the table now. Leans back and says, 'Oh, different kinds of girl shit. That bag has some weight. You got your vibrator in there?'

"I told him I carry extra batteries for a recorder I speak into, doing inventories at supermarkets. 'Twenty-four number-ten cans of apricot halves in heavy syrup.' While I'm telling him what a wonderful job it is—you know I did it while I was at school—I slip my left hand back into the bag to take off the safety and pick up the drink with my right."

Her dad stared at her, not saying a word. But then he asked, "Why'd he bring up his age? Wantin' you to guess how old he was?"

"I suppose 'cause most girls, scared shitless, told him he looked, oh, real young, something he loved to hear. I can't think of another reason. The bag's still on my lap and I ask him, 'You want to see my equipment?' He said, 'Your equipment, huh?' grinning at me. He said, 'Like the different parts that make you a hot chick?'"

"You're bringin' him along," her dad said, "but where you goin' with it?"

"We're there," Karen said. "Time to make the move. I said to him, 'What am I getting out of this deal?' He said, 'Honey, you get me.' 'Oh really?' I said. 'I hear you like to beat up girls.' He lost his grin and tried frowning, hard, wanting to know where I got that idea. I'm holding the Sig in one hand, the double whisky in the other, and I'm tempted to raise the glass and take a sip. So I did, and then I set it back on the table. Now I wanted a cigarette, but I'd better tend to business first. I said, 'Bob Ray, I'm placing you under federal arrest. Keep your hands in sight, flat on the table. You try to get up, I'll shoot you.' Now he put on a bewildered look, showing me the palms of his hands, saying, 'Honey, I'm sure not who you say I am. Bob Ray who?'

"I said, 'Bob Ray Harris. You win the prize for being my last takedown as a deputy U.S. marshal. You give me a hard time, I'll take my hand out of the bag and show you what I've got.'"

Her dad wasn't saying a word.

"The guy was shaking his head, telling me he wasn't who I said he was, trying to push the chair back. He leaned against the table, his hands going behind him to his back pockets, saying, 'Lemme get out some ID.' My bag, with my hand in it, was pointed between his legs. I see his hand come around with the knife, the blade snapping out of the hilt, while I'm aiming my handbag at him under the table. I fired, put a hole in my bag and grooved his thigh, and he howled. Three feet away he's trying to push to his feet to get at me, strike with the knife, and I shot him again."

Her dad sat there, staring at his little girl.

"In the balls, this time," his little girl said, "and put him out of business."

They both picked up their drinks from the bamboo table, her dad saying, "Your boss finally got there?"

"Milt arrived while they were hauling Bob Ray out on a gurney."

"You talked to him?"

"Milt? Yes, I did."

"He's taking you off court security, isn't he?"

"Yes, he is."

"And you want to stay with the marshals."

"If you don't mind," Karen said.

SECRET LANGUAGE

by YANNICK MURPHY

S HE ATE ONLY chocolate. Her mother, Adele, tried blending
together a concoction of fruits and vegetables, and eggs, and a
scoop of chocolate ice cream, but the daughter refused to even
put her lips to the glass. The next week Adele heard a noise in the
kitchen in the middle of the night. She walked in to find her daughter
sitting on the floor with the bottom freezer open and the chocolate-
ice-cream container on her lap, trying to scoop out mouthfuls of it
with the tip of a ballpoint pen—she was not yet tall enough to reach
the silverware drawer.

Late into the night they sat in the bath together, listening to Jesus,
the father, snoring from the bedroom. Adele took a wet, soapy cloth
and gently wiped the chocolate from her daughter's face, and then she
rubbed hard, trying to wipe away the blue pen marks as well. They
stayed in the bath a long time, and when Adele began to feel sleepy
in the warm tub water and yawned, her daughter giggled loudly and

stuck her finger in Adele's mouth. Adele nearly bit the girl, snapping her mouth shut, and the girl yelped. Jesus slept through it all. He always slept soundly after a day outside on the poles. Adele imagined that it was probably tiring for him to be in the high hot sun and the strong wind that sometimes came off the ocean and swayed the poles side to side and made him tighten his safety harness and shout into the receiver of his test phone in order to be heard. Adele imagined it was also tiring to be out on the poles on cold mornings that frosted the leaves of the trees planted in a line in front of the cathedral that Jesus could most likely see from his place high on the pole, and tiring, too, to be out in the rain that pocked the river water and drove the carp down deep so that you couldn't see them, not like you could on a warmer, drier day when their orange bony backs glowed brightly beneath the water's murky green.

The chocolate was Jesus's fault. He'd brought it to his daughter when she first refused to eat. When Adele protested, he'd say, "At least she's eating something," and then he'd pull out a chocolate from the leather tool belt strapped to his waist and pop it into his girl's mouth. Sometimes he would bring up from his tool belt red coiled wire or blunt-nosed cutters instead, to tease his girl, and she would fly at him. Her small fists pounding his chest, hitting the machine-stitched letters above the pocket of his uniform shirt that read JESUS BERNAL, TÉCNICO.

There were arguments. Adele screamed at him when he left the tool belt on the table and their daughter found it and dug into the leather pockets, fishing out so much chocolate that of course, Adele told Jesus, their daughter would not eat her dinner. She was stuffed to the gills on chocolate! But Jesus told Adele it did not translate. She was doing it again, he told Adele, trying to make her Americanisms work in his language, when they did not. Adele wondered, then, what *would* work? Was it "stuffed like a pig"? Was it "stuffed like a wine gourd"? "Stuffed like a sausage"? It was probably something like "stuffed like a seagull," because to Adele so many of Jesus's country's idioms did not make any sense. In this country, she had learned, people did not see out of the corners of their eyes; they saw out of the tails of their eyes. She thought of "stuffed like a seagull" because at the time she could see one flying by, dropping feces onto the clean sheets she knew she should have hung out to dry earlier in the day, before the dew fell. Any other housewife would have known better, she thought.

They not only fought over chocolate, they fought over eggs. Jesus wanted Adele to learn how to cook a traditional omelet. He wanted his mother to teach her how to do it, but for a long time Adele put it off. She wanted to learn how to do some things on her own.

Besides, Jesus's mother was irksome. She had the habit of pretending she didn't know how to do certain things when clearly she knew a lot. She knew, for instance, how to sew, but when Jesus asked his mother to teach Adele how to sew Jesus's mother said, "I'm no seamstress." Jesus shook his head, then. "Mother, no one knows better than you how to whip up a beautiful dress from a bolt of cloth," he said, and convinced his mother to sit with Adele and show her how to cut a pattern, how to thread the machine's needle, and soon it was clear to Adele that Jesus's mother knew a world about sewing. She was a very good seamstress after all, so good that Adele let her finish the dress they were making; she knew her own stitches would not be anywhere near as even if she tried to complete it by herself.

When Jesus asked his mother to show Adele how to cook an omelet, she said, "I'm no cook." Jesus told her there was no one better skilled at it that he knew of. "Please, teach Adele," he said.

"I really don't know very much, but I'll try my best," his mother said, and then she turned to Adele and said, "Just pick a day and I'll come."

*   *   *

Sometimes, before Jesus left the house for the poles, he gave her a list of things to do. "And don't forget to call and make me an appointment with the hairdresser," he might say, or "There's a rip in my pants, left knee, you'll see it," not even bothering to state that it needed repairing. After he left, and the door was shut behind him, she would imitate him. When her daughter heard her doing this she would begin to do it too. The two of them would stand by the door, shaking their fingers at each other. "And don't forget to move that boulder! And don't forget to drain the water from the ocean! And don't forget to stop that volcano from erupting!" they would say to each other, laughing at all the things Adele would never be able to do.

She met another mother at the park once. They were sitting on a bench together watching their daughters go down the slide. She and the other mother had marveled at the children's energy, at their ability to run up the stairs and slide down the slide over and over again. Adele had looked at the woman's high-heel shoes, with their wire-thin straps that went behind the Achilles tendon. She could not imagine herself wearing them to the park; she would have tottered on them like a drunk. But still Adele admired the woman for wearing them— she was not some housewife in wide-toed flats with rubber soles. She was beautiful. The woman, in turn, admired the scarf Adele was wearing. She reached out and touched the soft alpaca wool.

"Did you knit it yourself?" the woman asked.

"No, I can't do anything like that," Adele said. "I can't knit or cook. I'm a failure."

The woman laughed. "Oh, good—I can't knit or cook either. Let's be failures together!" She put her arm around Adele's shoulder and brought her closer so that Adele could smell her perfume, which smelled like the beach, like sand being warmed by the sun, and Adele swore that the smell went straight to her head and made her thoughts clear.

It was after talking to that mother in the park that Adele called Jesus's mother and asked her to come and teach her how to cook an omelet. If she failed to learn, it wouldn't be the end of the world, she reasoned. There were others like her in this country who could not cook either.

Jesus's mother spent hours teaching her about omelets. The first lesson was on picking the potatoes. They spent thirty minutes at the small, crowded market, picking up potatoes and smelling them, getting jostled as they held the potatoes close to their noses, the tips of their noses becoming dusty with traces of the potato field's dry soil.

"Choose one that your fingers and thumb can cover completely in your hand," the old woman said. "Never bigger, and not so small that the fingers can reach and overlap the thumb. Size is crucial."

But Adele could only seem to find small ones. She could make a tight fist around every potato she picked up. It was the old woman who had the knack for finding the right potatoes, the potatoes they finally brought home. And then, in the kitchen, when Adele reached into her silverware drawer and took out her peeler, Jesus's mother slid it from her grasp.

"No, we use a knife, always," she said. "Use this." And she handed Adele a small, sharp paring knife.

The next lesson was the amount of oil. "If you do not have that right, the dish is ruined," Jesus's mother said. She poured the oil into the pan, so much of it that it seemed to rise halfway up the sides.

"Okay, now I fill the pan halfway with oil," Adele said, wanting to remember the proportions.

"No," Jesus's mother said. "What if you're not using this same frying pan next time? You cannot think like that. You must put enough oil in so that when you add the sliced potatoes, they are slightly, just *slightly* covered by the oil."

"So if I don't have enough, then I can just add some more oil, right?" Adele said.

"No," Jesus's mother said. "You never add cold oil to a pan with the sliced potatoes and the hot oil in it already; you have to have oil that is the exact same temperature as the oil that's already in the pan. But that is impossible to achieve, so don't even bother." They hadn't even come to the eggs yet, and already Adele wanted to get out of the kitchen and be done with the lesson. She wanted to go with her daughter to the park, where she could swing her on the swing and chase her on the jungle gym, and have her reach for the monkey bars, and work up the girl's appetite so that maybe, just maybe she would eat something, maybe a slice of southern melon, a slice of northern ham. Maybe the beautiful mother in the high heels would be there. Maybe she would listen to Adele's stories about Jesus, because there were stories about countless things—the way he walked in front of her on the street, never waiting for her to catch up; the way, when she started talking to him about something she had seen or heard, he did not stay still to listen to her, but wandered through the rooms, making her follow him, making her make her voice loud to let it be heard over the sound of their footsteps.

The eggs, when they came to them, were just as trying. You had to beat them with a fork, of course, never a whisk. You had to remove the potatoes from the pan first, and dab them with a cloth to soak up the extra oil, and then they had to sit for three minutes. When Adele asked if she could just leave the potatoes in the pan and add the eggs on top of them, Jesus's mother shook her head sadly. For a moment, Adele thought her mother-in-law wasn't well. The oil heating in the skillet had made the kitchen hot, and Jesus's mother's face was flushed.

"Are you all right?" Adele said.

"I'm fine, dear," Jesus's mother said, but then she noticed the onion that Adele held in her hand and her smile disappeared.

Adele looked down at the onion. "I like onion," she said apologetically. "A little might be nice, and there's plenty of oil left. I thought I could sauté up some of the onion and then add it when I add the potatoes," she said.

Jesus's mother stared at Adele. There was something in her eyes that reminded Adele of a stuffed animal's eyes. They seemed scratched and dull, as if Jesus's mother had been dragged on the floor, facedown, from room to room. After a long moment, Jesus's mother finally said in a whisper, "You are the reason she refuses to eat. You are killing my grandchild."

Adele felt her face becoming red. She gripped the paring knife in one hand and the onion in the other. She gripped the onion so hard that juice began to be squeezed from it. She could feel it running through her fingers.

For a moment she hoped that Jesus had heard and would come into the kitchen to defend her, but that didn't happen. Jesus wouldn't have gone into the kitchen. The kitchen was for women. And plus Jesus's mother was blocking the doorway. The only way out was the open window with the clothesline and its pulley attached to the outside frame. Adele, standing there, imagined herself jumping onto the counter, grabbing hold of the clothesline and suspending herself over the alley, and then jumping down to the cobblestones below.

Instead she leaned against the cabinets, in the V formed by the corner, and slid down, letting her backbone hit the metal knobs on the drawers and hiking up her sweater as she sat on the linoleum floor. I'm just a failure, she thought, and then she remembered the beautiful mother in the park and how she had thrown her head back and laughed and touched Adele when she had said that before, how she'd said she was also a failure and that they would be failures together, and just remembering it made Adele laugh out loud too. Her laughter brought her daughter into the room. Her daughter squeezed past her grandmother and jumped into her mother's lap, wanting to know what was so funny, asking her in English, "What's so funny?" saying, "You can tell me, no one else will know." Because English was their secret language that neither Jesus nor the old woman knew.

When exactly Jesus's mother left the room, Adele didn't remember. She spent a long time with her eyes closed, hugging her daughter and whispering English words into her ear, telling her she was laughing because she had pictured herself traveling from one building to the next on the clotheslines of all their neighbors, and wouldn't that be fun? She said this to her daughter and her daughter agreed. "Take me with you. Let's go now," the girl said, trying to climb her mother's shoulders to stand on the counter and get closer to the clothesline and the open window and the blue sky.

Sometimes Jesus left the house in the middle of their arguments. He did not take his rigging with him when he left, or his safety harness or his belt. He would take one of his rayon dress shirts and put it into a bag, along with his razor and his aftershave. Adele would throw other things at him while he did this. "Take this, too! What if your whore's afraid of the dark?" she'd say, and throw a table lamp at him. "Or this," she'd say, "take this!" And she'd throw one of her own sweaters. "You don't want the whore getting cold in that ocean breeze," she'd say, because she knew from receipts she had seen in his pockets that near the ocean was where he often went.

The ocean was not so far away, in miles maybe thirty, in kilometers, who knew, she never was sure of kilometers. When she estimated distances for Jesus in kilometers she was always wrong. He took it as a sign of her failure to fully get rid of her Americanness. He viewed it like a coat, like something she refused to take off when she entered a room, even when the room was warm and the people friendly. She was stubborn for no reason, he said.

Adele would show her daughter photographs of herself as a child, with her parents, in America. She named the street for her daughter: Magnolia, she said. And she named the house: A colonial, she said, and she named the family car: A Ford, she said, and she named the parents Dorothy and John, and her daughter would recite these words back to her. After a few times her daughter knew all the words for the people and the things in the pictures and she would point to them and tell Adele the names. It was then that Jesus would ask if there wasn't something else the child should be doing.

"Shouldn't she be learning her letters? Learning to count? Learning to cook?" he said.

They would go to the ocean on Sundays. They would bring Jesus's mother. She would only go in the off-season, when it was cooler, and she and Jesus would not have to smell the suntan gel of the tourists and step on their ratty straw mats as they tried to cross the sand to the waves. They would go to the windy beach, too, because Jesus said the windy beach would be less crowded, so Adele wore a scarf on her head and wrapped one around her daughter too, but her daughter never kept it on—she would hold it out so that it flew away like a kite, way, way down the beach and sometimes over the water, blending in with the tops of the choppy waves.

They would not swim; the strong wind cooled them off too much and made the water less inviting. Instead they would sit and watch the whitecaps and Jesus's mother would go and sit in the car, saying that in there she could control the wind. She did not want too little or too much wreaking havoc with her hair, she said. Eventually Jesus would lie back and sleep, and Adele wondered how he could, with all the wind whipping about, but then of course she knew how easily he could sleep. He was always tired—he could sleep anywhere because of all the time he spent up on the poles. While he slept she would take her daughter and walk with her down the beach, stopping to pick up bits of shells that her daughter would put in her pockets.

Afterward they would stop for lunch at a restaurant and the girl would take out her shells and spread them across the tabletop. Jesus's mother would spend her time wiping the sand that had come with the shells off the table.

It was always a small, inexpensive restaurant they stopped at, the menu consisting of only two meals and no tablecloths covering the tables, so that the dark wooden tops were scratched with wear. When the food came and Jesus started to eat he would say, "Mother, you could have made this meal yourself, and it would have tasted ten times better."

Jesus's mother would wave her hand in the air then, and turn her head away, saying, "Don't be silly!"

"I bet you could have!" Jesus would insist, and his mother would say, "Maybe I would have added a pinch of sugar to the marinade, that's all."

Then Jesus would pound the well-worn table, whose unsteady legs would shake, and say, "That's the difference! You know exactly the small things to do to improve a dish. That's what makes you a great cook. Everything you make turns to gold."

Adele once insisted on ordering a meal for her daughter, thinking that if she had her own plate in front of her instead of always having to share, she would be excited to eat it by herself. But it wasn't true. The girl didn't like having the plate in front of her. It was in her way when she laid out her shells.

The receipts in Jesus's wallet were for expensive restaurants that overlooked the sea, or that were high up in buildings surrounded by glass. The receipts, always for two meals, listed razor clams and legs of lamb cooked with mustard and thyme, and wines from other countries.

Her daughter said, "Oh, how beautiful," when she saw the magnolias in bloom on the trees on Magnolia Street in the photographs, but Adele did not tell her daughter how sometimes, when they were past the bloom, the magnolias smelled like rotting meat and covered the ground in patches that turned brown and made you slip when you were walking.

It wasn't always her best sweater that she threw at him during a fight. The colors were sometimes faded with washing, the buttons loose and threatening to come off, the pockets stretched, holding the form of her clenched hands, the shape of her knuckles. She wondered, what could it matter? She should have thrown her nicest sweater at him. She should have thrown the plush cashmere at him, or the one sewn with hundreds of tiny pearlescent beads. She should have shown him how much she didn't care.

He would let the sweater drop, the buttons clacking on the hardwood floor. He would catch the lamp and toss it onto the bed, where it would bounce, the fragile filaments in the bulb breaking.

Their last argument, when it came, was about many things. It was about chocolates, and money, and the wind, but it was really about the visit. She had taken her daughter to the doctor for her yearly exam. "Ghostly thin," the doctor had said, and then he ordered tests. The blood test revealed a low iron count.

"Anemic!" Jesus cried when she came back with the news.

"No, he did not use that word. He said 'low iron,'" Adele said.

"Did you tell him how she won't eat your food? Did you tell him that?" he said.

"I told him how she prefers chocolate. I told him she fills herself up on the chocolates you bring her and that afterward there's no room left inside her for a meal," Adele said.

"So it's all my fault? That's what you told the doctor? That I made my daughter anemic when it's because you're a failure in the kitchen that she won't eat? Is that what you told him? Is it? Is it?" Jesus yelled.

Adele shook her head. *Anemic* was not the word. She wished he would stop saying it. *Low iron* was the expression the doctor had used, and what was so tragic about low iron? Who would want the reverse? Who would want all that iron in their blood?

He went to the bedroom first. She could hear the telltale signs of the closet door being opened, the hushing sound of his rayon shirt being slid off the hanger.

She missed the food stores back home. She would think of them while she was in the crowded markets, the aisles so narrow no two people could share them back to back. She longed for the simple green of a dollar bill. The proud receding hairline of George Washington. The sharp lines of the pyramid centered with the all-knowing eye. Bills here were bright and intricate, no two denominations the same color. After Jesus left she sat against the spackled wall in the bedroom and rested her head in her hands. The wall's plaster spackling hurt. It had been spread like cake frosting, with peaks, but the peaks were hard, and pricked her skin.

Earlier in the day, before the fight and the visit to the doctor, she had planned on making an omelet. She was going to do it exactly the way she had been taught. But since Jesus was gone, she did not see the point. Her daughter wouldn't eat it anyway, and Adele did not feel like eating at all.

"Come on, sweetheart," she said to her daughter. "Time to shop," she said, and they left the house.

They walked across the river's bridge. The sun was strong. The smell of the river rose up into the air, warm mud and carp. Adele thought how, on such a warm day, the beach was probably crowded, the tourist season in full swing.

The chocolate shop had the air conditioner on because of the summer weather. Adele stood in front of the cases and let her daughter point and smudge the glass. When they left they had a shopping bag filled with boxes and the saleswoman was coming out from behind the counter with a bottle of cleaning fluid and a paper towel to erase the fingerprints.

Adele let her daughter eat the chocolates as they walked home. At first Adele reached into the bag herself and handed the chocolates to the girl one at a time, but then she just gave her an entire box. The sun melted the chocolates quickly, and the stuff soon ringed the girl's mouth, but Adele didn't bother to wipe it off. She knew that her daughter wasn't finished yet.

At home she laid the open boxes on the coffee table. The girl sat on her knees and ate. Adele sat beside her, on the floor, leaning against the couch, feeling the cold leather against the back of her arms. After a while she got up and went to lie on her bed, leaving her daughter at the coffee table with the boxes spread out before her and half the chocolates gone. It was still early, but Adele was tired. The heat had made her slow, and so she slept, sprawling her legs out wide because she wanted to keep them apart in this heat and because she could, because Jesus wasn't there.

Her daughter's vomiting woke her a few hours later. The girl had made it to the bathroom, but not the toilet. She had used the bathtub instead, and inside of it were large splatters of vomit that looked, at first, so much like blood that Adele thought the girl had eaten shards of glass. But it was only chocolate.

She held the hair away from her daughter's face so the strands would not become soiled. She rubbed her daughter's back while the girl's body convulsed. Adele reminded herself that now was the time to act.

She used a clip to keep her daughter's hair out of the way and told the girl to sit tight. "Sit tight, Mama?" her daughter said, not under-standing the English expression and looking up at her mother with a very pale face.

"Yes, sit tight. It means relax. I'll be right back."

She went to the living room and saw that her daughter had eaten all of the chocolates except one. Back in the bathroom she wiped her daughter's clammy forehead with a towel and then told her that she had a gift, a surprise. She held her hand behind her back. The daugh-ter, who had been resting her head on her arms on the edge of the tub, lifted her head, her eyes half closed from her nausea and fatigue.

"Guess what I have," Adele said.

"Show me," the girl said weakly.

Adele took her hand from behind her back, keeping the hand in a fist. The girl reached for her mother's hand and turned it over, mak-ing Adele peel back her fingers. When her daughter saw the choco-late, melting in her palm, she started to gag again. "Don't you want some?" the mother said, and lifted her hand a little higher, a little closer to the girl's mouth. The daughter shook her head, then turned, leaning over the tub and gagging more. The sound of it echoed against the porcelain.

Afterward Adele wiped her daughter's mouth, noticing how the chocolates had coated her teeth and gums with a film of brown. Then she scooped the girl up in her arms and walked with her into the hallway, kissing her cheek, and told her that now it was time for them to sleep, that she would feel better in the morning. Her daughter was already asleep by the time Adele had brought her to the bedroom door.

The sun woke them. It streamed in the open window in a broad, hot shaft that fell on their uncovered legs. They had slept late. Already Adele could hear the neighbors hanging their laundry, pinning it to the clothesline, moving it along with the pulley, the rope squeaking with the weight of the load traversing the alley.

"It's a beach day," Adele said. "Come on, let's put on our suits and go."

The girl sat upright.

"Our suits? Really? We can swim?" she said.

"That's right," Adele said. "We'll go to the calm beach today, not the windy one."

In the car Adele talked of the supermarkets back home. She told the girl about the aisles of endless food. She described the bright photographs on the cardboard boxes in the frozen-food aisle, photographs that made your mouth water. She described the chickens slowly cooking on the rotisseries, behind glass cases that couldn't keep the wonderful aroma of the cooking chickens locked in, so that when you breathed you could taste the flavor in the air. The meat of those chickens, which had been cooking slowly for so long, was like butter, Adele said. It fell easily off the bone, hitting just the right place on your tongue before it slid down your throat.

Her daughter jumped up and down in her seat. "I want to go!" she said. "I want to try that chicken!"

"Someday I'll take you there," Adele said, and then, to change the subject, she said, "but first we must go to the beach!"

And she drove quickly, pushing hard on the gas, making her little car whine and whir as it had never done before, so that her daughter said, "The car is excited—it wants to go to the beach too!" And when they crossed the bridge, the girl asked her mother what direction she thought the carp were swimming in—"Are they swimming toward the beach too?" the girl said.

"Yes," Adele said. "Everyone wants to go to the beach today."

The tourists were there, just as Jesus had warned they would be. They were glistening with orange gel on their ratty bamboo mats, their eyes closed and their faces turned up toward the sun. The sea was calm and warm. There was no wind to send up white chop or spray. They swam for a long time, and then they lay down on their towels like the tourists, their chins tilted up, trying to catch the dazzling rays. Adele heard her daughter's stomach growl. "I'm hungry, Mama," the girl said, and Adele turned on her side and looked at her daughter and admired how white her teeth looked now that the girl's face was golden from the sun.

"Then let's eat!" Adele said.

She chose the restaurant she had seen the name of on the last receipt she had found in Jesus's wallet. It overlooked the ocean, and from inside you could see the fishing boats moving slowly from side to side, and the seagulls flying by, too, their heads turning in search of food.

Adele ordered the razor clams and the lamb with thyme and mustard. "Chicken! I want chicken," her daughter said, and so Adele ordered her the chicken. Her daughter ate great mouthfuls of it. Adele could see the bumpy outline of the meat behind her daughter's bulging, suntanned cheeks. The girl smiled. She talked with her mouth full. "This is good, Mama," she said.

There were other couples in the restaurant. She imagined finding Jesus sitting at one of the tables. What would she say if she saw him? She did not know. And then suddenly she knew.

On the plane she formed the words that she would say to him later, over the phone from halfway across the world. "I have our daughter and we are not coming back," she said, looking out the window of the plane, her daughter eating peanuts the stewardess had given her.

FIFTY WAYS
TO EAT YOUR LOVER

by AMELIA GRAY

1

When he buys you a drink, plunge a penknife
into his nose and carve out a piece.

2

When he asks you what you do for a living,
dig into his spine with a broken juice glass.

3

When he wonders aloud if you ever get that feeling
about someone, bite his tongue out of his mouth.

4

When he says you have a beautiful body,
scoop out a chunk of his Achilles tendon.

5

When he slides his hand under your thigh,
sliver off his earlobe with a box cutter.

6

When he persuades you to spend the night,
sink your teeth into his collarbone.

7

When he asks if you're on the pill,
squeeze your pelvic floor until his penis comes off.

8

When he wakes up in the morning, clip his eyelashes and snort them.

9

When he makes the bed, open up the vein
inside his elbow and fill your cupped hand.

10

When he stops by your place after work,
crush his skull with a tire iron and lick his brain.

11

When he gives you a book he likes,
make him step into a deep fryer.

12

When he asks you out again, stab him
with a letter opener and suck the wound.

13

When he wants to know what movie you'd like to see,
wrap a piano wire around his testes until they drop into your mouth.

14

When he takes a picture of you, grind his toes with a pestle.

15

When he asks where you've been all his life,
clamp your mouth to his sidemeat.

16

When he asks you if you're going to write about him,
push a corkscrew into his shin and chew what curls out.

17

When he takes you to meet his parents, smother him
with a pillow and eat his middle finger.

18

When he moves his books into your apartment,
take a cheese grater to his knuckles.

19

When he brings home a puppy,
shave the rough from his heels.

20

When he tells you he loves you,
papercut his fingertips and suck their blood.

21

When he asks you to marry him,
panfry his foreskin.

22

When he takes you to Paris,
wrench his wrist and gobble the tendon.

23

When he builds you a desk, use an awl
to tap a piece of bone from his hip.

24

When he asks you to do the dishes, wedge an oyster knife behind
his kneecap until there's space in there for your tongue.

25

When he brings home the wrong milk,
peel off a layer of his facial dermis.

26

When he slams the door, spread
citric acid across his nipples and latch on.

27

When he kisses someone else,
flay his abdominal skin.

28

When he says he's sorry, get his nose.

29

When he tells you that you don't love him,
rip a fistful of hair from his head and put it on your cereal.

30

When he wants to know if he's made himself clear,
press your thumb against his eye socket and slurp the goop.

31

When he says he's sorry you feel that way,
peel off his toenails and sprinkle them on a salad.

32

When he says he needs some time off,
jam his hand into a toaster oven.

33

When he shows up with flowers,
nibble the hair from his arms.

34

When he suggests that the two of you
take a walk, crush his elbow in a vice.

35

When he asks if you'll let him come back,
tuck your fingers under his lowest rib and pull.

36

When he draws you a bath, sever his smallest toe.

37

When he settles down beside you on the couch,
squash his neckflesh in your fist.

38

When he asks you to wear the dress he likes,
slice off a slab of his buttock and serve it on a plate.

39

When he wants to know if you think he'd be
a good father, broil his viscera.

40

When he marvels at how much time has passed,
gnaw the skin between his fingers.

41

When he asks you to take it down a notch at the Christmas party,
pour wine into his ear and drink what drains out.

42

When he teaches your kids to drive, masticate his chin.

43

When he takes you out for your anniversary,
squeeze his forearm until it bursts.

44

When he says you've looked a little pale this year,
open his throat with a rough wedge.

45

When he drives you to the doctor,
cut a knot of muscle from his upper thigh with a handsaw.

46

When he sits with you, chew off the tip of his thumb.

47

When he tells the nurse to leave you both alone,
work a metal tube into his larynx.

48

When he says you've had a good life together,
force your finger into his mouth and scrape out his soft palate.

49

When he says he'll miss you, dig a spoon into his belly button.

50

When he says goodbye, eat his heart out.

ANYTHING HELPS

by JESS WALTER

BIT HATES GOING to cardboard.

But he got tossed from the Jesus beds for drunk and sacrilege and has no other way to get money. So he's up behind Frankie Doodle's, flipping through broken-down produce boxes like an art buyer over a rack of prints, and when he finds a piece without stains or writing he rips it down until it's two feet square. Then he walks to the Quik Stop, where the fat checker likes him. He flirts her out of a Magic Marker and a beef stick.

The beef stick he eats right away, and cramps his gut, so he sets in on the counter while he writes on the cardboard, carefully, in block letters: ANYTHING HELPS. The checker says, You got good handwriting, Bit.

The best spot, where the freeway lets off next to Dick's, is taken by some chalker Bit's never seen before: skinny, dirty pants, hollow eyes. The kid's sign reads HOMELESS HUNGRY. Bit yells, *Homeless Hungry?* Dude, I *invented* Homeless Hungry. The kid just waves.

Bit walks on, west toward his other spot. There are a few others out, stupid crankers—faces stupid, signs stupid: some fifty-year-old baker with VIETNAM VET, too dumb to know he wasn't born yet, and a coke ghost with tiny writing—*Can You Help me feed My Children please.* They're at stupid intersections, too, with synced lights so the cars never stop.

Bit's headed to his unsynced corner—fewer cars, but at least they have to brake. Streamers off the freeway, working people, South Hill kids, ladies on their way to lunch. When he gets there he grabs the light pole and sits back against it, eyes down—nonthreatening, pathetic. It feels weird; more than a year since he's had to do this. You think you're through with some things.

He hears a window hum and gets up, walks to the car without making eye contact. Gets a buck. Thank you. Minute later, another car, another window, another buck. Bless you.

Good luck, the people always say.

For the next hour, it's a tough go. Cars come off the hill, hit the light, stop, look, leave. A woman who looks at first like Julie glances over and mouths, I'm sorry. Bit mouths back: Me too. Most people stare straight ahead, avoid eye contact.

After a while a black car stops, and Bit stands. But when the windows come down it's just some boys in ballcaps. Worst kind of people are boys in ballcaps. Bit should just be quiet, but—

Get a job, you stinking drunk.

That's good advice, Bit says. Thanks.

A couple of dimes fly out the window and skitter against the curb; the boys yell some more. Bit waits until they drive away to get the coins, carefully. He's heard of kids heating pennies in their cigarette lighters. But the dimes are cool to the touch. Bit sits against his pole. A slick creeps down his back.

Then a guy in a gold convertible Mercedes almost makes the light but has to skid to a halt.

I think you could've made it, Bit says.

The guy looks him over. Says, You look healthy enough to work.

Thanks. So do you.

Let me guess—veteran?

Yep. War of 1812.

The guy laughs. Then what, you lost your house?

Misplaced it.

You're a funny fucker. Hey, tell you what. I'll give you twenty bucks if you tell me what you're gonna buy with it.

The light changes but the guy just sits there. A car goes around. Bit shields his eyes from the sun.

You'll give me twenty bucks?

Yeah, but you can't bullshit me. If I give you a twenty, honestly, what're you gonna get?

The new Harry Potter book.

You are one funny fucker.

Thanks. You too.

No. Tell me *exactly* what you're going to drink or smoke or whatever and I'll give you twenty. But it's gotta be the truth.

The truth. Why does everybody always want that? He looks at the guy in his gold convertible. Back at the Jesus beds they'll be gathering for group about now, trying to talk each other out of this very thing, this reverie. Truth.

Vodka, Bit says, because it fucks you up fastest. I'll get it at the store over on Second, whatever cheap stuff they got, plastic bottle in case I drop it. And I'll get a bag of nuts or pretzels. Something solid to shit later. Whatever money's left—Bit's mouth is dry—I'll put in municipal bonds.

After the guy drives off, Bit looks down at the twenty-dollar bill in his hand. Maybe he is a funny fucker.

Bit slides the book forward. *Harry Potter and the Deathly Hallows.*

What's a *hallow*, anyway? he asks.

The clerk takes the book and runs it through the scanner.

I guess it's British for *hollow*. I don't read those books.

I read the first one. It was pretty good. Bit looks around Auntie's Bookstore: big and open, a few soft chairs between the shelves. So what do *you* read?

Palahniuk. That'll be twenty-eight fifty-six.

Bit whistles. Counts out the money and sets it on the counter. Shit, he thinks, seventy cents short.

The clerk has those big loopy earrings that stretch out your lobes. He moves his mouth as he counts the money.

How big are you gonna make those holes in your ears?

Maybe like quarter-size. Hey, you're a little short. You got a discount card?

Bit pats himself down. Hmm. In my other pants.

Be right back, the kid says, and leaves with the book.

I'm kind of in a hurry, Bit says to the kid's back.

He needs to stop by the Jesus beds, although he knows Cater might not let him in. He likes Cater, in spite of the guy's mean-Jesus rules and intense, mean-Jesus eyes. It's a shame what happened, because Bit had been doing so good, going to group almost every day, working dinner shifts and in the yard. Cater has this pay system at the Jesus beds— you serve meals or clean or do yard work and get back these vouchers you can redeem for snacks and shit at the little store they run. Keeps everything kind of in-house and gets people used to spending their money on something other than getting fucked up. Of course, there's a side market in the vouchers, dime on the dollar, so over time people save enough to get stewed, but Bit's been keeping that under control, too, almost like a civilian. No crank for more than a year, just a beer or two once a month, occasionally a split bottle of wine.

Then last weekend happened. At group on Thursday, Fat Danny was bragging again about the time he OD'd, and that made Bit think of Julie, the way her foot kept twitching after she stopped breathing, so after group he took a couple bucks from his stash—the hollow rail of his bed—and had a beer. In a tavern. Like a real person, leaned up against the bar watching baseball. And it was great. Hell, he didn't even drink all of it; it was more about the bar than the beer.

But it tasted so good he broke down on Friday and got two forties at the Quik Stop. And when he came back to the Jesus beds, Wallace ran off to Cater and told him Bit sold his vouchers for booze money.

Consequences, Cater is always saying.

I feel shitty, Bit's always saying.

Let's talk about *you*, Andrea the social worker is always saying.

When you sober up come see me, the fat checker at the Quik Stop is always saying.

Funny fucker, the guy in the gold convertible is always saying.

The bookstore kid finally comes back. He's got a little card, like a driver's license, and he gives it to Bit with a pen. There, now you have a discount card, the kid says. On the little piece of cardboard, where it says NAME, Bit writes, *Funny Fucker*. Where it says ADDRESS, Bit writes: *Anything Helps*.

Bit starts walking again, downtown along the river. For a while he and Julie camped farther down the bank, where the water turns and flattens out. They'd smoke and she'd lie back and mumble about getting their shit together.

Bit tried to tell Cater that. Yes, he'd fucked up, but he'd actually been selling his vouchers to buy this *book*, to get his shit together. But Cater was suspicious, asked a bunch of questions, and then Wallace piped in with *He's lying* and Bit lunged at Wallace and Cater pulled him off—rough about it, too—Bit yelling *Goddamn this* and *Goddamn that*, making it three-for-three (1: No drinking, 2: No fighting, 3: No taking the Lord's etc.), so that Cater had no choice, he said, rules being rules.

Then I got no choice either, Bit said, pacing outside the Jesus beds, pissed off.

Sure you do, Cater said. You always have a choice.

Of course, Cater was right. But out of spite or self-pity, or just thirst, Bit went and blew half his book money on a fifth, spent a couple of nights on the street and then shot the rest of the money on another. You think you're through with some things: picking up smokes off the street, shitting in alleys. He woke this morning in a parking lot above the river, behind a humming heat pump. Looked down at the water and could practically see Julie lying back in the grass. *When we gonna get our shit together, Wayne?*

Bit walks past brick apartments and empty warehouses. Spokane's a donut city, downtown a hole, civilians all in the suburbs. *Donut City* is part of Bit's *unified urban theory*, like the part about how every failing downtown tries the same stupid fixes: hang a vertical sign on an empty warehouse announcing LUXURY LOFTS!, buy buses that look like trolley cars, open a shitty farmers' market.

Very interesting, Andrea says whenever Bit talks about his theory. But we talk about *ourselves* at group, Bit. Let's talk about *you*.

But what if this *is* me? Bit asked once. Why can't we be the things we see and think? Why do we always have to be these sad stories, like

Fat Danny pretending he's sorry he screwed up his life when we all know he's really just bragging about how much coke he used to do? Why can't we talk about what we *think* instead of just all the stupid shit we've *done?*

Okay, Wayne, she said—what do you think?

I think I've done some real stupid shit.

Andrea likes him, always laughs at his jokes, treats him smarter than the rest of the group, which he is. She even flirts with him, a little.

Where's your nickname come from? she asked him one time.

It's because that's all a woman can take of my wand, he said. Just a bit. Plus I chewed a man to death once. Bit right through his larynx.

It's his last name is all, said Wallace. Bittinger.

That's true, Bit said, although I did bite a guy's larynx once.

You think you're so smart, Wallace is always saying.

And do you want to talk about Julie? Andrea's always saying.

Not so much, Bit's always saying.

We're all children before God, Cater's always saying.

But Cater isn't even at the Jesus beds when Bit stops there. He's at his kid's soccer game. Kenny the intake guy leans out the window and says he can't let Bit in the door till he clears it with Cater.

Sure, Bit says, just do me a favor. He takes the book from the bag. Tell him I showed you this.

Bit walks past brick storefronts and apartments, through nicer neighborhoods with green lawns. The book's heavy under his arm.

Another part of Bit's unified urban theory is sprinklers, that you can gauge a neighborhood's wealth by the way people water. If every single house has an automatic system, you're looking at a six-figure mean. If the majority lug hoses around, it's more lower-middle-class.

And if they don't bother with the lawns... well, that's the sort of shit-burg where Bit and Julie always lived, except for that little place they rented in Wenatchee the summer Bit worked at the orchard. He some-times thinks back to that time and imagines what it would be like if he could undo everything that came after it, like standing up a line of dominos. All the way back to Nate.

Bit breathes deeply, looks around at the houses to get his mind off it, at the sidewalks and the garden bricks and the homemade mail-boxes. It isn't a bad walk. The Molsons live in a neighborhood between arterials, maybe ten square blocks of '50s and '60s ranchers and ram-blers, decent-size edged yards, clean, the sort of block Julie always liked—nice but not overreaching. Bit pulls out the postcard, reads the address again even though he remembers the place from last time. Two more blocks.

It's getting cool now, heavy clouds settling down like a blanket over a kid. It'll rain later. Bit puts this neighborhood at about 40 percent sprinkler systems, 25 percent two-car garages, lots of rock gardens and lined sidewalks. The Molsons have the biggest house on the block, gray, two-story, with a big addition in back. Two little boys—one black, one white, both littler than Nate—are in the front yard, behind a big cyclone fence, bent over something. A bug, if Bit had to bet.

Hullo, Bit says from his side of the fence. You young gentlemen know if Nate's around?

He's downstairs playing ping-pong, says one of the boys, and the other grabs the kid's arm, no doubt heeding a warning about stranger-talk.

Maybe you could tell Mr. or Mrs. Molson that Wayne Bittinger's outside. Here to see Nate for one half-a-second is all.

The boys are gone awhile. Bit clears his throat. Shifts his weight.

Listens for police. He looks around the neighborhood and it makes him sad that it's not nicer, that Nate didn't get some South Hill fosters, a doctor or something. Stupid thought; he's embarrassed for having it.

Mrs. Molson looks heavier than the last time he stopped by, in the spring—has it been that long? More than half a year? She's shaped like a bowling pin, with a tuft of side-swooped hair and big round glasses. A saint, though, she and her husband both, for taking in all these kids.

She frowns. Mr. Bittinger—

Please, call me Wayne.

Mr. Bittinger, I told you before, you can't just stop by here.

No, I know that, Mrs. Molson. I'm supposed to go through the guardian *ad litem*. I know. I just… his birthday got away from me. I wanted to give him a book. Then I swear, I'll—

What book? She holds out her hands. Bit hands it over. She opens the bag and looks in without taking the book out, like it might be infected.

Mr. Bittinger, you *know* how Mr. Molson and I feel about these books. She tries to hand it back to him, but Bit won't take it.

No, I know, Mrs. Molson. He pats the postcard in his back pocket—picture of a lake and a campground. It was mailed to their old apartment. Bit's old landlord Gayle brought it down to the Jesus beds for him, what, a month ago—or was it three months now?

> Dad—I'm at camp and we're supposed to write our parents and I'm kind of mad (not really just a little) at the Molsons for taking away my Harry Potter books which they think are Satanic. I did archery here which was fun. I hope you're doing good too. Nate.

I respect your beliefs, Bit tells Mrs. Molson. I do. It's probably why you and Mr. Molson are such good people, to open your home up like this. But Nate, he loves them Harry Potter books. And after all he's been through, me being such a fuckup—Jesus, why did he say that—I'm sorry, pardon my... and losing his mother, I just... I mean... Bit can feel his face flushing.

Mrs. Molson glances back at the house. For what it's worth, we don't push our beliefs on the boys, Mr. Bittinger, she says. It's all about rules. Everyone here goes to church and everyone spends an hour on homework and we keep a close eye on what they read and watch. We have the same rules for all the boys. Otherwise it doesn't work. Not with eight of them.

No, I could see that, Bit says. I could.

Bit read the first Harry Potter to Nate when he was only six, even doing a British accent sometimes. Julie read him the second one, no accent, but cuddled up in the hotel bed where they were crashing. They got the books from the library. After the second one, Nate started reading them himself. Bit kind of wishes he'd kept up, before the dominos started going: before CPS came, before Julie got so hopeless and strung out, before...

We've been doing this a long time, Mrs. Molson is saying. We've had upwards of forty foster kids and we've found that this is what works: adherence to rules.

Yep, that's how we saw things, too, and I can't tell you how much I appreciate him having a stable home like this. I really do. My wife and I, we did our best, and we always figured that once we got every-thing back together, that, uh... but of course...

Mrs. Molson looks down at her shoes.

This wasn't what he meant to do, this self-pity. He wanted to talk like real people, but Bit feels himself fading. It's like trying to speak another language—conversational suburban—and it tires him out the way group does: everybody crying out their bullshit about the choices they've made and the clarity they've found. And he's worse than any of them, wanting so bad for Andrea to like him, to think he's fixed, when all he really wants is a pinch. Or a pint.

Bit clears his throat.

It's just... you know, this one thing. I don't know.

Mr. Bittinger—

Finally, Bit smiles, and rasps: Anything helps.

She looks up at him with what must be pity, although he can't quite make it out. Then she sighs and looks down at the book again. I guess... I could put it away for him. For later. He can have it when you can take him again... or when he's on his own, or with some other—

Thank you. I'd appreciate that. Bit clears his throat. But before you put it away, could you show it to him? Tell him his old man brought it for his birthday?

Sure, Mrs. Molson says, and then she gets hard again. But Mr. Bittinger, you can't come by here.

I know that, he says.

Next time I'll call the police.

He begins backing away. Won't be a next time.

You said that last spring.

Backing away: I know. I'm sorry.

Call Mr. Gandor and I'm sure he'll set up a visitation.

I will. Thank you, Mrs. Molson.

She turns and goes inside. Bit stands where he's backed up to, middle of the street, feels like he's about to burst open, a water balloon or a sack of fluid, gush out onto the pavement and trickle down to the curb. *When are we gonna get our shit together?*

Quickly, Bit begins walking toward downtown. He imagines the curtains parting in the houses around him. *Think you're so smart. Let's talk about you.* Jesus he wants something. He stowed his cardboard back behind Frankie Doodle's; instead of going to the Jesus beds and pleading with Cater, maybe he'll go get it. Hit that corner again. Tear it up one more night, like he and Julie used to do. Maybe the guy in the gold convertible will come by and give him another twenty. He tries to think of something good. Imagines the guy pulling up and Bit spinning his sign and it reading *Funny Fucker* and the guy laughing and Bit jumping into the car and them going to get totally fucked up in Reno or someplace. *Anything helps funny fucker! Funny fucker helps anything! You want to talk about Julie? Fuck funny anything helps! How long you been saving for that book, Bit? Anything funny helps fuck*

Dad!

Bit turns and there's Nate, stand-pedaling a little BMX bike up the street, its frame swinging beneath his size. Jeez, he's big, and he's got a bike? Of course he does. What thirteen-year-old doesn't have a bike? He remembers Julie waking up once, saying, We gotta get Nate a bike. Even fucked up Bit knew that not having a bike was the least of the kid's problems.

He tries to focus. The kid's hair is so short, like a military cut. Julie would hate that. There's something else—his teeth. He's got braces on. When he pulls up Bit sees he's got the book in its brown bag under his arm.

I can't take this, Dad.

No, it's okay, Bit says. I talked to Mrs. Molson and she said—

I read it at camp. This kid in my cabin had it. It was good. But you should take it back.

Bit closes his eyes against a wave of dizziness. No, Nate, I want you to have it.

Really, he says, I can't. I'm sorry. And he holds it out, making direct eye contact, like a cop. Jesus, Bit thinks, the kid's different in every way—taller and so... awake.

Take it, Nate says. Please.

Bit takes it.

I shouldn't have wrote that in my postcard, Nate says. I was mad they wouldn't let me read the book, but I understand it now. I was being stupid.

No, Bit says, I was glad you sent that card. You have a good birthday?

It seems to take a minute for Nate to recall his birthday. Oh. Yeah. It was cool. We went to the water slides.

And school starts...

Three weeks ago.

Oh. Sure, Bit says, but he can't believe it. It's not like time passes anymore; it leaks, it seeps. He wants to say something about the grade, just so Nate knows he *knows*. He counts years in his head: one after they took Nate, one after Julie, and one he's been trying to get better in the Jesus beds—a little more than three years the Molsons have had him. Jesus.

So... you nervous about eighth grade?

Nah. I was more nervous last year.

Yeah. Bit can barely take this steady eye contact. It reminds him of Cater.

Consequences, Cater's always saying.

I was more nervous last year, Nate's always saying.

I don't feel good, Julie's always saying.

Yeah, Bit says, no need to be nervous. He's still in danger of bursting, bleeding over the street.

You okay, Dad?

Sure. Just glad I got to see you. That *ad litem* business... I'm not good at planning ahead.

It's okay. Nate smiles. Looks back over his shoulder. Well... I should—

Yeah, Bit says. He moves to hug the boy or shake his hand or something, but it's like the kid's a mile away. Hey, good luck with school, and everything.

Thanks.

Then Nate pedals away. He looks back once, and is gone.

Bit breathes. He stands on the street. Feels the curtains fluttering. What if Julie didn't die? What if she got herself one of these houses and she's watching him now? *You ever gonna get your shit together, Bit? You gonna get Nate back? Or you goin' back to cardboard?*

Bit looks down at the book in his hands.

At the Jesus beds last weekend, after Bit explained to Cater how he was only a couple dollars short of buying this book for his kid, Cater stared at him in the most pathetic way.

What? Bit asked.

Cater said, How long you been saving for that book, Bit?

What do you mean?

I mean, ask yourself, how long you been a couple dollars short?

He supposes that's why he went crazy, Cater always looking at him like he's kidding himself. Like he's always thinking, How long has it been since you saw your kid, anyway?

Bit stands outside Auntie's Bookstore holding a twenty-eight-dollar book. Holding twenty-eight dollars. Holding a few fifths of vodka. Holding nine forty-ounce beers. Holding five bottles of fortified wine. Holding his boy. Civilians go into the store and come out carrying books in little brown bags just like the one he's got in his hands.

Here's why at the Jesus beds they can only talk about all the stupid shit they've done—because that's all they are now, all they're ever gonna be, a twitching bunch of memories and mistakes. Regrets. Jesus, Bit thinks. I should've had the decency to go when Julie did.

Back at his corner, Bit eases against the light pole. You think you're through with some things. But you aren't.

It's about to rain; the cars coming off the freeway have their windows up. It's fine, though. Bit likes the cool, wet air. The very first car pauses at the bottom of the hill and its driver, a woman, glances over. Bit looks away, opens the thick book, and begins reading.

The two men appeared out of nowhere, a few yards apart in the narrow, moonlit lane. For a second they stood quite still, wands pointing at each other's chests...

The light changes but the woman doesn't go. Raindrops have started to dapple the page, so Bit pulls his jacket over his head, to shield the book. And when he goes back to reading, this time it's with the accent and everything.

LOUELLA TARANTULA

by BENJAMIN WEISSMAN

AN ENORMOUS TARANTULA wandered onto my mother's face while she was taking a nap this afternoon. It was probably nine inches across, like the size of a dinner plate. It looked like it weighed twenty pounds but my dad said it was super light, maybe only three.

"Don't try to remove it," he said. "Just leave it there. It makes your mother happy." And a few seconds later he said, "Don't give me that incredulous look. She seems a lot calmer. More relaxed. It's her private thing. Quit judging shit."

"I can't believe that you just let a tarantula walk into the house and squat on Mom's face," I said. "It's one of the most horrific things I've ever seen in my life. Where did it come from?"

"It came from the neighborhood. And it's not squatting. That's its regular wide stance. She's very respectful. It's a she I think."

"You sexed it?"

"All tarantulas seem like women to me, son. Or females rather. It crawled in about seven o'clock this morning and it's already dropped her blood pressure, so it's a good thing. She's connecting with it. Whatever it's doing, it's working. They're bonding. Don't rock the boat with your negativity."

He was right. I have this terrible problem of throwing wet blankets on really fun, positive experiences like poisonous animals biting my sick fragile mom.

"Why don't you fry up some crispy potatoes?" my dad said. "Put a good smell in the house."

That night as I slept in my old childhood bedroom all I could think of was the tarantula. It was a terrible black sun hovering over my face. It cruised through the kitchen and dangled on the refrigerator, crawling over the notes that were held by magnets to the door. It tapped an all-night percussion session on a bag of potato chips. It rolled an onion down the hall. What can't it do, I wondered, lying in bed, staring at the ceiling's gothic shadowplay of odd shapes. At some point I was fortunate enough to fall asleep.

A few hours later, I was awakened by a tiny tickle on my chest. When my hand slapped down I felt a spill of cool jelly burst onto my skin.

It was a cockroach. In a panic, I sprang out of bed and swept the remains onto the ground, then reconsidered and put them in a cup. I drizzled a circle of boric acid around the entire bed.

The next morning, after feeding Louella the bashed cockroach, I drove my mom to the doctor for chemo treatment. She just stared straight ahead in the passenger seat. I turned on the radio, but she dropped the volume down to one decibel above off. When I said something about how scary these days were she remained silent, frozen in her statuary pose. What do you mean, she said several traffic lights later, and I said, The chemo and everything, you not feeling well, and she said, Don't talk like that around me ever again. She was staring straight ahead and she said it like a sullen cowboy, lips barely moving, her voice low, and then she turned the radio back up to drown out any additional words from me. I had a runny nose and made the mistake of rubbing it on my right sleeve. The clear snot became a long silver streak down the forearm of my black shirt.

My mother seemed to be struggling to breathe, or she was anticipating the day when she no longer could. She opened and closed her jaw like she was practicing to be a skeleton. She was nervous, terrified. I wanted to help her but I had no idea how. I couldn't soothe her in any way, couldn't think of a comment to cheer her. She breathed with obvious exertion. She pulled air into her lungs from the space around her as if the air was resistant or heavy and she was preparing to push it out so she could gather more, quickly. Sometimes she'd let out a wild burp as if it saved her life. She seemed grateful for it and would try to erupt another. In the past she'd always encouraged me to do the same. How about another, she'd say, encore. She had a Japanese appreciation for burps.

In the waiting room I pretty much just stared at people's feet: clogs, open-toed espadrilles, aqua-painted toenails within, suntanned ankles comfortably nestled inside wingtips, kelly green socks looking cheerful inside brown Converse low-tops, black Mary Janes, pink slippers with little roses on the tops.

After the chemo she asked if I'd drive her to the Christian Science Reading Room, a little place where she could pick up new literature. Amuse yourself for a few minutes, she said when we got there. I won't be long. Then she opened her door and, in super-slow motion, rotating her body to the right, rose out of the passenger seat with great exertion. Once she was out she gingerly stepped onto the curb and walked away, leaving the door slightly ajar.

I sat in the car in a loading zone and waited. The reading room was a sad little storefront on a super-fancy street in Beverly Hills. In a dusty window display there were a few sun-bleached books nestled on a yellow blanket with a little plastic spotted lamb standing by, looking lost, ever-faithful that someone will read to it. A sexy woman in white short shorts strode down the sidewalk like it was a porno runway, her vagina visible from thirty feet, nipple rings protruding from her chest, poking through her shirt like electrified sensors. Find my cock, I said to her massive rack and super-cool sunglasses. Locate here, in driver's seat of Honda CVR. Find my cock and smoke it. Since I was parked so close to his base of operations I addressed God directly and asked him to intervene. God, I implored, please don't underestimate the neediness of my cock, or the adventures it longs to experience in order to feel complete, to feel that it's had a fair chance on this earth, especially with the Beverly Hills ladies, who are sexually attracted to men with ten-inch snot streaks on their shirt sleeves.

All I've wanted to do since my mom's diagnosis is fuck. Couldn't this woman just stand over me and pretend that she was a peach or grapefruit tree and dangle her big fruit onto the eyelids of a blind man?

Louella gripped the headboard behind my mom's bed and waited for her to return. Once her head touched down on a stack of pillows, Louella made her way over to my mom's face. Assume the position, I thought, and let the spider transform you.

My mom reached for a pad of paper and pencil by her nightstand

and wrote *paint my toe nails black*. Then she gestured with her right hand toward the bathroom.

I found the cotton balls and a hand towel. "Mom," I yelled from the bathroom, "I can only find red nail polish. *Crimson vampire.* Do you want me to go to the store and get black?"

I walked back into the room. She nodded yes. The tarantula moved up and down with her. "I love you, Mom," I said, and stood close to her. I picked up her hand and held it. There was no way to give her a kiss. I got as close as I could, inches from her face, but it was all Louella and her amazing body. I was staring at the center bulb, into what I thought was Louella's face or mouth, but it could've just as easily been her anus. All of a sudden Louella kicked out a leg, like she was telling me to back off, so I did.

Downstairs, my dad was sitting on a stool, plucking away at a three-string ukulele, the one I'd broken two decades earlier, softly singing "You're the Top," a Cole Porter song.

You're the dam at Boulder
You're the moon,
Over Mae West's shoulder

At the market I also bought sunscreen and Ivory soap. The first girl that ever ravaged me with sex used Ivory soap and I'd been sudsing myself with it ever since. Back home here was a grasshopper in the driveway with Louella's name on it, so I got a coffee cup and a postcard and captured it. When I reentered the house I sat back down on Mom's bed. My parents slept in twin beds right next to each other, like in a hotel. I put a little cotton ball in between each of my mother's toes and commenced the delicate job of painting.

I had never really looked at my mom's toes before. They were narrow little things, hairless and long, surprisingly pretty, the second toes longer than the big toes. That seemed elegant for some reason.

My dad's toenails look like rhino horns now. They actually curl down and up. When I noticed I was surprised he could walk with them.

"I brought Louella some lunch," I said. "Or a snack. A really nice grasshopper. Very frisky."

My mom's eyes were closed, as they always seemed to be now. She was either sleeping or trying to will herself into sleep. Louella, her new muscular friend and guardian, seemed capable of lifting her right off the bed and carrying her away. Every once in a while Louella relaxed a leg and shifted her position. Most of the time she seemed to be moving ever so slightly in response to my mom's breathing. When my mom sighed, Louella copied that and caved in. Louella was all brain, just brains and legs, with a dark plan up her sleeve. She seemed more alien visitor than insect, like a divine elder from the Church.

I'd learned a few things about tarantulas from my parents' mailman, Andrew. They secrete poison into their prey. Once the prey is immobilized, Andrew said, the tarantula secretes digestive enzymes that turn the bird or frog into a kind of soup. Then it can suck up its meal using strawlike mouthparts. He also said tarantulas have something called book lungs, which are respiratory organs composed of many fine leaves. They're like layered pastry rather than the easily punctured balloons that we have.

I'd seen smaller tarantulas at school. A little one named Toby walked on my arm in science class, but Louella was triple the size, like a furry spaceship.

"I'm a big fan of tarantulas," Andrew said at another noontime exchange, handing me the mail. "Did you know that the tarantulas in Thailand are iridescent blue?"

"That sounds kind of sexy," I said.

"They enjoy sleeping on peat moss and coconut husks. The males have mating hooks that clamp onto the ladies."

"I need some of those."

"Don't we all," Andrew said. He was wearing a federally issued pith helmet. It gave him a cartoony cuteness.

"I see you're growing a beard," he said after a moment. "In honor of the tarantula?"

"Maybe so," I said, fading from the conversation.

"They can live to be forty," Andrew said, and after a few more strange seconds he said, "Okay buddy, please give your mom my best."

My mom's friend Hoss came to visit, a big perfumey woman with tons of jewelry. She got the name Hoss from her mother, a battle-ax from the old country turned Hollywood script supervisor who was also named Hoss. Hoss Junior had herself become a success, adapting Faulkner and McMurtry novels for the screen with her husband, who had ratted out colleagues to the House Un-American Activities Committee.

She clanked around my mom's bedroom in three dozen bracelets, a pile of necklaces, and fifteen to twenty rings (as many as four on one finger). "Hi Dollface," she yelled to my mother, as if she were in a play. "How are you feeling?" Hoss's head rotated in my direction, and in a softer, deeper voice, she asked, "How is she feeling?"

"I'm not sure. Not well. Or stable. She hasn't eaten anything all day."

"Darling, would you like some fresh tangerine juice?" Hoss yelled. And then, to me, more softly, "I've been doing some research on Louella. She needs to stay moist, just like me. Even though she likes her habitat dry and warm she also appreciates a good misting every day, like a fern."

Hoss hovered over my mom's head/Louella and gave the two of them a big squirt with this huge, fancy-green squirt bottle. After one misting Louella seemed to loosen her grip and relax, sinking her center onto my mom's mouth like she appreciated the climate change and was nap-ready. Hoss and I watched in amazement.

When my dad walked in carrying another horrifying bouquet of flowers Louella began to stir again. She walked over my mom's chin and down her chest and belly. She paused at my mother's crotch, then raised and lowered one of her sturdy little legs, and my mom seemed to smile.

"Mischievous is what they are," my dad said. "They're pranksters." Then the tarantula continued down to the foot of the bed.

"More like vagina inspectors!" Hoss shouted.

But Louella didn't stop there. She wandered to the edge of the mattress and then under the bed, burrowing into a pile of newspapers and pajamas and underwear.

"She likes to be alone sometimes," my dad said.

After my mom died, my dad and I took all her clothes off and carried her into the bathroom and lowered her into the tub, where we propped her up as straight as her body would permit and bathed her with her favorite minty soap. The soap came in a long plastic bottle and had a ton of writing on it from the hippie manufacturer, a full manifesto about free trade. We both scrubbed away with a couple big sponges: me working on the neck, face, and shoulders, my dad working on the rest. I gave her thinning scalp a long, super-sudsy shampoo, really getting all ten of my fingers in there, and then a cream rinse. When I was in college I'd had a job as a live-in helper for a quadriplegic artist who I cooked for, bathed, and dressed, so I was sort of used to this sort of thing except that the artist was tiny, like a ninety-pound decomposed astronaut. My mom was a lot meatier.

With the aid of henna she'd been a redhead in life, but her lower sexual hair was pitch black, and for some reason the first sight of it shocked me. Her pubic hair. It was something I'd never seen before and I looked away faster than I've ever looked away from anything. I had seen a few different colors and textures in my life; my last empirical encounter was with a Scandinavian muff that was nearly invisible, more like fishing line than straw. But my mother's triangular fur was different on so many levels. And then I thought, Duh, you were created there, buddy; that's the outside of your nine-month transport vehicle. Your exit strategy into the world was that vagina.

Neither of us cried, which was good since we had a lot of things to take care of. Where was it, the weeping? When would it hit? How could we both be so calm? I think my dad and I were more relieved than anything else; relieved that the big suffering had stopped. He is such a positive, optimistic guy. I'm kind of the opposite, more of a dark-cloud gloomster.

I lifted my mom's arms as my dad sponged around carefully, not missing a spot. She was sixty-one years old. There was a gnarly childhood scar running down her back from a surgical procedure to cure a ruptured abdominal organ. I had never seen it before. It was huge and raw, and long, like eighteen inches, and tender, like it had just mended. After toweling her off we got her into the simple green and white prairie dress she liked to wear when she was pretending to be a country girl, with lots of little buttons that went right up to her throat. She looked really great in it, modest and rural.

* * *

"You're an observant fellow," the extremely damp mortuary man whispered to me when I said that my mom's face looked pinker than usual. Rouge was his number-one cosmetic. His name was Cletus, a name I couldn't help associating with knives, Roman murder, and the anus. Cletus's skin looked like wet butter, the complexion of the coffin-ready. He had a blond ponytail and unnaturally plump lips that he pushed out when he was pretending to think, as if to encourage a kiss or to imitate a fish. He radiated a terrible kind of sex, as if cannibalism were the logical conclusion to a hug. It felt like he was salting me with his mind.

My mom had been observant, too. She was also cautious, afraid of so many things in the world and in our house, especially the kitchen. Cooking was a huge challenge for her. Dishes were haunted: they rattled of their own accord on the drying rack, and if one frying pan clanked against another while she was searching for something she'd become mildly hysterical and scream back at the cookware and bang pots and pans until she grew exhausted.

In my mom's prime, when I was maybe twelve, but also thirteen, fourteen, and fifteen, she would forgo a hot kitchen on summer nights and take me out to dinner, usually to the Farmers Market for fried chicken and spaghetti. On the drive home she'd detour through the bowels of Hollywood to *observe people*. It was her only form of recreation. She'd see a male hustler leaning against a lamppost and slow the car down to a crawl. Oh my god, she'd say, look at those leather pants, they're skintight. I wonder what he's waiting for? And the guy would inevitably look our way and my mom would shout, He's looking at you! and I'd feel the gaze burning a quick little hole in me. She'd drive on, turn a corner, and find another guy. Look at that walk, so swishy, she'd say. Or, Look at that man's crotch, you can see his penis through his jeans. And then, Oh my god, look, look, he's touching his thing, roll up your window, lock the door.

* * *

At the funeral I thought about how my mom used to cut articles about serial killers and mafia hits and other poignant cruelties out of the newspaper and send them to me when I moved away and went to college. It was her way of staying in touch, continuing our morbid discussion about Earth's most foul citizens.

In her casket my mom's face no longer held the brilliant rose color that had appeared in Cletus's workshop. It had turned a curdled yellow. But as eerie as she looked, there was still something very much alive about her. The body ceasing to function didn't convince me that she was actually dead. How could she be dead and look so comfortable? I kept thinking about her black toenails. I wished she was barefoot or wearing open-toed sandals so her friends could admire them.

There were sandwiches called Rollers at the post-funeral reception, which was at our house. They were these ham/turkey/cheese things rolled up in flour tortillas with a tiny tomato, a sliver of lettuce, and a smear of pink cheese. I ate five of them and a couple of shrimps in spicy red sauce.

"Who's going to take care of Louella now that your lovely mother has died?"

It was Hoss, a plate of olive pits in her hand.

"I don't think she would want another woman taking care of it," she told me.

Her heavily powdered face was reddened at both cheeks like an electric clown's. Her eyelashes had been brushed high with mascara and outlined in black. She wore a black turban wrapped around her head; big hoop earrings swung from earlobes that had endured a half century of decorative weight. Her body was tilted forward like she was pushing a cart.

"I would volunteer, but I don't think Folly would be so accommodating." Folly was her cat. "No, I think your mother would prefer a man or a boy. A gentle manservant from South America, maybe. Someone who understands the ways and means of an arachnid, someone with a good soul. Another woman wouldn't be right. Another woman... would be a kind of betrayal."

"I don't know why you say that," I said.

"Your mother was a jealous woman. I think she'd feel that she and Louella did things together that were once-in-a-lifetime moments. They shouldn't be repeated with a woman of the same sex, or another person, rather. Of the same sex. I don't think she wants some floozy-bitch-whore—I'm using your mother's words here, she liked the word *floozy*, especially when used in combination with *slut*, *whore*, and *bitch*—to show up with a cigarette dangling out of her mouth and be like, Yeah, I'll take some of that tarantula."

My dad and I looked at each other for several seconds like we were trying to keep each other's faces from twisting up. Hoss had always been an alpha shrew. When my parents first decided to get married Hoss threw a tantrum because they hadn't consulted her first.

"Maybe we should let Louella decide," I said.

"Precisely," Hoss shouted, and threw an arm down like a gavel.

A few days later my dad said Louella might need to move on. Without your mother she's no longer happy here, he said. She seems totally disinterested in us.

Louella did in fact seem limp, droopy, inert, ignoring the dazed cicadas and cheerfully wiggly earthworms we prodded toward her as she lay in her lair under my mother's bed. I brought her a little dish of water but the waterline never dropped. I tried misting her, but now she only recoiled and hissed. I wanted to be her new pal but I was not what the tarantula ordered. We decided to put an ad up on craigslist.

We got a tremendous response. Matt of big eyes and flat vocal register said he grew up with tarantulas all around him and would like to take Louella to New York City; Ulysses said he was shooting a documentary film about his male tarantula, Clarence, and he'd really like to find Clarence a mate. Epifano said he felt like he was part tarantula himself, that he'd dressed up like one for Halloween. Mongo Shelsh Kavetch was a rabbinical scholar who believed all tarantulas were Jewish and felt Louella belonged in Israel. The interviews went on for hours until finally a young Amish girl named Esther showed up dressed in handmade, earth-colored clothes. "I've come to see about the possibility of caring for a two-year-old tarantula named Louella," she said in a tiny child's voice that sounded like an angelic prayer. Esther said she had just graduated from art school and did volunteer work at a vet but didn't want to make a career of it because of all the animals they had to put down. "I'd like to take Louella to the desert," she said, "to Death Valley, where my family lives. I think she would have a good life there." And then Louella, who had been hanging out underneath my mom's bed since the funeral, crept out and went straight for Esther and climbed up her leg.

"Oh, she's beautiful," Esther said, and laughed as Louella tickled her. "Where did the name Louella come from?"

"From an old gossip columnist my wife used to read," my dad said.

"There really aren't gossip columnists anymore, are there?" Esther said.

"No, not really," my dad said. "Or maybe everything is gossip now."

Esther considered my dad's comment thoughtfully. She had a little pug nose with the narrowest nostrils I've ever seen on an adult. Her face was so soft that it seemed void of internal bones. She said, "I really like the idea of a gossipy tarantula. She is a precious gift to the world. I'm honored to have met her."

My last view of Louella was of her nestling into Esther's big shoulder bag. I peeked in and could see her scrunching around, getting comfortable.

After Esther drove away my dad put his arm around me and said, "Now that you and I are completely alone, two bachelors, both grieving in different ways, you as a motherless son and me a classic widower, I think we should go do something special. Something involving nature. I've always wanted to go to Africa."

"Yeah, but that's crazy expensive," I said. "And we don't have much money."

"What do you have in mind, Mr. Great-Idea Destroyer?"

"Why don't we just go outside right now, sit on the porch, and sip a whiskey?"

"Brilliant suggestion, my son, blood of my blood. Please put a couple ice cubes in mine."

So I grabbed two little juice glasses from the kitchen and a dusty bottle of brown stuff from a liquor cabinet that hadn't seen much use. The two of us sat down on a bench by the front door. My dad has the body of a heavyweight wrestler but you only notice it when sitting beside him. His forearms are dark brown and bulge with muscle and his thighs are ridiculous tree trunks.

When I was a wee lad I remember holding on to his shoulders as he swam through the water. He was like a big hairy manatee. As he dipped and rose via his rhythmic breaststroke I remember telling myself that he came from the sea, not from Brooklyn, and there was no disputing it.

By midnight there were several moths slamming their crash-test-dummy bodies into the bare bulb of my parents' porch light. The area surrounding the bulb was like a moth graveyard, powdered with their khaki residue, but maybe some of them were just resting. It was hard to tell.

"I really don't like the term *a better place*," my dad said. "It's offensive."

"People get nervous. They don't know what to say. When they say 'a better place' maybe they just mean better than excruciating pain."

My dad made a consenting groan. "Sure. But when people tell me that your mother is in 'a better place' I want to punch them in the face."

"I think Mom would've been happy if we'd each carried an iron skillet around at the reception and just bonked people on the head."

"She would've loved that. Here, we forgot to do this," my dad said, and raised his glass. I tapped it with mine.

The porch light glowed, an ugly beacon. There were several white opaque webs or nests the size of my fingernail bivouacked in a corner of the stucco wall, like climbers' bunks suspended on a rock face with tiny shells and wings and legs inside. The live bugs continued to engage in some type of light-bulb ecstasy ritual.

"They're amazing, aren't they?" I said.

We were staring at a loud orange-and-black-striped one that careened about like an old prop plane piloted by a berserker, slamming repeatedly against the sun.

"It's hard to know what moths want," my dad said.

"They seem very suicidal when they get around a hot light bulb," I said, "like they want to die every second."

"But you know that's not their real objective," my dad said.

"It could be that dying feels good to them."

"All moths lust after light."

"Yeah, and they want to stay in the blaze as long as possible, even as it nips at their wings."

"The Wagnerian moth," my dad said, and began to take a sip of whiskey, then hesitated. "Look who just called it quits in my drink?"

He tilted his glass toward me. A dead moth was floating in the whiskey.

"Would you call that a better place?" I asked.

"I would call that the best place," he said.

GIANT OF THE SEA

by ABI MAXWELL

*F*ANCY-MAKE. She and Kristina learned that from him. They met him down on the docks and he wasn't a Swede—they never did figure out just what he was—but to Eleonora and Kristina he said, "Ladies, ladies!" in English, and waved his hand toward himself. They listened. They were fifteen and no man had ever called to them like that.

He had letters sent from America that he would pull from his pockets and sniff and read aloud to them in that jagged Swedish he spoke. "Look here—blue sky you can't believe! Fancy-make yourself right up, nice dress, plait hair, you fit right in!"

Yes, he would touch his hand upon their heads, too, but wasn't that customary?

*   *   *

Dear Britt,

You can't believe the beauty here they keep a clean house pay is good it would be wonderful to share your bosom with you please come to America at once.

Love for you only,

Erik Lindholm

What made Eleonora and Kristina get into such mischief? The man on the docks who said he had crossed the ocean to America and back three times over had nothing to do with this letter the girls wrote. On their own they posted that cruel joke. When it arrived at Britt's house it was not believed, clearly it had been shipped from their very own village, but still there was some fuss. The girls witnessed it because without shame they knocked upon Britt's front door to ask her mother if now might be a good time to have a short visit.

"I'm afraid someone's gone and made a fool of my girl," Mrs. Hansson said.

"Awful," Kristina said.

Menace in that word. Eleonora heard it clear as day.

Britt had a dark purple birthmark that stretched down the length of her face; now, beneath her tears, it lit up like a streak of lightning. She was said to have been born with only one and a half ears, but no one knew the truth of that, for she kept her hair plaited frankly over the sides of her head. Erik Lindholm was the most handsome of their town and although he was of a high class he had no airs about him, which made his handsomeness shine all the more. He had left for America not one year ago, and all of the girls had felt that he'd loved each one of them alone. But if he were to choose just one to send for, it would not be Britt Hansson.

When they left Britt's house, Kristina, that small, skinny thing, doubled over with laughter in the blooming forsythia. Eleonora forced out a small laugh, but at night when her mother planted a kiss upon her forehead she let out one large tear. "I am not good," she told her mother quietly.

"Now, dear," her mother said.

But it was true. Eleonora had for all her life been good and now the shame grew and spread and over and over again through the night she repeated aloud, "I will not be wicked, I will not be wicked." Morning came and she felt unsure of how she might ever learn to live with the self she had become.

"That was wicked," she told her friend later that day.

"Wonderfully wicked," Kristina replied. Those birdlike eyes, how they darted and paused and shone.

Eleonora's father was a sea captain who died at sea on April 22, 1878. Albert Olasson, nothing fancy about him. He would not like to see the way this Kristina taught his daughter to cross her legs and pucker her lips. A poor man with a small house, but a house with a clean floor, for he was a sea captain, after all. A good, wholesome man who by the end had loved Eleonora the best. For a time she'd had a cough so sharp they'd believed she would die, but they had lost two children before and though it was misery it was not unthinkable. Still, to lose this daughter was a fear that had kept Albert sleeping on the hard floor by her bed for months. He hadn't loved her in any extraordinary way before the sickness, or hadn't appeared to. But the cough came and the one he favored was out.

That was when Eleonora was fourteen years old. She sat up healed one day and the next afternoon her father died, so perhaps it was his own death and not hers that he had smelled around the corner. *Ellie,* he had taken to calling her in those last weeks. *Our Ellie.* In spite of her mother's firm ways that short name stuck and it gave the girl the sense that she had been chosen, she alone.

As for Kristina, she had no special role at home. The rooms run over with children, under the beds and upon the tables, her mother so busy she's sweating even when the windows are laced with ice. Kristina could escape any old time. If she disappeared, would anyone even notice?

Big Old, the man on the docks liked to be called. Kristina batted her eyes at him.

"I could go to America," she said. It was dark, she had snuck out, but Big Old had a candle lit.

"Can you?" he said. When he spoke it was from the corner of his mouth. This gave him a look of disinterest, which pushed Kristina further. It had since the beginning. Full attention was what she was after. *Someone down at the docks loves me.* He was not an unattractive man. A full beard, but clean. Thick, rough hands. Store-bought clothes.

"Sure as hell I can." There, a curse. Wasn't she old and free?

He leaned in then. The boat he slept on rose up and down against the dock. Her father was out there somewhere, on the open water. When she angled her eyes downward she could see the tip of her own nose, translucent in the candlelight. Offshore the bell of the sea spoke back to the waves. The astonishing thing is that she didn't mind, wasn't scared.

Because he had given her the candle then. *Hold it here,* he'd told her. He'd undone his pants and there, she saw it, she was an adult now, that's what he said.

"Ain't that a show?"

*   *   *

Of course she didn't tell Eleonora.

"Come out at night," she said instead. "The mermaids, Ellie, they rise from the sea. They *glow*. Ellie," she said, "your father could be among them."

"Do you believe in mermaids?" Eleonora asked her mother.

Her mother did. Mermaids and gnomes and all the other beings of the sea and woods.

"And do you believe my father is still in the sea?"

Yes. Yes, of course.

Still, she nearly didn't go. But then there Kristina was at her window, calling, "Ellie, you've got to see it for yourself!" Through the curtains came a rope of cotton that looked like satin in the light of Kristina's candle. Eleonora looked down at her friend smiling alone in the night and then out toward the sea where her father would be and finally back to the room where her mother lay and as she heard the far-off hum of a fishing boat she grabbed hold. Down toward the docks they ran, their small soft hands clasped together.

Eleonora had never been out at night. How calm and full of love her village looked! She could feel the gentle breath of each of her neighbors. Up and down it rose, together. She was running across the back of a great beast who slept when his people slept.

Parked in front of the dock was a carriage, lit up from the inside, glowing.

"Hide," Eleonora said, and pulled her friend toward the trees. But Kristina only laughed in a way that Ellie had never heard before. Not with glee. The laugh was a devil that rolled right up the street. She pulled Ellie forward and stuck her own head right through that carriage door.

"Hello," she said, as though she knew just who would be inside.

(And so what if she did know? Did that mean she knew what lay ahead? She will let her dear Eleonora believe that she did not. And for the rest of her life, she will let most of herself believe the same.)

Big Old patted the leather seat beside himself and Kristina jumped in next to him. The horses were so black they were nearly invisible. Ellie backed up.

"I've got to get home," she said.

"Walk then," Kristina said.

Why didn't she? She could have. Back then she still knew the way.

"I do not want to walk alone, Kristina."

"In, then," Big Old said. "We take ride home."

This time when Ellie backed up Kristina reached forward and grabbed her by the shoulder and pulled. Into the carriage she went.

I want to go home, was all she said. And after some time on the road, after they've passed the church and the edge of town, she says it again.

"Say it one more time I tie kerchief on your face," Big Old says sharply. Kristina giggles in close to the man.

Ellie begins to cry. "Now, now," Big Old says. He opens his jacket and removes a green-tinted glass bottle. "Here," he says, and holds it out. Kristina reaches for it but he pulls it away. "Here," he says to Ellie again. "Take sip. Calm you down."

"Take it," Kristina says. She places her hand on Ellie's knee. There is a sudden steadiness about her, those eyes so open, nothing hidden in them now. This is the Kristina who has herded seven siblings and lifted Ellie through her father's death. Eleonora could fight back, but has she ever in her life? Not once. Of course Kristina knows this.

Just a sip. There. Ellie leans back in the carriage and the bottle slips to the floor. No problem. Her head is pillowed by one thousand clouds and behind the carriage trails her father. He is coming to save her. There is seaweed draped from him but she will be safe all the same.

When Eleonora opens her eyes, she is on the other side of the country. Around her there hangs a soft and purple morning.

"Copenhagen," she hears. "Ticket to Copenhagen," over and over again. She knows that name, Copenhagen—that is the place the ships for America depart from—but they can't be headed there, because isn't her head resting against her father's shoulder?

"My daughter very tired," he says. "Nothing serious. Yes, she can walk of course."

He puts her down and stands her up and her legs bend forward. She tumbles.

"Ellie, wake up!" Kristina says. Kristina. Yes, that's right. This is not her father here with them. Wake up, yes. Stand. Run. Ellie pushes her teeth together and puts her hands out in front of her. Look, she can do it. She is on two feet. Run.

"See?" Big Old says. "My daughter just sleepy. Like mother. Sleep through tornado, they do. Yes, right. Eleonora and Kristina Johnsson."

"No," Eleonora is able to say. In her own mind she's shouting but to those around her it is just night murmurs. No, no, but no one hears. She puts her hands to her face and lifts her eyelids up. There. Her last vision of home.

How many days is it before she is able to rise? Enough so that when she does, and goes on deck, there is only a strip of black in the distance. It could be anyone's land, or no one's.

"What will you do in America?" A little boy, perhaps eight years old, asks her this. Eleonora prays, but she does not speak. There's a strong, warm wind and she goes to the rail, leans over. The boy follows her, and in time he becomes a small thing for her to love. He has some watercolors and some paper and in the afternoons the two of them sit on the deck and paint pictures of their villages.

"Where will you be going?" she has the sense one day to ask him.

She saw Kristina and Big Old there together on the bed that first time she really came to. And since that time throughout most of each day the door to the cabin has been locked and Ellie has been ordered to stay away.

"Do you know the address?" she asks the boy, and has him say it and say it again. They make a small song of it: *14 Pleasant Street Lynn Massachoosits! 14 Pleasant Street Lynn Massachoosits!*

When the boy has to tend to his mother, Eleonora tiptoes along the ship. She has a stack of handwritten notes in her pocket: *Forgive me, I am desperate.* This to replace a stolen bottle of medicine, a wool hat, vinegar.

What if she could be this little boy's mother? His blond hair so bright it's like the sun on his very own head. And oh, the way he laughs so free and easy!

"What is your father like?" she asks him.

His father is already in America. He has not seen his father since he was a boy five years old. Nice, yes, surely he is nice! Generous? Yes. Couldn't a man not recognize a wife in that time? Couldn't he take another?

"Do I look as your mother looks?"

"Sorry?" he says.

"Your mother has blue eyes and hair like mine?"

"My mother is sick," the boy says, and picks up his paintbrush, spits on its tip.

Sick?

*　　*　　*

At night Eleonora curls up on her bunk and pushes toward the wall, small as can be. She holds her thumb to her mouth and lets the rest of her hand cover her nose to block the stench. One night when she feels a slender arm ease itself over her body, just above the curve of her hip, she knows it is her old friend nestled behind her. She freezes.

"America is better," Kristina whispers. She smooths Ellie's stringy hair and hums an old song in her ear. And this could be a comfort, Ellie could close her eyes and be carried by Kristina in this way.

Instead Eleonora whispers, "No." But the word is too quiet, and anyway it means nothing, all of it is hopeless. Everyone on this boat is hungry, and they all want only to get to America. There is not one single being who will trust and stand up for this tattered thief of a girl that Ellie has become. None but a boy not ten years old.

"I didn't mean—" Kristina begins. "I never wanted—" she tries. "Ellie, forgive me," she finally settles upon.

Eleonora pulls herself closer to the wall.

Her little friend takes her across the ship's porch—this is what he calls it, *Doesn't our home have a marvelous porch*, he likes to say—and down to his cabin. It is larger than the one Ellie stays in, with drawers and pillows. It is scrubbed down bare and smells of vinegar.

"Here," the boy says. "My friend Eleonora." He says her name lavishly, as though she is upon a stage. Ellie loves him there. She leans forward and the boy's mother tilts her eyes upward without moving her head.

"Bless you, dear," she says. She pats the bed beside herself and her boy gently sits. Ellie is still standing when the surgeon comes in. He puts a hand to the boy's face and pulls it away just as quickly. *Look, I got your nose.* Eleonora shudders at this small gesture—a remembrance of home. The mother's temperature is taken. It's high. The surgeon holds his stethoscope to her heart.

"And what about yours?" he asks the boy.

"I know mine," the boy cackles.

"And you, dear?" the surgeon says. "Shall we make sure your heart's still beating?" He pats the edge of the bed, but Eleonora will not sit.

"What is it?" the man asks. He is kind, yes. Decent. Now couldn't she tell her secret after all? Couldn't this be the person to get her home?

But instead she drops her eyes. Better to find her own way in the new world. On this boat Big Old will say she's gone mad, absolutely he will. She and Kristina have been warned as much. And there's the book Ellie read at school, written by a man of her own country. They'll lock you up in port if there's something wrong, she knows, never to be seen again.

"My heart beats fine," Eleonora tells him.

He chuckles in that kind, pure way that could make her tip right over with an ache for home. He is still chuckling in that way when she says, "Will she die?"

"Now, now," he says.

"Eleonora!" the boy says.

"Will she?"

With ease and assurance the surgeon places his hand beneath Eleonora's chin and lifts it upward. He grabs her gaze with his own. *Be good*, she takes him to mean. *You be good.*

When he releases her he pats the boy's head once more. "Rub at her feet and move the fever through her body, that's all you can do," he says as he leaves.

The boy sees the surgeon out, then sets to work on his mother's feet. Eleonora presses her body against the cold wall and slides away from him, toward the woman's face. In her pocket she has Big Old's small green bottle—from him she has dared steal only this. Now she wraps her fingers around it and thinks for a terrible moment as the boy is bent over the far end of the bed that she could just pour it into this woman's mouth. One drop will send her into a sleep as deep as the sea itself, but if Eleonora pours the whole bottle in it will kill the woman dead, Ellie knows it will. And then couldn't she take this woman's life, become her? Marry her husband and raise this boy who gleams pure as a seed just sprouted from the ground?

"I have been watching out for your son on board," Ellie says. She sweeps a hand over the woman's hair.

"Do," the woman says lightly.

"I was kidnapped," Ellie whispers to her. "I have no family and no home now. I believe I am to be sold." She has thought this over and she is sure she is correct. Sold as a prostitute—she has read about it, though her mother would not have approved. It was in the journal from the city that the boys at school showed her.

"Water," the woman says.

The boy leaves to get it, and here alone in the room Eleonora's hand returns to her pocket to let her fingers run over the bottle once more.

"Would you like to be my friend forever and ever?" she asks the boy when he returns. "Forevermore?"

But the boy does not answer, because he has seen that his mother's color has brightened. He sets back to rubbing and patting at her feet.

"There," the boy says. "We'll see Father soon. There."

"I have given your mother a drop of tonic," Ellie explains. "It will help her rest." And she is right, it does. As the mother sleeps Eleonora and the boy wash the woman's face with warm water and hold her hands and take turns warming her feet, and it is in this listless, safe stretch of time that Eleonora comes up with a new plan. She will keep this woman alive.

The woman is still not recovered by the time Kristina finds Eleonora on the deck with the boy and the watercolors. Her lip has dried blood on it and her face and arms are pocked with bruises.

"He wants you now," Kristina says.

Eleonora has expected as much. More than three weeks it has been, and how could she get off so easily? She has kept herself clean enough with the water for the sick mother and the vinegar in their cabin, but Kristina smells of urine and her hair is a ball of weak strings. She has taken the brunt of it, but still Ellie has grown old enough during her time on the ship to understand what it is a man like Big Old wants. She cleans the tip of her brush and stands.

"Do not talk to this girl," she says to the boy. "Go to your mother. Do not stay by this girl." It's not hard to convince him.

Later Eleonora will remember that she did indeed scan the room before she entered fully. Her eyes landed on that empty cistern and she made herself stand beside it while Big Old loosened his belt.

He is shirtless. "Aren't you lucky one?" he is saying. "Without Big Old, you never cross ocean. Don't you want to thank Big Old?"

"Yes," Eleonora says, and bends down. She puts her hands on the cistern.

"Empty," he says.

"I'll just fill it," she says, and lifts it up. "I know a place."

He is saying that now is not a good time. He thinks he has

something she can drink. He turns to find it and then turns back, comes toward her. Yes, she knows what is coming now. She lifts that cistern higher and as if she's practiced it she smashes it upon his head.

Big Old grunts and then he is on the floor, kicking his legs and my god, if he is to get up. She finds the bottle in her pocket, bends down. Into his mouth, just a few drops, whoops, these hands shake, there goes all of it. His life takes flight through the cracks in the walls. He is dead, absolutely he is.

Our Ellie. She can hear her mother say it. *Our Ellie has killed a man.*

Outside the cabin Eleonora tiptoes across the deck. There Kristina stands alone.

"Come," is all Ellie says.

Kristina does not resist. Instead she stares blankly at Eleonora, and clutches her hand. Down they go, Kristina trailing after Ellie like a child. It is only when Ellie opens the door of the cabin a crack and the two slide in that her old friend tumbles into a sickening, delightful laugh. She walks to the head of the man on the floor and there she kicks him.

"No!" Eleonora says. She knows he is dead but to kick his empty body seems evil and nothing more.

Kristina kicks him one last time, then picks up that dented cistern and smashes him on the head once again. When she is finished she squats down close to him, opens his shirt, listens for his heart. Of course it is silent.

"I'm sorry," Kristina says to heaven. "I have killed a man."

And as for Eleonora?

"Forgive us. Forgive my friend Kristina for killing this man."

*   *   *

"Our father is dead, someone has killed our father!" It's Kristina who's shouting now. Ellie would have been too terrified for such a plan. They're believed, anyway—why would two girls beat their own father to death, and how?

"We loved him with all our hearts," Kristina says when the men carry him to the edge of the boat.

The men ask if Eleonora too would like to say something before they drop him over, but instead Kristina speaks again, says, "If it weren't for my father, I, Kristina Johnsson, would not ever make it to America." She smirks at Eleonora and the men tilt their arms so that Big Old rolls off and before she can hear him hit the water Eleonora runs away as fast as she has ever run before.

Kristina makes another friend on the boat after that. A single woman whom Eleonora has seen on deck at times. Because of this woman Kristina will ride in a carriage all the way to Chicago, where she will work as a prostitute until a man claims love for her and brings her west to Montana. There she will land with a baby in her belly and no man to speak of. An Indian girl will take pity on her and let her in. It's because of Kristina's nature—she can make any person laugh. By the time the baby is grown Kristina will be gone again and the child will never know where he got that strange first name of his, or that blond, blond hair.

America! When they see land a band appears on deck and Kristina and her new woman dance for nearly two days. Not Eleonora. That clump of darkness on the horizon will not ever make her rejoice.

Her things are ready. She has torn a strip of bedsheet and folded it into a sack and in it she has placed her stolen goods: one wool hat, a pair of shoes, four coins, a blanket. But to get through the gates will be a marvel beyond her imaginings. Instead what Ellie sees ahead for herself is a locked cell for the rest of time. Still she fashions a smile for the boy and follows him down to the cabin to tell his mother that land is in sight. This alone gives the woman more strength than she's yet had.

"Up," she tells herself, and with concentration breathes three slow, deep breaths. "Up, up." She claps her hands. Finally she rises and dresses and so taken is the boy that he does not see Eleonora duck out.

Here they are, Eleonora and Kristina, tags on their hats.

"Our dear father died on board," Kristina says.

"Yes," agrees Eleonora. "My father died at sea." Because, see, she has vowed to never again tell a lie.

They are let through. Miraculously they are. 1880, New York City. Surely there are lice in their hair. Probably Kristina has some other disease. Fifteen years old and already there is a pain between her legs too terrible for any man to comprehend, ever.

He was still breathing when Kristina began clubbing him, wasn't he? Eleonora decides that he was. He had taken that tincture before— he would have kept on.

Kristina has gathered money. She's been stealing along the way. "Take," she says to Eleonora, shoving a small bundle into her old friend's pocket. There are people swarming about them now. The buildings are tall, like monsters, like nothing Eleonora has ever dreamed.

"Go, Ellie," says Kristina. The woman she herself will go with stands behind her. "Don't follow me." She tilts forward, and holds Ellie's face firmly between her hands. Upon her friend's forehead she places one long kiss. "You can still make a good life," she says.

*   *   *

What can Ellie say?

"My husband sent for me," she says when she knocks on the door of 14 Pleasant Street, Lynn, Massachusetts. In New York she wandered the streets repeating this address until a dear woman recognized the words and led her to the station.

"What is his name?"

Oh, doesn't it feel good to speak her own language while the smell of warm bread falls upon her?

She is crying. Not for show but out of utter loss. So much loss that she nearly believes her own story.

"Erik Lindholm," she says.

Why his name? Why didn't she just make one up? Had she not said it, young Eleonora who used to be so good might have found a way to return home. She has murdered, yes, but that was self-defense. It is only after she's said that name that she knows she cannot go back. She cannot stand before her mother and feel anything but a sickening shame that will become a shark to eat every last drop of her. She says it, Erik Lindholm, and now watch as poor young Ellie lets that man's life be taken away.

"Why, Erik Lindholm is a member of our church."

The words fall out before she has a chance to catch them: "He doesn't want me. He never met me at the boat. I have come here alone. I have no roof, no food."

"And you don't have his address?"

"I have been there. He has sent me away."

Eleonora is ushered in. "Eleonora!" the boy exclaims. His mother is lovely now, clean and pink. Vaguely the woman remembers this girl who stands before her. Oh, if she could have remembered Ellie's true story.

"I am Eleonora Johnsson, I am just arrived, here is my proof," she says in the hallway, handing over her identification card. "I can cook and sweep and clean and teach the boy letters." She sits at the kitchen table with her hands on her lap. Please take me in. I will be good, I will be good. Please. "It is no trouble. I do not require an ounce of pay."

"Well," the father says. He places a cup of coffee in front of her. "Erik Lindholm is a good man, trusted at the church."

But wait, the boy's father thinks. Erik Lindholm is the treasurer there, in fact. For three years I have been entrusting a portion of my paychecks to this man's hands. And isn't the church missing a sum of money? Thirty dollars, to be exact?

"She looks like a girl from my home, but Johnsson is not the name I remember," Erik Lindholm says. "I will search for accommodations for her, but I assure you she is not my wife."

Eleonora says nothing except yes. Yes, she will take this offer. Which means that in the end Erik Lindholm finds the girl a position in the house of a rich man come over from England with his mother, but it does not clear Erik's own name. He is asked to leave his post as treasurer, and eventually, with all his community filled with mistrust, Erik Lindholm leaves Massachusetts for the land of Minnesota.

Eleonora never contacts her family. Such shame, no, she can only start anew. In time she meets a man and together they have four children, and she bears all that pain of childbirth without a word. She bears everything that comes her way. Her penance. She will be good. She punishes herself with work and on the first day that her eldest daughter bleeds, Eleonora tells her plainly to beware of womanhood. She says that she herself used to be called Eleonora Olasson, and that on April 22, 1878, her own father died. This was back before she learned to fight for herself, she says, and because of that something unfortunate happened back in the old country.

And there, in the old country, her family tells a story too. *Our Ellie*, they say. *Our Ellie was swallowed by the giant of the sea.*

CARLOS THE IMPOSSIBLE

by J. T. K. BELLE

"A bull's *querencia* is the spot in the bullring where the bull feels safest. Each bull will find its querencia in a different place in the ring, though not uncommonly near the gate where it entered. As the bull tires from the fight, it will seek to return again and again to this comfort zone. The skilled matador will turn the bull's querencia to his own advantage, luring the bull into a tenuous security before preparing for the final blow."

—*Book of Bulls: The Official Matador's Handbook (Second edition)*

"*Querencia* is the mirage of a corner in the roundness of a ring."

—Hernando

1

Once, outside of Ulysses, Kansas, by the banks of One Hundred Mile Creek, near the source of the Pequot River, in a field of slanted sunflowers laid low by grazing cattle, a bull calf was born to the cow Esmeralda. The calf was large, much larger than one might expect considering its humble lineage. Later, as the legend grew, they would say the bull was born with six-inch horns to the sudden clanging of the nearby church bells. Or that it emerged smoldering from a ribbon of dry heat lightning. Or even that this was no bull at all, but the offspring of an Indian elephant and a Jersey dairy cow. These types of apocrypha will attach themselves to budding legends and gather details like a tumbleweed of untruth. But here now are the true and simple facts of this taurine tale.

Though large, the bull calf was born sickly, at the Plumpkin Ranch, and soon afterward Esmeralda died of the bovine pox. From then on the calf was fed from a bottle by ranch hands and even by Plumpkin himself, a gentle soul who grew attached to the animal, holding its head in his hands as it drank. Plumpkin injected the calf with antibiotics morning and night, and by its twentieth day the calf was standing on its own, drinking full buckets of milk and devouring eight-pound bags of grain.

Its health restored, the calf began to gain pounds and inches by the day. By six weeks, it reached twenty hands high. By ten weeks, it had outgrown the calving pen. By six months, it stood as tall as a plow horse. By two years, from horn to hoof, the animal towered over the smokehouse, its hulking frame casting a shadow that stretched from the meadow at the near bank of One Hundred Mile Creek to the limestone bluff on the farther side.

The bull was named Son of Carleton after the seed bull, and the ranch hands came, with some irony, to call him by the diminutive Carlito. Eventually, when he outgrew even this, they called him Big Carl.

Plumpkin, meanwhile, calculated the poundage and counted the money in his head. When the day came—the day Big Carl was led to the slaughterhouse to be destroyed—the farmer took measure of his impending fortune with a mixture of wonder and remorse. Enough, he expected, to pay for an entire winter's expenses.

The proprietor of the slaughterhouse was equally impressed by the giant bull, though he frowned when the chute scale crumpled under Big Carl's weight. And so an agreement was made without an official measurement.

Plumpkin held his hat in his hand and frowned as the animal was led to the door of shed number five, where the stunner gun was loaded with bolts. The barrel was placed against Big Carl's head. And then, after a moment, the shot was fired.

Big Carl did not fall. The stunner was reloaded, and another shot was fired. Carl tilted his head, eyed the stunner with innocence and suspicion, squinted. Two bullets now sat lodged in his forehead, just above his left eye, beneath the root of the horn.

The gunman proceeded through the process as he had done a thousand times before. Stepping into the stall, he thrust his long knife forward to the carotid, where it scraped on Big Carl's hide and swerved sharply sideways. Recoiling, the man tried again, more forcefully this time. The knife snapped at the middle and fell clanging to the tile floor.

This bull cannot be killed, the man said.

The slaughterhouse workers stared at Carl. Carl stared back at them, seeming to sympathize, by his sidelong look, with their confusion and disappointment.

With nothing else to do, the rancher led the bull back into the cattle truck and drove him home to the slanting-sunflower field beside One Hundred Mile Creek, where the bull spent the following year idly grazing on bluestems and watching the creek's gently flowing waters pass between the limestone bluffs and press on down to the mighty Pequot River.

And then one day a man arrived at Plumpkin's door.

I hear you have a large bull, the man said.

Yes, said Plumpkin.

A very large bull, the man said.

As big as a smokehouse, said Plumpkin.

The man introduced himself as Douglas Button, a rodeo promoter from Kansas City. Plumpkin led Button to the field where the bull stood, eclipsing the afternoon sun.

Button gasped.

I'd like to bring him to Kansas City, he said. To the rodeo.

He won't buck, said Plumpkin.

He's four thousand pounds if he's a feather, Button said. He could lie on his belly in the shade and they'd still come from miles away to see him.

Carl sensed them, then. He was used to being spied. He sidestepped slightly and turned his head to see them, allowing the sun to rise slightly over the horizon of his shoulders. Button took in the enormity of the animal.

My goodness, he said.

In Kansas City, the crowds did come at first. But soon they dwindled, to Button's dismay. Without bucking, there was little other than Carl's size to draw an audience—no brave riders, no narrative to sell. They did not, in fact, come from miles away just to see the giant bull sitting in the shade. The sums the rodeos were willing to pay declined in short order.

I have another idea, Button said to Plumpkin.

And what is that?

Bullfighting.

Bullfighting?

Think of the draw!

At the rodeo?

No—in Mexico. I know an agent in Mexico City.

And who would fight this bull?

Someone will.

He can't be fought, Plumpkin said, shaking his head. He hasn't the temperament.

2

Hernando despaired at the new age of bullfighting: younger men (younger than he), without technique but full of bravado, fighting ever-smaller bulls in poorly orchestrated contests. Worst of all was the delegating, the wearing down of the bulls left to the *banderilleros*. All while commanding enormous sums for fancy capework and little more. Gone were the days of Arruza, his hero; Jamie Bravo, his mentor; and Manolete, oh Manolete!

Often he thought to himself, I am the last of a dying breed. The last of the true matadors.

When he was younger it wouldn't have bothered him, but Hernando was now thirty-five years old. Fighting bulls had cost him a marriage (a brief one, to a starlet of TV Azteca), the services of his agents and managers (none had lasted more than a year), and countless friendships. And these younger men, with their lesser skills, were earning nearly equal his wages, a king's ransom, tricking uneducated crowds into believing them worthy of it.

Today, it seemed, half of Mexico City was in attendance. The drunks in the sun seats *huh-huh*'d as the bulls stirred in their pens— the two matches before Hernando's had not satisfied their appetite for drama. They wanted only to see the master. The Legend of the Fiesta Brava.

Truth be told, he despised them, mostly. They did not understand the thing that unfolded before their eyes, did not comprehend the noble act or its intentions. Did not appreciate the difference between a courageous bull and a difficult bull, or award him ears or hooves based on anything more than a few flourishes of the cape and a few predictable passes.

Give me one-tenth the ticket sales, he would say, and forget the rest. We would all be happier. Before each corrida, when he knelt to pray to the Virgin of the Macarena, he would genuflect casually and ask the Lady not for Her protection and a well-behaved bull with courage and broad shoulders, but only for a knowledgeable crowd and a windless day.

Hernando's bloodline had been spilled in the sand by a long family history of middling matadors. His great-grandfather, who was called El Gaucho, was known for his luck and recklessness until he was gored nearly to death by the bull Ozomatzin and became a shoemaker in Aguascalientes. His grandfather El Zapatero was killed by the blue roan Zorrito, which his father Juan then had beheaded and mounted above the television in the family home, where it stared down over Hernando's truculent youth like a mounted siren calling the boy to the bulls. Juan, who went by El Pescador, fought for fifteen years, first as a *picador*, then in *ferias* in the South, then in the bloodless contests for the cruise-ship tourists in Baja, before retiring to the guava orchards of Ronda.

And then there was Hernando. From a young age he was possessed of a seriousness, an artfulness, not conferred by the Ages on his lineage. He was, they said, touched by the Taurine Fates, raised up from mediocrity by the angels of the corrida. Even now, at the sunset of his great career, these expectations weighed on him, punctuated his every victory with a lingering question mark. How much closer to the horns can you go? How many ears, hooves, and tails are enough? What more can you give them before bravery turns to foolishness and luck turns cold? Who can outrun the horizon?

It is true, the story they tell, that in his youth he fought two bulls at once. This was during the Feria de la Exuberancia Juvenile, after a poor season when he felt the need to do something grand, something to redeem his lesser efforts of the year before. Now, of course, in the towns around Ronda, where he was born, they will look you in the eyes and tell you he stood in their very *plaza de toros* and took on ten bulls—they will tell you they were blessed to witness it. What bravery, what honor! Hernando!

He would earn ninety thousand pesos for this fight. More and more, in the ring, he found himself thinking not of the work before him, or the pacing of the *veronicas*, or the tendencies of the bull as it came at the cape, but of his newest home in Zihuatanejo, high on a bluff overlooking the warm Pacific. Another year of this, another house. The next one in Cabo San Lucas, possibly a penthouse in the city. Granite countertops in the chef's kitchen. Parquet flooring...

In his prime—and the drunks in the sun seats would argue he was past it—he would have chased these thoughts from his mind in an instant. But after twenty years, from Tijuana to Cozumel, he was growing bored. The challenge was diminished. His stature was assured. Perhaps, just perhaps, it was time to—

The bull charged out through the gate. Smoothed sand kicked up under its hooves. This one was a fine animal, from the famed Don Fausto Meza breeding ranch in Tlaxcala. Full of courage, and, Hernando's men assured him, it would gallop straight and true as a train on rails. Perhaps a little smallish, but thick-necked, broad-shouldered, with horns spread wide and curved forward. Its glassy pelt waved over sun-drenched muscle and shimmered in the afternoon sun.

Hernando's focus returned. The old instincts flooded back, his senses heightened; he smelled the carnitas of the vendors walking the *tendidos*, heard the horses' quickening breath and the peanut shells hitting the dusty floorboards, saw the *presidente* of the plaza leaning over to whisper to his companion in the owner's box as the late-afternoon sun faded. The thin breeze raised the shaved hairs on the back of Hernando's neck.

Through the First Act, the matador stood back and critiqued the work of the *peónes* who ran the bull about, waving capes and testing the animal's bearings. Fine, thought Hernando. Nothing peculiar with this one. The picadors approached on horseback; the bull pawed at the sand, then charged. With a thud, the Tlaxcalan put its left horn up into the padded belly of the nearest horse. The stricken animal sidestepped, and then fell. Shuffling peónes with a thick black tarp quickly covered it over. After this, the remaining picadors had little difficulty, wounding the snorting Tlaxcalan with several sharp thrusts of their lances into the thick muscle between the shoulders.

In the Second Act, Hernando, full of theatrics, set the *banderillas* himself. Jumping, stabbing deep into the shoulder muscle with two heavy fists, then dancing away to the delight of the crowd. The colorful sticks bobbed from the animal's back and fell at its flanks as it skipped forward, snorting and coughing in the direction of the great matador who walked on his toes, head high, back turned, hand on hip. Not much longer, Hernando thought.

By the Third Act, the bull had slowed. Its head was held low now, drooping, its bulging shoulder muscles exposed, nearly spent but not yet ready for the sword. Each pass yielded a thunderous *Olé!* The bull still charged. It required little goading.

Olé!

Another pass. And another.

Olé!

Olé!

Hernando stood, feet together, pulling the *muleta* back gracefully as the bull's horns glided past his navel. The Tlaxcalan slowed further still, and retreated toward the gate on the far side of the ring, seeking its querencia.

Hernando paused for the benefit of the crowd.

Take him, Hernando!

He's ready, Great One!

Hernando allowed the bull to gather its courage. He pushed the muleta forward, slowly, clicking his tongue. He waited patiently, pulling gently again and again at the smaller cape, allowing the calls from the crowd to grow louder.

This will earn him a tail, he thought. His third of the season.

The bull lunged. Hernando stood on his toes and presented the sword with his signature arching of the back (they called this "the Hernando") before stepping forward and plunging the weapon high in between the shoulders of the exhausted bull. With a snort, the animal fell to its knees and collapsed, a little fountain of blood rising from its back and spilling into the sand. Hernando leaned-to and spread his arms like winged victory. The crowd erupted with chants of his name.

After the corrida, Hernando and his men retired to drink tequila at Café La Mancha and discuss the day's events.

What did you think of Ordoñez today, matador? one of the peónes asked.

Ordoñez? the matador huffed. The man knows nothing of bulls. Did you notice how he went to it in its querencia? Sheepish. Like a schoolboy to a spanking.

And Jiménez?

Technically competent, but cowardly at times. Terrible with the kill. He will soon need a longer sword to reach the bull!

This went on. Names of other matadors of the day were recalled, and Hernando batted back each one with candid derision.

Tito Suarez? A bore.

La Rosa? Awkward, angular, like a cactus with happy feet.

Villacorta? He dances like a chicken.

Diego Caron? Brave, I suppose, but stupid. He will be dead inside a year.

And how do you rate your performance today, matador?

Hernando paused, and considered the question with a frown.

Average, he finally replied, with a casual wave of the hand. The bull today was on the small side. They are bred too small, these days. Breed them larger, I say. We will see who remains in the ring then.

Hernando's words hung in the air. The first peóne squinted, and turned the tequila bottle in his hand.

Matador, the man said. There is something you should know.

Yes?

There is a bull fighting in the South.

Fighting? If you are a bull, you fight only once.

Jaripeos, the peóne said. And street fights. All manner of amateurs. They say he ran the Humanatlada, then fought in Sincelejo the following day. I understand he is now running in the *capeas* in your hometown of Ronda. This bull has fought ten times and killed thirty-nine men.

Ten times? What do you take me for?

It's true. They say he is as big as a cathedral.

Ha!

And made of stone.

There is no such bull.

They say the earth moves under his hooves.

Do they?

I assure you, it's quite true. This comes from Caron's men.

Caron?

Yes. He intends to fight the bull. He says the capeas are no place for such a beast. I'm sure you'll agree. Caron is in negotiations with the owner. He will promote him to the plaza and kill him honorably.

Herando snorted. Caron is a child and a cape waver, he said. If this bull is as difficult as you say, he will be gored before the trumpet blows.

A week passed. The stories filled Café La Mancha nightly, passing from table to table, the tumbleweed growing larger.

This bull they call Carlos fights in the capeas. Have you been to Ronda to see?

No, but he killed a cousin of my wife's. They say he took off and swallowed the poor bastard's arm.

And still the bull lives?

He goes on fighting, he can't be killed. He's tall as an elephant, with a hide twice as thick.

Another week.

Did you hear? Caron has been to Ronda.

And?

They say he is having second thoughts.

Hernando clenched his teeth, made a fist, and slammed it to the countertop.

Find me this bull's owner! he yelled.

The room went quiet.

I will guarantee him ten times Caron's price, Hernando went on.

I will do this as a favor to Caron, and as a gift to the aficionados who deserve the return of honor to the corrida. And their money's worth, at that!

The following evening, Button appeared. Standing in the doorway of Hernando's villa in Las Lomas, straw cowboy hat atop his head, he smiled a toothy smile.

Over iced tea in the madrone-paneled drawing room, Button and Hernando discussed the bull.

I am told this bull is big as a cathedral, Hernando said.

Two thousand kilos, give or take, Button said, nodding.

Impossible!

So he's been called. I don't blame you for your skepticism. You must see him to believe it.

These are the tales of drunks stumbling home from the festivals.

Ha! Well, there are enough of those.

And so you would confirm them, then? These reports? He has killed fifty men?

The number is twenty-three. But don't be fooled; this is no Miura bull. A giant, yes, but he is somewhat passive. Most were trampled crossing under him like calves.

Trampled? How many gored?

Only two have been gored, and only as they went for his eyes.

Hernando shook his head.

What you say disgusts me. The capeas are for butchers and cowards.

I agree. This bull belongs in the plaza.

With a professional. To have the fight brought out of him. To die nobly at the hands of a true matador.

Well, then, matador, Button said. Do we have a deal?

Hernando put his fingers to his cheek and scratched upward absentmindedly against his day's beard. A faraway look came over his emerald eyes.

It will be an honor to kill him, he said at last.

And so the deal was struck. It was arranged that the *empresario* for the Plaza Mexico would buy the giant bull from Button; come the Fiesta de la Fuerza Irresistible, the Great One, Hernando, would meet the bull born of a thunderclap with smoke pouring from his cavernous nostrils, the bull with six-inch horns that could not be killed in a Kansas slaughterhouse, the bull who had taken a hundred lives in the capeas of Ronda with not a drop of his own blood spent in the effort— the bull who they said would not quite fit through El Arco de Cabo, and who had come by now to be known to the aficionados as Carlos the Impossible.

3

They came by Metro, and by bus. They came on foot and in white-topped Beetle taxis, drinking from cola bottles and smoking *puros* and fanning themselves with broad-brimmed hats and taurine magazines. A swelling crowd of aficionados, fifty thousand in all, snaking toward the bull-statued gates of the Plaza Mexico. Everywhere they looked, on storefronts and bus stops and bulletin boards in market squares, hung red and yellow posters that cried:

HERNANDO

WITH THE GIANT BULL OF PLUMPKIN!

ORDOÑEZ AND SUAREZ
WITH THE BULLS OF DON FAUSTO MEZA

The fat-lettered posters showed Hernando enveloped in shadow, his emerald eyes transfixed by the enormity of the passing bull, one horn brushing his thigh, cape held out on a stiff right arm, his feet locked firmly to the sand.

Five o'clock in the afternoon. Murmurs circled up and around the great amphitheater. A brass band stirred. As the sun crossed over the roof of the upper stands and held directly above them, three gold-suited matadors came into the ring, flanked by their men—Hernando centermost, to the delight of the expectant aficionados.

While Hernando drank in a long ovation, Carlos stood up in his too-small pen beneath the pulsating plaza stands and listened as the band struck up a *pasodoble*. He liked the sound of the tuba best. Of all the noises that came in with that *paseo* music, it was that instrument's low boom that lifted him most.

The ceiling above him rattled with the foot traffic of the spectators taking their places in the shaded seats. Dust fell on his back and he knocked it off with a swipe of his tail.

The pasodoble ended.

Trumpets blew.

And then every few moments, a dark-eyed man under a felt sombrero descended the long ramp to the corrals beneath the stands to let loose another bull from another pen and watch it charge in a craze up the ramp.

Whenever this happened, Carlos heard trumpets give way to mild applause, then a handful of scattered *Olé*s, and then, again, mild applause.

Soon enough, the dark-eyed man approached Carlos's pen with a grimace. Gently, steeling himself deep in his boots, he slid back the rust-chipped bolt. With a loud creak, the gate swung open, and the man called loudly, Huh-huh! over his shoulder as he scampered up the ramp and back into the arena. Carlos, after a moment, squeezed through the opening and double-stepped upward after him, toward the sunshine and the trumpets.

When he reached the top, he paused in the gate jamb (which had been widened just so, to let him pass), and then slid through it slowly, scraping his shoulders as he went. The crowd stood, craning necks and leaning on toes toward the *callejon*. The bull's shadow unfurled before him like a Zapotec rug cast onto the orange sand. The crowd gasped.

Que enorme! they cried as he came farther out from the shadows.

It's true, they exclaimed, as he strode into the sunlight. *He is a monster!*

He must be an elephant! they declared as Carlos settled into the ring, twenty steps from the gate, turning his head from side to side, the better to survey the tittering crowd.

Across the ring, Hernando's men grew nervous. Despite the doubling of their wages, their misgivings remained. Their eyes went from the bull to the shadow, which seemed to draw forward to engulf them in the unshaded half of the bullring.

Only their leader remained calm. Your head will look fine above my television, toro, the matador thought to himself. Forever from this day, they will talk of the glorious afternoon when the Great Hernando took down the impossible bull.

He drew himself up. Someone, a journalist from the local paper in Ronda, or possibly it was *El Norte*, had once asked him the secret of his ways. Hernando would not divulge it, not to a *journalista*, not to a lover; but to the men in his *cuadrilla* he would tap the side of his head with two fingers and declare, It is simple, boys—you have only to think like a bull.

And so as the giant beast stood there, long white horns like crescent moons eclipsing the afternoon sun, Hernando sought to divine the thoughts of the massive animal.

Carlos did not charge. He took in his surroundings with a tranquil confidence, disinterestedly noting the men with the capes shuffling toward him. He scanned the height of the plaza, then walked himself around in a tight circle to survey his rear. He seemed to sense this was no capea, but rather something much more... pleasant.

A peóne leaned into Hernado's shoulder and said quietly, I don't like this, matador.

Hernando's eyes remained fixed on the giant bull. Settle the horses, he said in his cold, calm way.

Carlos walked another tight circle. No, this was not like the capeas, with their unstructured violence and frenzied mobs. No silly young men darting across cobblestone alleys and *huh-huh*ing over their shoulders as they skittered past his horns. There was a rhythm to this, a precision.

The First Act, though, was unenlightening. The terrified peónes with their quivering capes failed to provoke the bull, or discern anything of use about its tendencies.

It's no use, jefe! they cried. *He won't run.*

The picadors' efforts came to much the same. They did not damage the animal, did not so much as break his hide with their lances. To the observant aficionados, the bull seemed merely curious: studying the thick-padded horses prancing in the ring, the men with long *pics* mounted atop them, thrusting their weapons toward him awkwardly and from too great a distance, the lone man with bright green eyes standing near the sideboards, sizing him up, taking him in.

Send the horses closer, Hernando said.

The men in their saddles urged their animals forward, slapping them on their withers. The horses whinnied, pulled up short, then high-stepped sideways, away to the fence.

Laughter circled the plaza.

Never mind the horses! Hernando called out.

The matador came forward, waving the picadors back. A shower of hurrahs greeted him there. And now Carlos, too, came forward, leaning into a half step, the better to see Hernando's eyes—emerald green eyes that grew wide and electric and dared him to run.

Olé! the drunks shouted in mock celebration.

Carlos's eyes dilated like a blooming black rose.

Finally the burning intensity of the matador's green glare pulled Carlos to him. The giant bull felt some old mystical impulse, and at last divined that to play his part correctly he must present himself.

The bull made a passive attempt at a charge.

And another.

As Carlos caught on to the cues, his charges, deliberate and reserved, began to shake the earth. With each measured pass, the plaza crowd let out a series of slow-rolling *Ooooooo-lé*s. After several successive charges, Hernando's confidence grew further. He inched closer to the gliding horns, for the benefit of the crowd and for the sake of the Fiesta's redemption.

Carlos began to quicken the pace, sensing now what was expected of him.

Olé!

Take him wide, Hernando!

But no. This was too sloppy. Hernando resigned himself to a quick kill, forgoing any further gracelessness. When Carlos came at him again, his head lowered, Hernando drew his sword, reached up, and plunged the weapon as best he could into the giant bull's back, high up between the shoulders in the spot they call the *morillo*. This required a little jump-step, an unflattering concession to the scale of the beast, but so be it.

The sword, hitting flesh, bowed in the middle, then broke at the tip and snapped upward into the air. For a moment it hung there, in the held breath of the puzzled crowd. Then it landed on the sand, ten paces from Hernando's feet.

Fifty thousand mouths went all agape.

Carlos remained still, calm, looking up only briefly into the sun seats where the drunks laughed with swollen red faces.

Hernando wiped his brow with his silk suit sleeve and decided he'd struck bone. He stepped back, retrieved the damaged sword, and walked to the *relichero*, where he was handed a replacement. He tested it against the sideboard with a heavy *thwack*, and then marched solemnly back toward the center of the ring.

Carlos followed the matador with his eyes.

Hernando took position, inciting Carlos again with the cape.

Casually, the bull walked forward and made an effort to catch the cape with his horn. Emboldened, Hernando waved the cape again and stepped around to Carlos's rear. Curious, Carlos circled with him.

They did this several times, until the crowd grew restless.

Basta! they cried.

To the end! they cried.

Lowering the muleta, Hernando set Carlos's head low and went to plunge the sword between the shoulder blades. He jumped, he thrust, and again the sword bowed and snapped, shooting upward and out of the matador's hands, arcing end over end and falling to the ground.

The drunks in the sun seats howled. Hernando's invectives circled the ring, echoing up into the warm, still afternoon air.

You will need an elephant gun! someone cried.

From behind the *barrera* a drunk tossed an empty bottle that shattered somewhere in the outer ring, causing both Carlos and Hernando to turn their heads at once. The bull's left horn, coming around, caught Hernando high up on the thigh and threw him heels over head through the air. Blood sprayed into Carlos's eyes. The matador's body thumped to the sand.

Two peónes darted through the slits in the barrera and pulled their man toward the railing, blood trailing behind them in a long black tail. Hernando struggled to free himself, clawing for the sword. The picadors grabbed his feet more firmly, but he slashed at them until they held up their hands and backed away. Freed, he flailed wildly in the direction of the bull, pulling himself on his elbows, lines of blood now crisscrossing the sand.

Carlos stood motionless, red-tipped horns held high, watching as Hernando, his sword held back, ready but unable to strike, at last lost consciousness at the bull's front hooves. The wide-eyed peónes rushed forward again and took the man up. Hernando's blood dripped down from his opponent's nostrils.

As they raised the matador over the rail and hoisted him onto a stretcher, Hernando came to just long enough to pardon the bull. *Save this one,* he said. *I will meet with him again.*

Hernando spent forty-three days in hospital, in a suite once occupied by a twice-gored Jamie Bravo. His slowly improving vital signs were reported daily in *El Norte*.

The Great Matador's recovery was complicated by infections and malaise. His suite overlooked a circular garden filled with well-kept zinnias, dahlias, and marigolds, and in his narcotic hallucinations what he saw there was a bullring: a magical ballet played out in cloud shadows and blowing leaves, marked off by long-stemmed aficionados blowing kisses and applauding him with rose petals. Hernando saw himself fighting the giant bull with a duvet for a cape and a maguey frond for a sword, dragging both wearily behind him as he desperately circled an impossible beast. Sweat poured from his forehead as he was weaned from the intravenous morphine and finished the last of the antibiotics.

On the forty-fourth day, Hernando left the hospital, emerging from the halogen halls and squinting into the daylight. He walked with the assistance of a crook-handled acacia cane. A throng of paparazzi stood waiting at the curb.

How do you feel, matador? the throng barked from behind flashing bulbs. *Will you fight again?*

Hernando responded only with silence, and made his way to his chauffeured sedan. As it departed, he thought only of the day he would rejoin the impossible bull in the ring, and put it to its overdue death.

A year passed. Gradually, Hernando regained his footing, dispensed with the crook-handled acacia cane, and at last sat for a Televisa interview that was broadcast on the eve of the following season:

JOURNALIST: How grave were your wounds?

HERNANDO: Not too serious, really.

JOURNALIST: But you spent forty days in hospital.

HERNANDO: For exhaustion, it seems. And dehydration.

JOURNALIST: I understand the horn discovered the femoral artery.

HERNANDO: They tell me it was grazed, yes.

JOURNALIST: With three trajectories!

HERNANDO: I did feel a tickle down there.

JOURNALIST: Will you retire from the ring?

HERNANDO: I think not.

JOURNALIST: So then what is next for you, matador?

HERNANDO: I intend to return to the plaza and kill the giant bull come November.

JOURNALIST: You mean to say you are planning for a rematch? With the very same bull?

HERNANDO: I prefer to think of it as a continuation after intermission.

Carlos spent the Mexican winter lying in the cool shade of a calabash tree on a rolling cactus-hilled breeding ranch in Tlaxcala. Hernando knew the owner, the famed Don Fausto Meza; as a favor (and for his own sport), the matador would often test the ranch's young bulls for bravery and form in the private sessions they call the *tientas*.

On Carlos's first day there, the ranch's herd of twenty calves receded in unison to the far side of the field to escape the enormity of the imposing stranger. When Carlos approached them with his nose to the ground, his morning shadow coming at them like a blackened cape, they parted and then fled with stuttering gaits, looking over their shoulders as they went. Don Fausto feared that Carlos would so unsettle the young bulls as to sap their courage, and so he instructed his *vaqueros* to build a new fence of mesquite wood and river rocks in order to cleave the field in two. One side for Carlos, where he could idle away the long days alone under the winter sun, and one for the suspicious little toros, who would keep well back of the barrier that separated them from their fearsome cousin.

The ranch hands were no less spooked than the baby bulls. Don Fausto told them only half in fun that he thought the giant bull was the reborn spirit of the evil one they called Huay Chivo, and not to look the thing in the eyes.

4

La revancha! In September, the rematch between the great matador and the impossible bull was set for La Fiesta de la Objeto Inamovible, eight weeks away. Red-lettered posters announcing the event appeared on shuttered *tiendas* and busy bus stops and graffitied, papered-over walls throughout the city. Across cantina tabletops, in street cafes and tequila bars from Tijuana to Vera Cruz, aficionados debated the merits of man versus bull. They debated with the fevered logic and foul language of fanatics. They argued at work and at home, on television and on the radio, over cold meals and under warm sheets.

Inevitably, the gambling houses began accepting wagers. But how? Who had ever taken odds on the bull in a bullfight? As the debate wore on, the betting line hopped like a jumping bean from side to side; it was only in the last placid week of November that the odds finally settled at three to one in favor of the bull.

The day arrived under calm blue skies. Ah, pulsing butterflies, budding gooseflesh, and the high adventure of an afternoon at the corrida! Hernando spent more than his usual few passive moments in the plaza's chapel that morning, praying with studied efficiency to the Virgin of the Macarena. Afterward he ran through his routine of superstitions for good measure—massaging his earlobes and the soles of his feet, touching the wallet-worn picture of his first bull, Hamartia, and the one in profile of the great Arruza, as well, then silently reading that old poem of Lorca's.

When he finally took to the ring with a deep breath and a signing of the cross, the crowd rose to its feet and roared in defiance of the betting line that so favored the bull. At this, Hernando puffed with pride, and his stomach, which had betrayed him with flutters, calmed once again.

While Hernando drank in his ovation, Carlos stood up in his too-small pen and listened as the brass band played "The Spanish Gypsy Dance." He listened fondly to the familiar booming tuba. When the refrain came around, he held his head high and his black nostrils flared wide and rang in the chorus with the tuba bell. The gypsy dance grew louder. The floorboards above him shook under the long parade of those taking their seats in the shade. Dust settled on his snout and he removed it with a lick of his salty tongue.

Soon enough, a slightly built man with his hair in a ponytail approached Carlos's pen on the balls of his feet. The rust-chipped bolt was slid back, the gate swung open with a creak. The man called, Ah-ha, ah-ha! as he backpedaled up the ramp and into the arena. Carlos double-stepped after him, toward the soothing sounds of the tuba.

Trumpets blew. The crowd leaned in. When Carlos emerged from the shaded chute, the spectators stood again and roared and jeered at equal decibels. In all the corridas de toros of Mexico and far beyond, never had there been such a reaction to the entrance of a bull into the bullring.

Carlos took in the crowd happily, not at all perturbed by the noises swirling in the round. Where was the tuba? He scanned the great amphitheater from right to left, and then from left to right. Fifty thousand round faces looked back down at him. The one belonging to the presidente of the plaza was long and mustached and glowed with delight. The presidente's companion's face was tight, the corners of her mouth pointed downward. The drunks in the sun seats slapped their hats and frothed with glee; the ladies in the shade either clapped their hands politely or fanned themselves with their programs. Carlos observed one and then another along the long rows behind the barrera without much interest. But when his eyes settled on the man who stood on the sand twenty paces before him, they widened with a soft glow of recognition.

Hernando's eyes darkened. His fingers tightened around the handle of his sword. He put out of his mind the foot-long scar that meandered upward from his knee to his groin like a crack in a dry riverbed.

No picadors appeared. No banderilleros were called in. Hernando's men sat stone-faced behind the barricade, prepared, on order of the matador, to intervene only in the event of his demise.

As a hush drew over the plaza, Hernando made a circle around the giant bull. Carlos followed him with his head and shoulders until Hernando reached the rear of his right flank. Then the bull turned his head to the other side to await the man's emergence again from shadow.

Hernando's thoughts were drawn to Lorca:

Now the dove and the leopard wrestle / at five in the afternoon...

But Carlos did not charge. Hernando closed the distance between them with a straight back and a stiff neck and presented the red cape.

Carlos sat down on his hindquarter.

Someone yelled *Olé!*, drawing a crescendo of laughter. Hernando spat in the sand and cursed under his breath.

Arsenic bells and smoke / at five in the afternoon...

Minutes passed. Hernando willed the giant bull forward with little gestures. Mocking *Olés!* showered down on him like tiny banderillas.

The bass-string struck up / at five in the afternoon...

Finally the burning intensity of the matador's eyes pulled Carlos to him. The bull made a passive attempt at a charge. And another.

It was five in the afternoon...

Enough of this, Hernando thought.

On the next pass Hernando dropped Carlos's head with the cape and jumped, landing the sword precisely at the spot he intended—just between the shoulders, at the centermost point of the giant aorta that ran beneath.

It was five in the afternoon...

Suspended in the air, his hand removed from the sword, Hernando felt a moment of joy like no other. Before gravity took hold—before it could return him to the dry sand below, as he hung there like a golden specter of the Fiesta Brava, held aloft by the whistles of the faceless crowd—the corners of his mouth began to lift into the beginnings of a smile.

Groups of silence in the corners / at five in the afternoon...

And then, too soon, he began to fall. As the matador landed, Carlos's right hind hoof stepped directly onto Hernando's turned-out ankle, snapping the bone. A revolting *pop!* could be heard all the way to the rafters. Hernando screamed.

Bones and flutes resound in his ears / at five in the afternoon...

Carlos quickly lifted his hoof and moved away with a halting, sympathetic limp. The matador fell with a thump to the ground and twisted wildly in a half circle. Sand caked together on his cheek and in the sweat above his brow.

Horn of the lily through green groins / at five in the afternoon...

Panic crossed hotly over Hernando's face. Glancing toward his men in desperation, he pushed himself up to his knees. And then, with a full, devastated breath, he stood and hopped gingerly to a position ten paces away from the bull.

I will finish him on one ankle! Hernando fumed through his pain. He barked at his men to throw him another sword. Carlos, sword-tip buried shallowly in his hide, trotted forward.

Now the bull was bellowing through his forehead / at five in the afternoon...

Gathering up his muleta quickly, Hernando leapt again—inasmuch as he could. But with only one leg to propel him, he failed to gain the height he needed. He landed awkwardly, twisted his remaining good ankle, and crumpled in his suit of lights to the ground.

Aaaaay! he screamed.

Carlos pulled up and turned to see the matador writhing.

The wounds were burning like suns / at five in the afternoon.

Ignoring his flailing arms, Hernando's men leaped over the barricade, distracting Carlos unnecessarily with a great waving of capes, and carried the matador to safety. The bull, in turn, settled gently on his hindquarters and watched them from the center of the ring.

It was five by all the clocks! In the shade of the afternoon!

Despondence. Hernando convalesced at his beach home high on a cliff overlooking the crop of black rock formations in Zihuatanejo Bay. He sat silently for much of each day, his leg elevated on a leather pillow perched atop a wicker ottoman, watching the occasional puff of cloud cross the watery horizon.

Uninvited voices haunted his waking dreams. *Is he up to the task?* they said. *Why not let it go? You'll get a pass. Fight a smaller bull, a normal bull.* Hernando heard them shouting from the plaza seats, heard them chuckling on the Metro, heard them in their homes talking back to their television sets.

One voice rose above the rest. Was it Fortune? Was it Fate? Our Lady of Surrender? Manolete, whispering from the grave? Was it whispering of defeat? Of humility? Or ignominy? What sound does Providence make?

Hernando chased these thoughts from his restless mind like so many autograph-seekers at the plaza's back gate. When he squinted into those melting Pacific sunsets, he saw bulls in the fat red clouds.

*   *   *

As Hernando grew stronger and practiced his footwork—at first against an assemblage of charging, bent-at-the-waist, finger-horned peónes, and then with the baby bulls at the ranch of Don Fausto Meza—Carlos spent the year idly, pacing the dry hills of Tlaxcala, dreaming of sunflower fields and limestone bluffs and the gently flowing waters of One Hundred Mile Creek, near the source of the Pequot River.

5

The third fight between Hernando and the bull was scheduled for the following Fiesta de Conflicto Eterno, on the last day of the bullfighting season. Hernando's ankle, though pronounced by his doctor fit to bear weight, swelled in the rain and throbbed like an *acordeón*. This match brought more gamblers than the last, and the odds settled quickly at ten to one in favor of the bull.

This time, the contest stretched on for more than five hours. For those five hours, Carlos played his part as if he were bred for it, gaining speed with each veronica. Hernando, his ankles swelling with each thundering pass, made thirty-five attempts to find the spot between the bull's shoulders, and could not. After three hours, the crowd began to thin, and showered the ring with catcalls and the balled-up butcher paper they peeled from their *tortas* as they went.

The stalwarts remained until the sunset turned to darkness. Only the drunks stayed until the end, to witness the Great Matador collapse from exhaustion near to midnight.

Was there ever such comeuppance? Hernando passed the off-season ignoring the laughter of the public. Ignoring the slights from breathless journalists and bemused passersby, ignoring the gossiping *garnacha* vendors in the marketplace. He went for long stretches without the company of women. Pride leaked through his pores like helium through a festival balloon.

The voices persisted. *What is this business? This messing about with bulls? Tell me again the point. What good ever came of it?* They came like unholy spirits in the night and loitered in the outer ring of Hernando's convalescent ego.

As for Carlos, he passed the off-season dreaming of red capes that waved between sunflowers, pawing soft dirt under the steady watch of an emerald green eye as cold, clear waters flowed from an unknown source to an unknown destination.

Despite summer months filled, for Hernando, with endless tactical sessions and a coterie of paid advisers, the fourth meeting (in the first fight of the season) saw the oddsmakers start the betting at one million to one in favor of the bull. This, said the oddsmakers, was necessary in order to attract any bets at all for the matador.

One million to one? thought Hernando. Can it be? Can this bull be truly indestructible?

The sentiment among aficionados was that Hernando would never regain his swagger, never regain the very bravado that had destined him for fame. Hernando himself knew all too well what becomes of ruined matadors. He'd not known his grandfather but had long felt the cold spell of the blue roan that killed him as it stared out into the parlor above the static halo of the family television. He had seen his father go weak in the knees when he returned to the ring after his brush with the end at the horn tip of the bull Conejhero. Juan's passes became quick, jumpy. Not to mention Suarez, Villacorta, Ordoñez, all of whom had lost their nerve in the ways he so despised: the muletas bent back by tentative elbows, the footwork reduced to a frantic shuffle.

No, Hernando said, it is all in the head. This bull will die by day's end, and the *pinches* in the tendidos will go silent with awe. The whole of the plaza will roar with the chants of *Hernando! Hernando!* once again.

But, as the Fates had evidently designed, this fight ended as did the others: with Carlos sitting dejectedly on his tail as Hernando lay unconscious in the sand. By rights, Hernando ought not to have survived, said those who witnessed things firsthand—but again he summoned the strength to pardon the bull before he collapsed into extended darkness.

He spent the year in a partial coma. Though he began to respond to certain stimuli almost immediately (long and guttural *huh-huh*s caused his fingers to twitch), it was not until the following November, when Caron took two tails in the first two weeks of the season, that Hernando sat upright in his bed and declared that he would fight again.

When he returned, the plaza would not take him. He offered to front the ticket sales. They said, You should take this act to the Circus Atayde!

All season long, he called on every empresario of every bullring large and small, from Tijuana to Cozumel.

We're full up, they said.

Try farther south, they said.

So sorry, Great One, they said. Perhaps you might fight another bull?

And so Hernando bought Carlos back from the empresario of the plaza for two hundred pesos and a half bottle of Oaxacan mezcal. With nowhere else to turn, he sold the villa in Las Lomas and bought for himself and for Carlos the smallish but respectable bullring in his hometown of Ronda, where his name still echoed in the ancient rafters and the feats of his youth were both remembered and imagined.

*   *   *

That fourth year, they claimed, the bull became sympathetic to the matador. Even the rheumiest *gabachos* in the upper seats could see that Carlos had studied the man's passes with a critical eye. The bull had developed an attachment.

Was it ever so? Carlos, it cannot be disputed, had become an accomplice in the Spectacle Without End (as the newspapers now called it), and enjoyed the exercise and the company, if not the awkward conclusion of each fight. It seemed that the animal sensed, however faintly, a purpose, if not a meaning, in his part.

The gambling ceased. There was not an aficionado in all of Mexico now who would part with his money on the confidence of the matador, no matter the odds.

Small crowds came to the bullring in Ronda, at first for the fight, and then for the man—and then only for the bull. And then simply to mock and jeer at the great bullfighter in his shame.

After the fifth year, Hernando could no longer employ a cuadrilla, even with above-market salaries and a light workload. He sold the condominium in the city.

And then the crowds simply stopped coming at all. *This is the man who fought ten bulls at once? The Great One? The Legend?*

For many years they fought like this, Hernando's spirit, like his reputation, growing tattered as an aged *capote*. His heart as empty as the plaza's seats.

The matador's only chance at redemption had ever been in killing the bull. But at each *faena*, the tragedy ended as the last—with broken banderillas, fractured swords, and an exhausted Hernando conceding defeat, unable to pierce the shoulder blades of the ever-more-accommodating animal.

As time went on, and the contests lost the last pretense of formality, it was Carlos who shouldered the uneven weight of the performance. By now he was settled fully into this daily routine: up with the sun each morning, a breakfast of corn and grain (or now and then the remains of tamales wrapped in banana leaves left at the gate by the wife of Don Fausto Meza), a leisurely stroll around the ring under the watchful eye of the matador. Then through the motions with a series of well-practiced charges, until he was pardoned with an exhausted wave of the matador's hand, and back to his pen where he settled into his bed of hay.

Twelve hours later, as the sun crept over the wet sands of the ring, Hernando would drag a feed sack into Carlos's pen, open the door, drop the sack on the sand in front of the bull, and say, *Eat, toro, this is your last meal on this earth.* Carlos would dutifully nod his snout and paw at the sack excitedly until it spilled open onto the ground. And then Hernando would turn his back and walk up the callejon, to practice his veronicas to the roar of the empty seats.

If your demons offered you a truce, would you take it? If your monsters put forward a middle ground, would you meet them there? Hernando would not. After seven years, the matador's anxiety became acute. His prize money, his entire life's savings, dwindled to little more than a peóne's wages. One by one, his remaining homes were taken from him, sold at auction. And so, eventually, he made a home of his bullring—aside from Carlos, the last of his possessions.

*   *   *

For ten years more it went on this way. Seasons passed like strangers. Hernando's beard grew long and white and tangled. His dementia advanced like the afternoon shade. As the matador slowed, Carlos compensated with brisk, vigorous charges, on each pass placing his horns just within reach of the man's torso, but only just so. He followed Hernando as a calf follows a cow.

At the end of each day, Hernando sent the bull back to his stall with a familiar refrain:

Toro, you torment me.

[*Carlos snorts.*]

You can't know the pain you have caused me.

[*Carlos burrs.*]

I'm of a mind to set fire to you and be done with it.

Hernando's heart came undone like a cow hitch slipping its knot. Carlos, for his part, basked in the familiar routine of feeding, running, and sleeping under the matador's ever-present emerald eyes. He grew content with this life, though when he slept he dreamed almost always of the same orange and yellow sunflower field, the same towering limestone bluffs and the same gently flowing waters of the Pequot River.

Hernando dreamed only of killing the bull.

And then the fighting stopped. Matador and bull would meet in the afternoon only to siesta; Hernando on his back basking in the sun, Carlos pacing the ring freely until he made a bed for himself in the shade. On occasion he would nuzzle Hernando with his snout, careful with the horns so as not to mistakenly puncture the man.

At night Hernando sat behind the barrera and watched the shadows play out generation-old performances by Arruza and Manolete, cheering them through the echoes of his own febrile laughter.

Only rarely was the matador now recognized by the public. Only rarely would he be acknowledged. When he was, they would say with genuine surprise, *Are you still fighting that bull?* And then they would laugh at the thought of a fifty-year-old man, who looked twenty years older still, dancing with a bull who seemed to regard the corrida as a sublime but humble amusement.

6

It was in the twentieth year, long after the public's attention had evaporated like morning dew from the plaza sands, that Hernando succumbed to his madness in full. He slept in the pens or on the bullring floor. He pawed the sand as he walked, twisting his head and snorting—his long beard hiding oats and hay, his rotten teeth hiding the corn feed he shared with Carlos.

On his last day, he prayed to the Virgin of the Macarena for a knowledgeable crowd and a windless day, crossed himself twice, and closed his eyes. When Carlos emerged from the callejon, stretching lazily under the morning sun, he found Hernando slumped sideways over a horse's saddle, motionless, dew rising up around him.

The bull recoiled. His heart contracted, then slowed. Pain filled his chest. Adrenaline poured through him like a hundred toros running blindly through narrowing streets as he stepped toward the body of the matador, knelt, and nuzzled the cold back of the man's neck.

*   *   *

Days of melancholy followed days of despair. What to do with this bull? Hernando's creditors asked themselves. The plaza we will keep. But the bull? Too old now to slaughter even if he could be slaughtered, too old to breed.

And what now for the bull to do?

Carlos paced the ring, ate little, sleeping much of the day and all through the night. The doctors said, This animal is under a great deal of stress.

Carlos began to thin. The giant bull dropped a thousand pounds within a month, another thousand pounds the next. Ribs pressed out from his softening skin and into the sand of his pen like the ship timbers of a scuttled galleon. Even the ancient bolts trapped in his skull became visible in bright light.

In his fitful sleep, he dreamed a full palette of colors: orange and yellow sunflowers, red flashing capes, the once-sharp look in Hernando's eyes lit in piercing emerald green.

The end comes, not with a flash of the muleta, not at the end of a pic. Carlos, having played his part, drifted toward his querencia, unrequited. Some would say it was the two bullets in his skull that finally did him in. Others would say that for a bull of that age, well, it was simply time. The poets of the obituaries proposed his soul was twinned with the great matador's like a *nahual*, and argued the denouement was fitting.

Hernando finally killed his bull, they said.

No, the doctors said. This animal was healthy in all other respects. He simply lost the will to live.

Hernando finally killed his bull, they said.

*   *   *

Tumble, tumble, tumbleweed. These are the last true facts of this taurine tale:

The arrangements fell to Don Fausto Meza. Left to divine the eternal wishes of the matador, Don Fausto had spread Hernando's ashes among freshly planted trumpet lilies beneath a calabash tree on a hill near his breeding ranch in Tlaxcala, where forevermore the great matador might test the young calves for courage and form. Now, Don Fausto thought to himself as he considered the deadweight of Carlos's remains and the difficulty of their transport, what to do with the carcass of an impossible bull?

And so Carlos the Impossible was buried where he fell, below the sands of the plaza de toros in Ronda, slightly off from the center, where to this day, when a bull with particular courage finds himself strangely in need of comfort, as though he could will himself away from the *toreros* and the crowd, he will look for a corner in the roundness of the ring, and back into that very spot. And there he will find a slight breeze and a gentle water current and the swaying of orange and yellow sunflowers beneath his hooves, and he will stay there for a while, as he gathers up his wits or has them drawn out for him, before he lowers his head and charges through the *Olés* toward the man with the cape.

CONTRIBUTORS

TOM BARBASH is the author of *The Last Good Chance*, a winner of the California Book Award, and *On Top of the World*. He currently teaches in the writing program at California College of the Arts.

J. T. K. BELLE lives in Seattle with his wife and two kids.

ROBERTO BOLAÑO was born in Santiago, Chile in 1953. He grew up in Chile and Mexico City, where he was a founder of the Infrarealist poetry movement. His first full-length novel, *The Savage Detectives*, received the Herralde Prize when it appeared in 1998, and the Rómulo Gallegos in 1999. Bolaño died in Blanes, Spain, at the age of fifty. "The Neochileans" is taken from *Tres*, published by New Directions.

BENJAMIN COHEN lives with his family in Pennsylvania, where he is a professor at Lafayette College. He is the author of *Notes from the Ground: Science, Soil & Society in the American Countryside*, and was once the film critic for the *Granville Sentinel*.

STEPHEN ELLIOTT is the author of *The Adderall Diaries*. He directed the movie *Cherry*.

DAVID-IVAR HERMAN DÜNE records music as Herman Dune or Yaya Herman Dune. He has shown his drawings, in black ink and gouache, on both sides of the Atlantic.

AMELIA GRAY is the author of *AM/PM* and *Museum of the Weird*. Her first novel, *THREATS*, is due out in March 2012 from Farrar, Straus and Giroux.

VÁCLAV HAVEL is a Czech politician and playwright; he served as the last president of Czechoslovakia from 1989 to1992, and as the first president of the Czech Republic from 1993 to 2003. His books include *Open Letters: Selected Writings 1965-1990*, *The Garden Party and Other Plays*, and *To the Castle and Back*.

LAURA HEALY has translated two collections of poetry by Roberto Bolaño, *Tres* and *The Romantic Dogs*.

JULIE HECHT is the author of two story collections, *Do the Windows Open?* and *Happy Trails to You*, and a novel, *The Unprofessionals*. She is also the author of *Was This Man a Genius?: Talks with Andy Kaufman*. She is currently working on a new book, *May I Touch Your Hair?*

MARCO KAYE's writing can be found online at *McSweeney's Internet Tendency*, *The Rumpus*, and *The Morning News*.

AVERY LEE performs improvisational comedy in Chicago with the groups Classy D and 98.6.

ELMORE LEONARD has written more than forty books during his career, many of which have been made into movies, including *Get Shorty* and *Out of Sight*. He is the recipient of the Lifetime Achievement Award from PEN USA and the Grand Master Award of the Mystery Writers of America. *Justified*, a TV drama based on Leonard's character Raylan Givens, was the recipient of a Peabody Award in 2011.

ABI MAXWELL is from New Hampshire. "Giant of the Sea" is her second published story, and the first in an unpublished collection of linked stories titled *The Lake's People*.

DICKY MURPHY's writing has appeared in the *San Francisco Panorama* and *Lady Churchill's Rosebud Wristlet*.

YANNICK MURPHY's latest novel is *The Call*, based on a short story that first appeared in *McSweeney's 29*. She lives in Vermont with her husband and three children.

E. C. OSONDU was born in Nigeria. He is a winner of the Caine Prize for African Writing, and the author of a book of stories, *Voice of America*. Currently, he is an assistant professor of English at Providence College, in Rhode Island.

ELIZABETH SANKEY is a writer from London. She also sings in the band Summer Camp.

JENNIE ERIN SMITH is the author of *Stolen World: A Tale of Reptiles, Smugglers, and Skulduggery*, and a frequent reviewer on natural history for the *Times Literary Supplement* and the *Wall Street Journal*. She lives in Germany.

TABITHA SOREN left a career in television in the late 1990s to start another as a photographer. Her work is in the collections of the New Orleans Museum of Art, the Ogden Museum of Southern Art, and the Oakland Museum of California.

FLAGG TAYLOR is an assistant professor of government at Skidmore College and the editor of *The Great Lie: Classic and Recent Appraisals of Ideology and Totalitarianism*.

JESS WALTER is the author of five novels, most recently *The Financial Lives of the Poets*. Among his other books are *The Zero*, a finalist for the National Book Award, and *Citizen Vince*, a winner of the Edgar Allan Poe Award.

BENJAMIN WEISSMAN is the author of two books of short fiction, most recently *Headless*. He teaches at the Art Center College of Design and Otis College of Art.